A *Rake* BY ANY OTHER NAME

MIA MARLOWE

sourcebooks
casablanca

Published by Sourcebooks Casablanca, an imprint of Sourcebooks,
Inc.
P.O. Box 4410, Naperville, Illinois 60567-4410
(630) 961-3900
Fax: (630) 961-2168
www.sourcebooks.com

Printed and bound in Canada.
WC 10 9 8 7 6 5 4 3 2 1

For the Norwegian Hunk, my hero always.

One

Where one stands on a matter depends upon where one sits. When someone else is holding court on one's settee, spreading delicious falsehoods, one is tempted to brand them a liar. When one finds oneself on the same settee, practicing deception, one considers it being economical with the truth.

—Phillippa, the Dowager Marchioness of Somerset

June 1817

"WHAT THE DEVIL DO YOU THINK YOU'RE DOING?" Richard Barrett demanded as he climbed down from the hired carriage. He pushed open the garden gate and thundered up the overgrown walk.

The young woman wielding a pair of shears was annihilating a runaway rosebush with evidence of malice aforethought. Prickly cuttings spilled from the basket at her booted feet. Peeping from under the broad brim of her straw bonnet, the girl glanced over her shoulder at Richard and then turned back to her pruning.

Without a word! Richard was usually benevolently neglectful where servants were concerned, not bothering to notice them most of the time. But he certainly wasn't used to *them* ignoring *him.*

His friend Lawrence Seymour ambled after him, hands in his pockets, whistling tunelessly. Lawrence was only along on this trip for moral support. If Richard wanted to dally on his way home to Somerfield Park with an unscheduled stop at Barrett House, he knew Seymour wasn't one to complain.

Dallying was one of the things Seymour did best.

"I said," Richard spat through clenched teeth, "what are you doing?"

"What's it look like?" she muttered. "Writing a book?"

If she knew who he was, she'd never be so disrespectful. Richard was about to give her a blistering dressing down when she looked up and held his gaze with a pair of astoundingly blue eyes.

"Do forgive me," she said in a slightly more conciliatory but not at all deferential tone. "I simply despise being interrupted when I'm working on something."

Her voice was low and strangely musical, with an unusual lilt he couldn't identify. She certainly didn't sound like one of the local girls who went into service on his father's estate. But then she ruined her quasi-apology.

"In case you're not as bright as you look," she explained, "I'm trying to undo years of neglect."

Richard bit back the smoldering set down she deserved. If he were honest, he'd have to admit the irritation he felt didn't have anything to do with roses or cheeky gardeners. His life had been upturned by a letter, and the changes it portended set his teeth on edge.

"In case *you're* not as bright as you look," he said, "may I point out that you're cutting the bush back too far?"

Ordinarily, he wouldn't care, but Richard's grandmother, whom he adored, had planted that bush, or at least had ordered it planted—the dowager marchioness might arrange cut blossoms in crystal vases, but she drew the line at any activity which involved perspiration.

"You're going to kill it," he warned.

"Perhaps." The young woman shrugged and tucked away the straggling lock of dark hair that had escaped her bonnet. "But at least it won't be sending bloomless shoots up the drain pipe any longer. If it lives, it'll be loaded with blossoms later in the season."

But Lady Antonia and her family were coming *sooner* in the season. Richard ran an appraising gaze over Barrett House as if he were seeing it for the first time. The two-story house was usually reserved for pensioners who retired from Somerfield Park's service. It used to be the dower house on the estate. Richard's grandmother had ordered a much more opulent residence built for herself when it came time for her to occupy Barrett House. Still, by most lights, the place was considered quite charming.

At least, it used to be charming.

The roses weren't the only things crying for attention. Though Richard had met his family at their town house in London fairly often, several years had passed since he'd been to their countryseat. While he'd grown to manhood, finished his education at

Oxford, and gone on an extended Grand Tour of the Continent, Barrett House had crumbled. More than a few slates were missing from the roof, and the listing chimney was in serious need of repointing. The heavy front door, once a deep bottle green, had faded to the shade of old grass clippings.

Surely the butler who looked after Barrett House could explain its state of decay. "Where's Porter?"

The young woman continued to brutalize the bush, snipping away with abandon. "I have no idea."

"Well, don't just stand there, girl. Run and fetch him."

She stopped at that and turned to face him, shears still held in her gloved hand.

A bit menacingly, Richard thought.

There was a smudge of dirt on her cheek, but it was a lovely cheek nevertheless, with a soft hollow beneath the bone. Richard usually considered that feature the mark of a beauty who would age well. However, her expression was far from lovely. Her dark brows lowered over those disconcertingly blue eyes.

"Of the two of us, only one is being useful at the moment," she said as if she were his equal. "Since you're the one who wishes to speak to Mr. Porter, I suggest *you* run and fetch him."

"Who the dickens do you think you are?" he demanded.

"I don't merely *think*," she said with a withering glare. "I *know* who I am, my lord. For all your fine trappings, can you say the same?"

He was Richard Barrett, Lord Hartley by courtesy, since it was one of his father's lesser titles. As son and heir to the Marquess of Somerset, he was a heartbeat away from being a peer of the realm, by God. No dirty-cheeked chit was going to speak to him so. But Richard was saved from sacking her on the spot by the arrival of Mr. Porter, who bustled out the green door.

With his nervous energy and high tenor voice, Porter reminded Richard of an overgrown cricket, his arms and legs slightly bowed, yet still longer than they needed to be. His wiry, gray eyebrows waved like myriad antennae above pale eyes. Porter rubbed his hands together and hurried down the front steps.

"Ah, Lord Hartley, you'll have had news of the sad event then."

"Only the barest information." Richard had been in Paris when word of his father's accident reached him. His mother's cryptic letter pleaded for him to come home and take up the reins of the estate during his father's incapacity. "I gather Lord Somerset isn't improved."

"Oh, it'd be a wise man as knows that. He keeps to his chambers most days, I understand, but welcome home in any case, your lordship," Porter rattled on. "Er…ahem, I don't mean welcome exactly. Not under these circumstances. But it is ever so good to see you, my lord. And you too, sir, Mr. Seymour, isn't it?"

Porter bowed politely to Lawrence. Despite his resemblance to a humble insect, the butler had a prodigious memory and could call every visitor who'd ever darkened Barrett House's door by name—probably knew where to find them listed in *Debrett's Peerage* too. "Would you care for tea before you go up to Somerfield Park?"

"Don't bother," Richard said. "We'll have something at the inn."

Stopping in the village of Somerset-on-the-Sea was a stalling tactic. Between slow mail and a delayed Channel crossing due to dicey spring weather, it had been a full month since Lord Somerset's accident. Another hour or so could hardly make a difference. Besides, none of the changes in Richard's world would seem real until he set foot in Somerfield Park.

And he wasn't ready for them to be real.

"See that Barrett House has a proper turn out, will you?" Richard said. "I'm expecting guests, and I want the entire estate shown in its best light."

Mr. Porter blinked slowly at this. "You mean to entertain, your lordship?"

"No, of course not." It would be the height of disrespect to his father to host a house party when Somerfield Park was in crisis over Lord Somerset's condition. "The people I'm expecting are more like family. Or at least, I expect they will be. It's the lady I plan to marry, along with her parents."

Porter glanced at the young woman with the shears and relaxed visibly. "Oh, well, in that case, I should inform you that—"

"Lord Hartley," the girl interrupted, "despite our disagreement over how to trim roses, allow me to tell you how distressed I am over your father's unfortunate accident."

Her manners might be missing, but her somber expression declared her words sincere and surprisingly well-spoken for a gardener. Then she picked up the basket and, with a beguiling swish of skirts, breezed into Barrett House through the faded front door.

Richard stared after her with consternation. Despite

her smudged prettiness, she was proof that the quality of the help at Barrett House had deteriorated along with the property.

"Off you go too, Porter," Richard said. "And tell that girl to mind her tongue and use the back door from now on if she wants to keep her position."

Porter's eyes bugged out a bit at that, but he scurried away to do Richard's bidding.

"If she loses her position here, I can think of a few I'd like to see her in," Lawrence drawled. "Nothing wrong with that little gardener that a bath wouldn't fix. Come to think of it, a bath is something I'd enjoy assisting her with immensely."

"Stow your gab, Seymour," Richard said. "There's enough on my plate without having to fret about you despoiling the help."

"The help? No need to worry on that score. I seem to recall you have three nubile sisters at home."

Richard punched Seymour's shoulder as they climbed back into the carriage. "Meddling with my sisters is a serious offense. I'd have to borrow that tasty little gardener's shears and apply them directly to your manhood."

"Ouch." Seymour winced and then cocked his head at Richard. "Tasty little gardener, eh? The way you've been doting on the angelic Lady Antonia of late, I didn't think you'd notice a lesser mortal."

"I'm planning to marry, not enter a monastery."

Richard barked an order to the driver, and they rattled down the road toward Somerset-on-the-Sea and the one and only inn in the village. Even though Richard hadn't been home in years, he was very like his father. Many of the residents seemed to recognize him as the carriage rumbled past. The men doffed their caps in respect. The women dropped quick curtsies.

Richard had expected to have another couple decades with his father at the helm of the Somerset marquessate. Now that Lord Somerset was unable to perform his duties, Richard's carefree days were gone. These were *his* people. His responsibility. Every soul in the village, every crofter on the surrounding farms, even the vicar and sexton in the local church were beholden to the Somerset estate for their livelihood in one way or another.

The invisible weight on Richard's shoulders grew heavier with each turn of the carriage wheel.

☙

Millicent Goodnight let the parted curtain fall together and skittered away from the front window of Barrett House lest her daughter accuse her of eavesdropping on her conversation with that surprisingly good-looking young man. Sophie handed off the basket of clippings to a waiting servant and sank onto the slightly threadbare settee before the fireplace.

Chin resting in her hand, Sophie sighed.

Any other mother might suspect her daughter had fallen head-over-giddy-heels with such a present-able fellow after even so short an acquaintance. But Millicent knew Sophie.

The sigh meant she was bored.

It's my own fault, Millicent decided. She should have come home as soon as Sophie was born, but she couldn't bear to leave her husband, Henry, in India. After allowing the girl to grow up wild as a mongoose in the bustle of Bombay, amid exotic temples and petty princes' decadent courts, Millicent supposed the British countryside seemed pretty bland to her daughter.

"Good heavens, child, don't keep me on pins. Was that him?"

"It was," Sophie said.

"He's quite striking, isn't he?"

That was an understatement. His hair was the color of dark honey, but there was nothing sweet about Lord Hartley. Tall, broad-shouldered, and raw-boned, he was blessed with masculine symmetry in his strong features and dark, deep-set eyes that hinted at an even darker sensuality behind them. He was bound to turn feminine heads everywhere he went.

Though Millicent was intensely devoted to her husband of some thirty years, even her heart had skipped a beat over Lord Hartley's handsome face. She fanned herself quickly and hoped Sophie attributed it to the frequent flashes of heat that plagued her now. "I knew Lord Somerset's heir was young, but I didn't expect he'd be nearly so—"

"So rude," her daughter finished. "He didn't say a single civil word to me."

"Well, when you go about dressed like a charwoman, what do you expect?"

"Forgive me, Mother. Next time I feel like gardening, I'll be sure to wear my pearls." Sophie rolled her eyes. "A gentleman's courtesy shouldn't be dependent upon my wardrobe."

"But it is, dearest. When will you accept that the world sees people for the way they present themselves?"

"There may be something to what you say,

Mother. Lord Hartley presented himself just as I suspected he would—as a spoiled, self-important..." Sophie paused and Millicent could almost see steam coming from her daughter's ears. "He's probably the most horrible rake too. After anything in skirts. Titled fellows usually are, I've heard."

"Sophie!" Where had she heard such things? Mrs. Goodnight decided to take another tack. "Granted, this wasn't the most auspicious of meetings, but surely you can find *something* good to say about the man."

"He seems terribly...English."

"Well, of course he does." If that wasn't damning Lord Hartley with faint praise, she didn't know what was. "Because he is English, and so are you."

"No, I'm not. I don't belong here, Mother. I can't fit into these ridiculous column dresses. Do you know I can't even stretch to my full stride when I go walking in that blasted blue thing?"

"Language, dear. Restrain yourself."

"If only you knew how much I *am* restraining myself." Sophie snorted. "I can't fit my mind into the narrow rules of this place. I shall run to madness if I try."

Millicent sighed. It really was her fault. She should have guarded Sophie's attachments more closely as she was growing up in India. She ought not to have allowed her to mingle with so many people of different backgrounds. It had given her queer notions.

Millicent glanced at the ormolu clock on the mantel. She wished again that Henry hadn't insisted that they stay at Barrett House instead of in guest rooms at Somerfield Park. The pensioners' house was sitting empty, he'd argued, and they had much more privacy than if they'd taken up residence at the big house. Millicent would have traded her privacy all day to live in such a grand place as Somerfield Park, but her husband assured her that it wasn't good business to spend too much time with those with whom one is attempting to negotiate. "It's not too early for you to bathe and dress for dinner. Everything must be perfect this evening. If you would be taken for a lady, you must dress the part."

"And have a father with deep pockets," Sophie said tartly as she rose from the settee and stomped off to her room. "That seems to be counted a lady's best feature in this benighted country."

❧

Mr. Porter had already ordered the proper turn out Lord Hartley demanded, and the thorough airing of Barrett House had begun days ago. Fortunately, the inside of the place was in better shape than the outside. Of course, the patches of damp rot would take some carpentry and fresh paint to fix, but there was time for that. Now that the heir was back, things would turn around.

They simply had to.

Porter set off for Somerfield Park, trotting up the long lane leading out of the village as fast as his bowed legs would carry him. Chest heaving, he burst into the grand manor's kitchen with the news that Lord Hartley was taking tea at the village inn and would likely be home in less than an hour.

"Well, who don't know that?" Mrs. Culpepper didn't look up from the pot of stew she was stirring. "The kitchen boy from the Hound and Hare beat ye here by a good five minutes. Careful with that hen, Eliza," she said to the girl who dipped a freshly killed chicken into a pot of boiling water to loosen the feathers. "That has to stretch for supper for all of us below stairs, mind. Won't do to have ye dropping it on the floor. That'd put Himself on a right proper tear and no mistake."

"But does Himself—" Porter stopped and cleared this throat. It irked him that Mrs. Culpepper bestowed the honorific of "Himself" on Mr. Hightower. The fellow was the butler at Somerfield Park, not God Almighty. Porter was a butler too, albeit in a much smaller household, but no one ever called him "Himself." "I mean, does *Mr. Hightower*—"

"He's alerted the Family to the news and is assembling the staff in the great hall as we speak. There's not much we can count on in this world, but one thing certain is that Himself will see everything done good and proper." The cook wiped her hands on her apron and turned a kindly eye toward him. "Have ye had tea yet, Mr. Porter?"

"No, Mrs. Culpepper, that I haven't."

"Well, then, sit ye down and I'll sort ye out."

Porter watched as the round woman sliced bread and set out jams and a pot of clotted cream for him. While he sipped the aromatic blend and thanked her, he was pleasantly mindful that the *Mrs.* before Mrs. Culpepper's name was only a formality. There wasn't now, nor had there ever been, a *Mr.* Culpepper.

Not that Porter was likely to ratchet up his courage to do anything about it, of course, but still… It was enjoyable to contemplate such things while a man ate a woman's bread and drank her tea.

❧

As the carriage approached, the last rays of sunlight glinted off the upper windows of Somerfield Park. If Richard half closed his eyes, the four-story Georgian manor seemed to twinkle like a jewel on its green, velvet lawn.

"There they are," he said, "spilling out of Somerfield like bees from an upturned hive."

It was tradition. When one of the family had been gone for an extended period of time, everyone came out to greet them. In deep blue Somerset livery, the servants lined up on the right side of the big double doors.

Richard frowned. There seemed to be less than half the usual number.

"Something amiss?" Seymour asked.

"No. It's fine. Everything will be all right." If it wasn't, he'd have to make it so. And pretty quickly too. After all, Antonia and her family would be there tomorrow, and he needed to put his best foot forward.

Only three figures assembled to the left side of the door.

"One of my sisters seems to be absent. Probably Petra," Richard said. "We never could keep her out of the haymow. She'd hide there from her governess all day, squirreled away with a few apples and a book."

"A book? What a waste of a perfectly good haymow," Seymour said dryly. "Perhaps someone should show Lady Petra what a roll in the hay is like *sans* reading material."

Richard skewered his friend with a glare. "I wasn't joking about those shears."

Two

Secrets are the most delicious morsels, but only when one is gobbling them up. Keeping them down often gives one the most frightful indigestion.

—Phillippa, the Dowager Marchioness of Somerset

"Stand up straight, David," Mr. Hightower said under his breath while the son of the house climbed down from the carriage to greet his mother and sisters.

Two of his sisters, at least, David thought.

David Abbot resisted the urge to shift his weight from one foot to the other. Someone was going to catch it because Lady Petra had gone missing again. He was bound and determined it wasn't going to be him this time.

Like the military man he'd once been, Mr. Hightower ordered in a rough whisper, "Eyes straight ahead."

David straightened his spine and tried to watch from the corner of his eye as Lord Hartley leaned to kiss his mother's cheek. Her chin quivered, but she didn't dissolve into tears of joy over the return of her firstborn.

The Barretts weren't that sort of family. There was no excess, no superfluous displays of affection.

Lord Hartley's sisters were only a little more demonstrative. Lady Ella, the eldest and acknowledged blond beauty of the bunch, returned her brother's kiss on the cheek. The youngest, Lady Ariel, gave him a grin and a quick hug. But on the whole, the Barretts were like a flock of swans on the trout pond, long necks dipping in unison, moving in unhurried concert.

Nothing disturbed the tranquility and dignity of the Somerset name.

It was so different from David's distant memories of his own mother and her wild swings between tender overindulgence and foxed neglect. He gave himself a brisk shake and tucked the past back into the deepest corner of his mind. In many ways, his real life had begun when he came to Somerfield at the age of six to serve as his lordship's bootblack boy. Now some twenty-odd years later, David had worked his way up through the below stairs ranks to become a footman.

Not bad for a boy of no background from Brighton.

"It's so good to have you home, Hart," Lady Somerset was saying. "At last."

The big double doors carved with the marquessate's coat of arms opened behind them. David heard the squeak of a wheelchair, but on pain of another censure from Mr. Hightower, he didn't turn to look. Instead, a tingle of apprehension danced down his spine.

"Mr. Witherspoon," Lord Hartley said. "I expected

to see the doctor wheeling my father around, not his man of business."

"We have much to discuss, my lord," Mr. Witherspoon said. "And unfortunately, it cannot wait."

David's belly tightened at that. Every day for the last month, he'd all but tiptoed around the great house. At any moment, he expected his lordship to recover well enough to tell someone what *really* happened the day he fell off the roof.

With a sick taste in his mouth, David wondered would happen to a boy from Brighton then.

❦

"But what was Father doing on the roof in the first place?" Richard had been steered into the parlor by his mother and Mr. Witherspoon so they could talk without the household looking on. His father was there as well, but the marquess hadn't contributed a thing to the conversation. Richard poured a jigger of Scotch for himself and offered one to Mr. Witherspoon. The man of business declined with a shake of his head.

So, this is definitely not a social call.

"Oh, you know how your father is," Lady Somerset said. "He loves to look at the sea from the parapet."

"But the leaves are out now. The ocean is only visible from Somerfield Park during winter, when the trees are bare."

Lord Somerset smiled vacantly at him. Then he gazed down at his hands in his lap, examining the signet ring on his forefinger as if he'd never seen it before.

Richard's chest constricted and he was forced to look away. "What does Dr. Partridge say?"

"He's frankly baffled," Lady Somerset said. "The doctor believes that your father's faculties may return. He may even walk again someday, but we have no way of knowing when. Dr. Partridge says we're to count ourselves fortunate your father survived the fall. He's at a loss to explain how he lived through it."

"Oh, I can tell you that. He was saved by good gardening."

Richard turned at the sound of his beloved grandmother's voice. Phillippa, the dowager marchioness, appeared at the doorway dressed in a rich gown at least twenty years out of date, with a rope of gray pearls at her wattled throat. She advanced into the parlor, her back ramrod straight, leaning only slightly on her ivory-headed cane. To the rest of the world, she was the indomitable dowager, but to Richard she was just plain Gran.

"Your father tumbled directly onto my lilac bush, the simply enormous one at the southeast corner of the house. It cushioned his fall." Gran sank into a tufted wing chair as gracefully as her years allowed. "My son was spared. The lilacs, however, will never be the same. Isn't it a mercy that I didn't leave the thorny old gorse bush in that spot? Now don't just stand there, Richard. Come and give us a kiss. And bring me a whisky while you're about it."

Richard was quick to obey. "Gran, your charm hasn't dulled one whit."

"Perhaps not, but my joints aren't at all what they used to be." She presented her papery cheek for him to kiss, took a quick sip of the amber liquor, and sighed. "Well, Mr. Witherspoon, have you told him yet?"

"There's more?" Richard's stomach swirled

downward. It was the same sinking feeling he used to get before an exam for which he had not studied.

In measured tones, Mr. Witherspoon gave a chilling account of the estate's finances.

"I don't understand." Richard paced the room, nervous energy crackling from him. His father had never failed to send sufficient funds while Richard was larking about the Continent with Seymour. There was never any hint of this kind of trouble. "How can the money be gone?"

Mr. Witherspoon spread his hands. "An unfortunate set of circumstances. As you know, we had hardly any summer last year, due to that volcanic eruption in the South Sea Islands. The ash cloud affected the climate worldwide, I collect."

"Pity those islanders couldn't keep their ash in their own hemisphere. Beastly of them to spread the misery around," the dowager said with a sniff.

"My lady," Witherspoon said, "they can hardly be blamed for that."

"Whyever not? Do we trouble them when we have more rain than expected?" The elder Lady Somerset banged the tip of her cane on the floor. "Indeed we do not. We slip on our Wellingtons and keep the mud to ourselves."

Witherspoon's mouth opened and closed a few times, but he couldn't seem to find an answer for the dowager. He turned back to Richard. "At any rate, it actually snowed in July here. Crops failed. Lord Somerset's tenants couldn't pay even a fraction of the rents owed."

"But none of them were evicted, surely," Richard said.

"Of course not," his mother put in. "We've always had a partnership with the families who farm the estate's lands. Some of them have been here for generations."

"So your father decided to take what funds he held in reserve and invest in a whaling vessel. I advised against it, of course. Any maritime venture, of necessity, involves risk," Mr. Witherspoon explained. "But if the ship had come in loaded with ambergris and oil, the Somerset balance sheet would have been the envy of the *ton* for soundness."

"Unfortunately, the *Betsy Ross* had the poor grace to sink off Nova Scotia in a squall." Gran held up her glass in an unspoken request for another drink. "*Betsy Ross*, indeed. Should have known we couldn't trust a Yank."

"Nature and Americans, it seems, conspire against us." Richard refilled his grandmother's jigger, watering the whisky this time. "What's been done?"

"We adopted alternative financing in order to help the tenants with the planting this year and keep up with other expenses. The estate is mortgaged to the rafters. So far, the crops look only fair. Even if the harvest is moderately acceptable, we will still be in dun territory and unable to meet our obligations next fall."

"Intolerable." The idea of being indebted and unable to pay was as abhorrent to Richard as contracting a case of the French pox. "Surely there must be some way of restructuring the debt."

"There isn't," Witherspoon said. "If we don't have an immediate infusion of cash, your creditors will be flocking to Somerfield Park within a couple of weeks to make an inventory of the artwork, the furnishings, your mother's jewelry…"

Lady Somerset made a small noise, a cross between a sob and a squeak. "It sounds as if not even the silver service is safe."

Witherspoon nodded grimly.

She dabbed at the corners of her eyes with a lacy handkerchief. "Are we to be reduced to eating with our fingers?"

"Well, my dear, they *were* made before forks." A second whisky on an empty stomach always made Gran uncharacteristically agreeable.

Hands fisted at his waist, Richard stood at the window. The grounds of Somerfield Park stretched to the forest on the horizon, spring green and fresh in the deepening twilight. For generations, his family had claimed this land. They'd carved it out of nothing during the time of the Conqueror. They'd held it through the vagaries of despotic kings and warring factions. The original castle had crumbled, and the current manor house was raised up, but no matter what, there had always been a Lord Somerset tramping over the meadows, hunting in the woods, and keeping watch to the east when the trees were bare and the sea foamed in angry gray swells.

He couldn't lose Somerfield Park.

"There must be an asset we haven't tapped yet."

"Actually, there is," Mr. Witherspoon said. "It's you, your lordship."

"Me?"

"Your name, your title, your"—Witherspoon slipped a finger into his tight collar and gave it a tug before he continued—"your troth."

"Now, wait a moment. Are you suggesting—"

"That you marry well. Exceedingly well. Yes, my

lord," Witherspoon said. "I'm not only suggesting it. I'm telling you it's the only thing that will answer."

In silence, Richard's father sat in his wheelchair, running the tasseled ends of the lap rug through his fingers. No help would come from that quarter. Richard turned to his mother.

"My affections are already engaged," he said. "I very nearly proposed to Lady Antonia Pruett in Paris."

"How nearly?" Gran asked before his mother could reply.

"I asked for and received her father's permission."

"But you have not asked her, and even if her father unwisely told her of your intentions, she'll have to consider them revoked," Gran said sternly. "Lord Pruett will not be able to produce a sizeable enough dowry for our purposes. He's always been a wastrel, flush from winnings at the poque table one week, poor as a church mouse the next. You must write her this evening and cry off."

"I wouldn't know where to send the letter," Richard said. "She'll be here tomorrow, you see. I invited her and her parents to come stay."

"But we have already—" His mother clapped a hand over her mouth.

"You recall I mentioned alternative financing," Mr. Witherspoon said. "The gentleman from whom we borrowed funds to keep going is in residence at Barrett House now, along with his family."

"I take it you use the word *gentleman* loosely."

Witherspoon nodded sheepishly.

"Who is he?" Richard asked.

"Mr. Henry Goodnight."

"A commoner?"

"Yes, but he's possessed of an absolute pasha's ransom in cash," Gran said, lifting her empty jigger again.

Richard decided to ignore it.

"Please," his mother said to Gran, "there's no need to be vulgar."

"Oh, my dear, if we expect our darling Richard to marry a fortune with feet, we are well past the point of vulgarity and might as well accept it." Gran stood and went for the whisky herself. "Remember the family motto: *Frangas non flectes.*"

"'Thou may break but shall not bend me'? The motto doesn't fit this situation." Richard raked a hand through his hair in frustration. "You're expecting me to do plenty of bending."

The dowager waved his objection away. "Oh, well, it was a stupid motto in any case, picked by one of the bloodthirsty barbarians in our past. Pay it no heed." She downed her third shot. "Perhaps it won't seem so bad if we think of this course of action as adventurous instead of desperate."

"I'd rather we didn't think of it at all." Richard all but growled. How dare they plot to part him from Antonia? "What do we know about this Mr. Goodnight, aside from the condition of his pockets?"

"At present, that is all that need concern us." Mr. Witherspoon pressed doggedly on. "He was with the East India Company for most of his adult life, where he made an incredible fortune."

"How nice for him."

"For us as well, I should think," Gran said as she returned to her comfortable chair with only a slight wobble in her step. "He has a daughter of marriageable age."

"Of course he does." The noose of family responsi-bility tightened around him. Richard plopped into the seat opposite his grandmother.

"An *only* daughter and no sons. Which means however untutored the young woman in question may be, she is well gilded. That compensates for a great deal in our present circumstances." Gran stifled a soft belch from too much whisky in too short a time, though she'd deny to her last breath that a dowager marchioness was capable of such a thing. "Raw gold is still gold. We can work on polishing her up later."

Richard spared the nameless heir to the Goodnight fortune a moment of pity. Being polished by his grandmother was not a fate he'd wish on anyone. He leaned forward, balancing his elbows on his knees and holding his head in his hands.

"All this talk of money is so distressing," Richard's mother said. "And it's tiring your father as well."

She rang the bell pull for Lord Somerset's valet, Mr. Cope. He and the footman David appeared to carry the marquess's chair up to his chamber on the second story. "Put his lordship to bed, Mr. Cope. He needs rest if he's to meet our guests for dinner tonight."

Richard looked up at his mother. "Guests?"

"Yes, dear, the Goodnights are coming to dine."

"And while we dine, chew on this," Gran said. "Your family is depending upon you, Richard. Think of your sisters. Think what parceling out Somerfield Park will mean when you try to arrange matches for them. For that matter, think what it will mean to me. Without my portion from the estate, I doubt I'll be able to keep Somerset Steading."

Somerset Steading was the current dower house. It was large and ornate enough to serve as the main manor on most estates. No doubt it took at great deal to keep his grandmother in the style to which she was accustomed. At her age, she wasn't likely to settle for less with good grace, and heaven knew his mother wouldn't welcome having her mother-in-law move in with the rest of the family if any another option were available.

"And the folk of the village and your tenants. Don't forget them, my lord," Mr. Witherspoon said.

His mother put a hand to his cheek. "Don't feel you need to do anything immediately, son. Just meet the young lady. You know I would never allow you to be forced into something you don't feel is right."

Richard was tempted to abandon hope. Nothing would ever feel right again. How could he betray Antonia—his beautiful, laughing Antonia?

On the other hand, how could he let Somerfield Park wither and die? Or worse, be chopped up by creditors as ruthlessly as that girl at Barrett House had chopped up the roses?

He was coming home to a disaster of biblical proportions. And he hadn't even met the grasping commoner his parents expected him to sell himself to yet.

❧

As soon as the footman left his dressing room, Hugh Barrett, the Marquess of Somerset, threw off the lap rug and stood, stretching hugely. "Put that wretched chair in the corner, Cope," he told his valet. "It sickens me to look at it."

His wife slipped into the room, taking care not to open the door wider than necessary, lest someone chance by and see that a "miracle" had occurred and the marquess was on his feet.

"You must keep your voice down," she hissed at him and then turned to his valet. "Mr. Cope, does anyone else suspect?"

"No, milady. Not even Mr. Hightower knows his lordship is recovered."

"Well, I daresay, that *is* quite a coup. Mr. Hightower knows if a mouse hiccups in the stable. Keep up the good work, Mr. Cope," she said briskly. "That'll be all until it's time for his lordship to dress for dinner."

The valet gave them each a quick bow and slipped out of the room as carefully as Lady Somerset had slipped in.

"Are you sure this is necessary, Helen?" the marquess said.

"It was your mother's idea, remember. Hart is so stubborn. She didn't believe our son would come around to our way of thinking if he wasn't made to feel the weight of things. So long as you're holding the reins of the estate, he's not responsible."

"I suppose I'm fortunate that *Maman* didn't suggest I abdicate in a more permanent manner." Hugh slipped off his shoes and paced the floor, taking care not to tread too loudly. He was used to being an active man and made use of the time he was alone to exercise as much as he could. "Pretending to a debility is one thing. Pretending to my death would have been quite insupportable."

Helen chuckled. "I suspect it didn't occur to her

after your accident, or she might have recommended it. The dowager is difficult to turn once she gets an idea in her head. I suppose that's where Hartley gets his stubbornness. But I think she's right this time."

"There's an astonishing admission." He drew her into his arms. Helen's waist was a little thicker than it had been when he first married her, but she'd given him four healthy children and still fit wonderfully into his embrace. "You and she are usually at loggerheads. I thought the best I could hope for was an armed truce."

"We're allies in this. For good or ill, Hartley must marry Miss Goodnight, and this is the best way to help him see that he must."

"So in the grand scheme of things, my falling off the roof was a bit of good fortune."

"Bite your tongue."

"I'd rather you did." He claimed her mouth with a kiss full of passion despite years of practice. Helen still lit a fire in his belly. Just looking at his wife made him feel pleasurably male.

Hugh had been insensible for two days after his fall, and even now he couldn't remember exactly how the accident had happened. Someone else had been on the roof with him. Perhaps two someones. He was nearly certain of it, but for the life of him, he couldn't see their faces clearly in his hazy recollections. His memory of earlier times in his life was riddled with holes as well. He hoped it would all come back to him eventually. It was important that it did. Nothing was worse than a marquess who didn't have full command of himself and his own mind.

A mad king was enough for England to bear without a lunatic lord thrown in for good measure.

"So," he said when he broke off their kiss, "how long do you think I'll have to keep up this charade?"

"You may safely plan on dancing at our son's wedding, but not before."

"That long?" He fiddled with the buttons marching down the bodice of her day gown. "How about if you and I do a horizontal waltz before dinner, so I can keep in practice?"

Her brown eyes glowed warmly at him, and her lips parted in that sensual smile he loved so well. "You have one hour till the dressing gong sounds and not a minute more."

"Madam, I shall try mightily not to take a minute less."

Three

Oh, the horrible importance of first impressions. It sets the tone for all future discourse. Try as one might, it is devilishly difficult to undo that initial effect.

—Phillippa, the Dowager Marchioness of Somerset

"CHEER UP, OLD SON." LAWRENCE SEYMOUR FELL INTO step with Hartley as they trudged down the grand staircase. "If I were set to marry a great heiress, I'd try not to meet her for the first time with such a Friday face."

Hartley adjusted his cuffs and flexed his fingers. "That's just it. I'm not set to marry this girl. I'm being forced to it."

"No one is holding a pistol to your head."

"No, they're holding something much more lethal—my conscience. They think they've arranged matters so that I can't say no. In truth, I don't know which way to turn. If I say yes to the Goodnight chit, I lose Antonia. If I say yes to my love, I lose Somerfield

Park. Either way, I lose everything that means anything in my life."

Lawrence thought Hartley was being a bit melodramatic, but he didn't see a good way out either. However, when a man is faced with no other choice, he might as well look for the strawberry in the situation.

And a wife with a dowry large enough to fund a small country was one delectable strawberry.

"You're thinking about marriage all wrong. For a woman, it's different. It *is* everything," Lawrence explained. "To a man, marriage is merely a part of his life, as large or as small a part as he chooses to make it."

Hartley shoved his hands into his trouser pockets. He might fool most people with his show of outward calm, but Lawrence knew him well enough to recognize barely contained frustration simmering in his friend.

Too much restraint was bad for digestion. Lawrence thought his friend would benefit from taking up pugilism to relieve the pressure of his tightly controlled temper. Punching his fist through a plaster wall might be hard on the house, but the release might help Hartley out of all knowing.

"Perhaps I'd feel differently if my parents' marriage wasn't a love match," Richard said. "I've seen what it can be. And I'm not ready to settle for half measures."

"Are telling me Lady Antonia is your love match?"

Hartley nodded.

"That puts you in a very slim minority, you know. Most of us wouldn't recognize our true love if she bit us on the bum." Lawrence chuckled. "Though a lady would get my undivided attention that way, I assure you."

"This is serious, Seymour."

"Well then, seriously, here's some advice from one who believes in love as much as he believes in faeries. A man marries to get an heir, more lofty connections, or—let me see if I remember your grandmother's words as you relayed them to me—for 'a pasha's ransom in cash.' Love doesn't signify in the slightest."

"But what about Antonia?"

"What about her? As a wise man once said, you intend to marry, not enter a monastery," Lawrence said. "With your new wife's wealth, you can set up Lady Antonia in a snug little love nest on the side."

Hartley glowered at him. "I'll try to forget you said that."

"But I predict you won't. The delicious seed will take root in your imagination and blossom at a later date. You may thank me then."

They stopped on the landing as a party entered the foyer below and was announced by Mr. Hightower in stentorian tones.

"Mr. and Mrs. Henry Goodnight."

If the butler, who was a stickler for observing the rules of precedence, felt any unease at announcing a couple whose blood was no bluer than his own, he gave no outward indication.

Mrs. Goodnight was a handsome woman with fine-boned features and a necklace of glittering emeralds above her modest décolletage. Judging by dress alone, she might have been a duchess, but Richard had met his share of duchesses. This woman's smile was too sweet, and she was too quick to drop a deep curtsy to Lord and Lady Somerset, who waited at the foot of the grand staircase to welcome them. Or rather Lady Somerset did. Slumped in his wheelchair, Richard's father was once again fascinated by his own signet ring.

If Mrs. Goodnight displayed the marks of graceful maturity, then Mr. Goodnight, on the other hand, showed signs of deteriorating health. His skin had a waxy pallor, and the whites of his eyes were yellowed. But he when he turned to the young woman who followed them into the foyer his face lit with a proud smile.

"And Miss Sophie Goodnight," Mr. Hightower finished, his voice reverberating through the imposing foyer, whose ceiling soared up to the flying buttresses that supported the roof skylights.

The young lady pushed back the lace-trimmed hood of her pink pelisse, revealing a head of dark hair twinkling with gem-encrusted pins. When she removed her pelisse and handed it to Mr. Hightower, Richard saw that her matching gown was cut to bare her shoulders. Her skin was flawless in the light of the candelabra suspended from the distant ceiling. As if she felt his eyes on her, her blue-eyed gaze traveled up the stairs to where Richard stood transfixed.

"I say, isn't that the tasty little gardener?" Seymour whispered.

Richard nodded grimly.

"What did I tell you?" Lawrence said out of the corner of his mouth. "Nothing wrong with her that a bath wouldn't fix."

"Yes, there is." Richard forced himself to start down the stairs. *She's not Antonia.*

～

Look at him. All lordly and aloof and hardly deigning to glance at me. Sophie wished she were skewering Lord Hartley instead of stabbing her fork into one of the beef medallions on her plate. They were both being coerced into this. The least he could do was acknowledge a fellow sufferer's presence. *Even if my parents weren't trying to force him on me, I'd despise him.*

Mr. Seymour had been mildly diverting during the soup course as he tried to flirt with Lord Hartley's sister, Lady Ella. But Lady Petra kept deflating his remarks by pointing out that her sister's eyes weren't actually the color of bluebells. Anyone could see they were a changeable hazel, and was there something wrong with Seymour's vision that he couldn't tell the difference?

Mr. Seymour confessed to color ignorance and dedicated himself to his plate after that.

Since the marquess was incapacitated and his son seemed disposed to monk-like silence, the ladies were left to carry the conversational ball.

"After all those years in the East, how do you find England, Miss Goodnight?" Lady Ella asked.

"Empty," Sophie fired back.

"Oh." Lady Ella blinked slowly, not sure what to make of Sophie's assessment.

"By 'empty' do you mean lacking in substance, that its society is frivolous and silly?" Lady Petra asked.

Sophie decided this bespectacled Barrett sister might just have a brain in her head. But before she could answer, her mother leaped into the fray.

"What my daughter means is that compared to India, there are far fewer people here. You can't imagine the press in the cities in the East. One can scarcely breathe."

That wasn't what Sophie meant, and her mother knew it.

Dinner limped along, punctuated with uncomfortable silences filled only by the soft clink of silverware on fine china. Lord Hartley's sisters were subdued after that near conversational misstep, even Lady Petra. They discussed the weather, always a safe topic, with dogged determination.

Probably been threatened with the prospect of no new gowns ever again if they put a foot wrong.

Their wardrobe, its care and increase, was the main concern of most English misses, so far as Sophie could see.

"And what about you, Mrs. Goodnight?" the dowager marchioness said to Sophie's mother. "However did you bear living in such an inhospitable place as India?"

Turning the conversation in this direction was another mistake. Sophie's mother was the charitable sort, dedicated to easing the suffering of the downtrodden. Recounting the plight of cholera victims and the squalor of the bazaars was not conducive to pleasant dinner conversation, let alone anyone's appetite.

Then the topic took a decided turn for the worse. Mrs. Goodnight launched into a recitation of her daughter's finer qualities. It was the low point of the evening.

Especially since she didn't deserve a bit of it.

❧

Sophie Goodnight said nothing while her mother praised her. She didn't meet Richard's gaze across the table. And she plainly wasn't enjoying her meal, since she used her fork more to rearrange the food on her plate than to eat any of it.

"And of course, we saw to it that Sophie received a thorough education, despite being so far from England," her mother was saying. "In addition to the usual subjects of study, she's an accomplished artist."

Richard didn't think stacking beef medallions and rearranging asparagus shoots was evidence of an artistic temperament.

"Perhaps she'd like to see the gallery. We have a rather large collection here at Somerfield," his mother said. "Hartley, why don't you take Miss Goodnight to see the portraits after dinner?"

"Why wait?" Richard pushed back his chair. "It's clear Miss Goodnight is finished eating. Shall we?"

She looked up at him, her gaze sharp and inquisitive. There was a hint of gratitude in her eyes as well. In a perverse way, he was comforted by the fact that she seemed as uncomfortable as he.

Richard came around the table and offered her his arm. She stood, rested her gloved fingers on his forearm, and allowed him to lead her from the room. Quite the proper lady when it suited her purpose. After their meeting over his grandmother's roses, he'd not have guessed her capable of such civilized behavior.

Once they cleared the threshold, she dropped her hand but continued to walk at his side.

"Thank you," she finally said. "I was beginning to think that deadly dinner would never end."

His thoughts exactly. "I always try to rescue damsels in distress."

"Oh, I'm not in distress, but it's clear you are. What have they threatened you with to bring you to heel?"

He nearly choked in surprise. The mating dance

done for profit was performed in drawing rooms all over England, but no one ever admitted to it outright. "It would be ungallant of me to say."

She chuckled. "Poor man. Trapped as surely as if your foot were caught by steel, and you're worried about being ungallant."

"Very well. If you insist on brutal honesty, Somerset's coffers are bare and my family looks to me to fill them with your dowry, Miss Goodnight."

"That's better. So long as we don't pretend this association is anything other than what it is. I can abide anything but deceit." She took his arm again and began walking. "You don't need to stand on ceremony with me. I shall call you Richard, and you may call me Sophie."

His grandmother was the only one who called him Richard. Even his mother called him Hartley or Hart. He heard his Christian name so seldom, it almost didn't seem to belong to him anymore. "That's rather intimate for so short an acquaintance."

"Yet not so intimate as our families would have us be." She shook her head and sighed.

A unique scent tickled his nose—attar of roses with a spicy undertone of warm woman. The bodice of her gown was cut low enough to display the rounded tops of her breasts. Nestled in the shadowy hollow between them was cabochon sapphire pendant big enough to choke a horse. It drew his eye to her cleavage and he found himself wondering if her skin was as satiny as it appeared.

If he hadn't met Antonia first, he could have done much worse than Sophie Goodnight.

"Not that you're right, but what is it that makes you think I'm in distress?" he asked.

She lifted one expressive brow. "You have the look of a cornered stag. The hounds have you surrounded, and the hunters are lining up for the kill."

"And I suppose you're the chief hunter?"

"Lud, no. I'm the wily vixen who slips away in the confusion, glad to escape her own hunt till another day."

She doesn't want to marry me.

The astounding thought rattled through his brain. He'd had to fend off countless debutantes who'd set their caps for him during the Season he'd spent in London. Until he met Antonia, he'd walked warily around the young ladies he met on the Continent, not wanting to give them a chance to ensnare him in the parson's mousetrap. Now he was being trussed up and delivered to this one like a gaily wrapped parcel.

And she didn't want him.

He laughed so loudly the help must surely have heard him below stairs.

"What's so funny?" Sophie asked.

"Everything. Nothing." He patted her hand, surprised to feel camaraderie with her over their mutual dislike of the union their families were plotting. "Why are your parents so set on this match?"

"My father has amassed enough riches to buy anything he pleases, yet what he really wants isn't for sale."

"And that would be…"

"A grandson who'll be a titled lord."

Most maidens would blush at the mention of

having a child, but Sophia Goodnight's cheeks didn't pink in the least.

"If you don't want to marry me—"

"Dear me," she interrupted, "do you think there's an *if*? My manner must be far more accommodating than I intend."

He scowled at her. "Then why are you going along with them?"

"Who says I am?" Her eyebrow quirked again. "But if I was, well, you've seen my father. I'm afraid he'll never make old bones—he's given up quite a bit to provide for me and my mother. While we toddled off to enjoy the cool summers of Kashmir, he sweltered in the malaria-ridden cities of the south. It ruined his health, but he never complains. I try not to either, no matter how unpalatable my options."

Unpalatable? She thought him unpalatable? What on earth could she have to complain about in him? Plenty of women would jump at the chance to have him. They'd eat the future Marquess of Somerset up with a spoon.

"As a great heiress," he said through clenched teeth, "surely you could have your pick of suitors."

"You'd think so, but my father is nothing if not diligent in his study of a market, even a marriage market. Of all the great houses under financial duress with an eligible heir, yours is the highest ranking. Why should my father's fortune bring down an ordinary beast when it can bag a trophy stag?"

"Back to the stag metaphor again. Remind me never to go hunting with you." They turned a corner and entered a long, high-ceilinged hall. "Here is the gallery."

Row upon row, his ancestors stared down at them from age-darkened canvases. Some were in medieval dress and suits of armor. There were cavaliers in plumed hats alongside stolid-looking reformers. A few sported the powdered wigs and lace-trimmed cuffs of the past generation.

Sophie peered up at each one, her brows drawn together in concentration. "There are some fine works here."

"There should be. My ancestors believed in hiring the best." Scattered among paintings by lesser-known artists, there were portraits by Holbein the Younger, Van Dyck, Joshua Reynolds, and Gainsborough.

"But none of your progenitors look terribly happy, do they?" Sophie said after she'd walked the full length of the room and back.

"I believe the point of the portraits is to impress the viewer with the power and prestige of the subject, not to give a window to their souls."

"Pity. Since their souls are all that still exist."

"That's not true. Somerfield Park still exists. Everything they bled and worked for is still here."

"And you intend to bleed and work for it too. Dead men's bones and dead men's dreams." She cocked her head, considering him like a kestrel eyeing a field mouse. "I do believe you've never had an original goal in your head."

If she'd been a man, he'd have laid her out for that insult. "Of course I have. You may as well know that my plan right now is to marry another woman, one my parents have not chosen for me."

"Really?" She cast a genuine smile at him then, a

sudden burst of such luminous glory that it nearly took his breath away. "There may be hope for you yet."

Then she spoiled the effect by arching that one brow again.

"But it's only a plan," she said. "I wager you've never actually *done* anything unexpected."

He'd show her. "You lose."

He'd give her unexpected. Richard snatched her close and covered her mouth with his. He meant to shock her, to silence her goading tongue. Now that little pointed tongue of hers was all tangled up with his in a sudden, desperate exploration.

He pinned her to the wall, her spine pressed against the flocked wallpaper next to a rather lugubrious rendering of his grandmother.

Her hands found his hair, raking her fingertips past his temples. She palmed his cheeks and slid her hands down his neck, her touch cool at first, then hot as she smoothed her fingers down his chest and around his waist.

God help him, she made him hard as iron.

Then the kiss changed. Yielded. Her breath poured into him, warm and sweet.

Trusting.

She made a soft sound, as if she were melting, like sugar in a saucepan. The little sigh went straight to his groin.

Then he slanted his mouth over hers, determined to make her sigh again.

Her lips were supple. Giving.

She answered his kiss with longing, with urgency, with a small tremble that he'd give anything to still. But he wasn't able to make her sigh again.

When he finally released her, he had to fight to master his breathing lest she see how deeply she'd affected him.

He was shocked to his soul at what he'd done. He was devoted to Antonia. Besides, no matter how sorely he was provoked, he wasn't the sort to ravish a young lady he'd just met as if she were a common trollop. What had gotten into him?

"Where does a virgin learn to kiss like that?" he whispered.

Sophie Goodnight smiled at him again. She could command angels with that smile, and they'd obey without question. Then she slipped out of his arms and headed for the door. She hesitated at the threshold, turned, and winked at him.

"What makes you think I'm a virgin?"

Four

A hostess always wants her guests to wish a dinner party would never end. However, sometimes the best thing one can say about an evening is that it did, in fact, sputter to a conclusion.

—Phillippa, the Dowager Marchioness of Somerset

ELIZA DOVECOTE HAD SAUNTERED DOWN THE EMPTY gallery. As the kitchen maid, she wasn't allowed in the upstairs portion of the great house except to lay fires in all the hearths during the early morning hours. Even then, she had to scuttle right smart to make sure she wasn't seen by any member of the family.

But Eliza couldn't resist sneaking peeks at the upstairs world when she could. It fair tickled her fancy, with its polished brasses and gleaming hardwoods and ceilings painted with scenes so beautiful she ached to lie on the floor and imagine she could float up into the cherub-filled clouds.

Few people ever entered the gallery. Other than the

maids, who straightened the occasional pillow tucked into side chairs and kept the picture frames and the bust of someone named Cicero free from dust, Eliza often thought she was the only one in Somerfield Park who visited the long row of artwork for pure pleasure.

She lingered over the ornate dresses in the portraits and wondered what the stiff lace had felt like against a lady's neck, or imagined how her insides might go all squishy if a fellow like the one in the hat with the long plume ever gave her a courtly bow.

Eliza was sure she'd faint dead away.

When she'd heard Lord Hartley and that Miss Goodnight approaching, she'd barely managed to scurry away to hunker behind the servant's door. But she'd been careful not to latch it. The chance to be a wee mousey in the corner was too tempting not to take. She couldn't pull away from watching the fine people in the gallery. What she heard and saw shocked her to her curled toes.

What makes you think I'm a virgin?

That was more wicked than Eliza had ever imagined. Miss Goodnight hadn't even blushed.

And such a kiss the scandalous Miss Goodnight and Lord Hartley had shared! Eliza had never been kissed herself, but she'd imagined what it might be like plenty of times. Now she'd have to reinvent her own daydreams to live up to the kiss she'd just witnessed.

Lord Hartley was still in the gallery, staring after Miss Goodnight as if his boots had been nailed to the Turkish carpet. He—

"I say, Eliza." Mr. Hightower's voice made her jump. "What are you doing here?"

She twirled around, leaning back on the hidden door so that its latch caught with a soft snick. "Nothing, Mr. Hightower. Truly, sir. I was just going up to my room to fetch—"

"Never mind that now. It's time for supper. You don't want to keep Mrs. Culpepper waiting." The butler started down to the below stairs common room. "And don't let me catch you loitering on the back staircase again."

"Yes, sir. I mean no, sir. Thank you, sir." She rabbited around him on the narrow steps, anxious to obey. Her mum had been delirious with joy when Eliza was first given a position at Somerfield Park. Mrs. Dovecote would be devastated if her daughter somehow lost it.

Eliza skittered into the kitchen.

"There ye are, girl. Where've ye been? Oh, never mind. Once ye start on a story, it takes forever for ye to finish and won't amount to spit in any case," Mrs. Culpepper said as she filled a tureen with chicken stew that was mostly potatoes with a chicken tracked through it. "Here. Take this into the commons."

Eliza hefted the ornate tureen with a built-in platter beneath it. The piece was fine, with hand-painted curlicues and a bit of gilt here and there. It had been used upstairs, until a clumsy footman chipped one of the porcelain handles.

The tureen was still in service. The footman was not. Mr. Hightower did not suffer mistakes that reflected badly upon the house.

The rest of the Somerfield servants had already gathered around the long table in the common room.

Mr. Hightower had taken his place at the head, with
Mrs. Grahame, the housekeeper, at the foot. Between
them, Mr. Cope, who was Lord Somerset's valet, and
Miss Minerva Gorny, lady's maid to Lady Somerset,
took their seats wherever they had a mind to.

And why shouldn't they? Eliza thought. They were
second only to Mr. Hightower and Mrs. Grahame,
respectively, in below stairs society.

The senior housemaids, Sarah and Drucilla, filed in
and collapsed into a couple of empty places along with
the rest of the housekeeping staff. Sarah was young
and lively, always ready with a smile and a kind word
for Eliza, despite the fact that she was only a kitchen
maid. Drucilla was a thin, pinched sort of woman with
her hair scraped back into a bun so tight Eliza thought
it must give her headaches. Her hair was dusted with
enough gray to show her to be on the downhill slide
of forty. Drucilla was too mindful of other people's
business to have any of her own.

But Sarah and Drucilla worked well together. Not
only did they help clean the great house to within
an inch of its life every day, but between the two of
them, they contrived to serve as lady's maids for Lady
Ella, Lady Petra, and Lady Ariel as well.

"It's a mercy that Lady Ariel is still in the schoolroom,"
Sarah often said. "Don't know as we'd manage elsewise."

Lady Ariel's age, about thirteen as nearly as Eliza could
guess, meant that her governess, a dour-looking stick
of a woman named Miss Constance Bowthorpe, was
responsible for her appearance and deportment most of
the time. As a governess, Miss Bowthorpe was neither
fish nor fowl. She wasn't invited to dine with the family

unless the numbers of the party required another female. Yet she was technically above all the other help and not comfortable eating in the common room.

Or especially welcome there, come to that.

Eliza would take a tray to her room on the second floor after she served the rest of the staff. Miss Bowthorpe's chamber was one level down from the rest of the servants, but not in the same wing as the family.

Mr. Hightower led the gathering in a brief prayer of thanks, his sonorous voice ringing a benediction of blessed stillness. Eliza's life was filled with constant trotting to fetch and carry, and run errands for others. It was restful to stop for even a few moments and let Mr. Hightower's words roll over her.

He should have been a preacher, a voice like that, Eliza thought as she began ladling out the stew, mindful of trying to make it stretch for the entire company.

"What did you make of Miss Goodnight?" Drucilla asked Mr. Hightower.

Wish someone would ask me what I made of her. I'd give them summat what would curl their hair.

Of course, Eliza knew better than to speak before she was spoken to in the common room while the others were dining. She was ever conscious of her place as the servant of servants. It was important to do things correctly if she hoped to get on in the big house. With any luck at all, she'd work up to being a chambermaid soon. She could wear a smart uniform and not have to sneak around upstairs.

"Drucilla, I find the question grossly impertinent," Mr. Hightower said. "It is not our place to comment on the guests of this house."

"Not even if that guest is about to become Lady Hartley," Drucilla muttered.

"That's enough, Dru," Mrs. Grahame said before Mr. Hightower could get up a full head of steam. "We none of us have a window to the future, so let's not be getting ahead of ourselves. The Family invited the Goodnights, so we must show them Somerfield's best face and not fret over what changes may be coming."

"Speaking of changes," Toby Welch, the second footman, said as he breezed in and plopped down next to Sarah. "Since Lord Hartley is back, he'll be needing a valet, Mr. Hightower. Have you decided whether it'll be me or David?"

"I have not yet made my decision," Mr. Hightower said with a frown.

Toby was always pushing himself forward, Eliza thought. But if a chap didn't toot his own horn, who would?

"Better let us know before he's ready to turn in for the night."

Mr. Hightower sent him a frosty glance. "This is not the appropriate venue for that discussion."

Toby's chair must have been a bit too close, because Sarah scooted hers a few inches away.

If Toby Welch sat down next to me, I wouldn't scoot away.

Toby was tall and well favored with light brown hair that glinted with gold and russet highlights. He was handsome after the manner of footmen. They were always the most presentable young men in the house. Eliza had to tear her eyes from him, lest he mark her interest and begin teasing her.

"A kitchen maid shouldn't get above herself," Mrs. Culpepper always said.

But I can't very well get below myself either. There's precious little beneath me, Eliza had thought furiously at the time but didn't say. Sometimes she wondered if unspoken thoughts would build up in her, and someday she'd burst from all the ones she hadn't let escape out her mouth.

Toby helped himself to the bread basket in the center of the table. "Well, either way, it's an advancement for me," he said with good cheer. "If David's made Lord Hartley's valet, that means I'll be first footman, won't I?"

"You'll be the *only* footman, Toby," Sarah said. "There's a difference."

"Well, be that as it may, this was a different sort of dinner party tonight, weren't it? Mr. Goodnight's naught but a glorified shopkeeper. My father runs the dry goods shop in the village," Toby went on with a laugh. "Do you suppose his lordship will ask him to tea one of these days? By God, this house is becoming positively republican."

Tension roiled off Mr. Hightower like a pot near to boiling as he glared at Toby, who was too busy slathering butter on his bread to notice. Finally, the footman realized that the rest of the company had laid aside their spoons and were waiting in silence for what must surely come. He glanced at Mr. Hightower, whose face had flushed an unhealthy shade of puce.

"The occupations or stations of the guests of Somerfield Park have no bearing on how we treat them, Toby," the butler said evenly. The softness of his tone did little to disguise its menace. "If you cannot remember that, you may shortly find yourself without a position in this house."

Eliza's breath hissed over her teeth. Since a number of their fellow workers had been shown the door since "the troubles" began, it was no idle threat.

"Mr. Hightower, I beg your pardon. I meant no disrespect and I hope you didn't find fault with my work this evening. I never give less than my best," Toby rattled on. He was worried now, the smile completely gone from his voice. "But surely you, sir… I mean, your reputation for adhering to good form is legendary. There's nothing the least traditional about this match in the making. Surely you can't like what's happening here."

Mr. Hightower would like it even less if he'd witnessed the little scene in the gallery that I did. And her admitting to not being a virgin—like she was proud of it.

Eliza was confused by Miss Goodnight right enough, but she did admire the girl's confidence. She carefully placed the tureen in the center of the table, so latecomers could help themselves, though there was precious little chicken left among the potatoes and broth.

"I don't have to like what's happening to support it," Mr. Hightower said through clenched teeth. "Much as it pains me to think of Lord Hartley and—" He interrupted himself and tugged his waistcoat down. "Nevertheless, we must trust the Family to do the right thing, whatever that may be in order to ensure that Somerfield Park continues. If it means some traditions must be…modified somewhat, we must be accommodating."

Eliza could be accommodating. While he was speaking, she filled Mrs. Grahame's teacup with her favorite blend. If only the housekeeper would notice how well she was coming along, how willingly she'd don a maid's crisp uniform and work her heart out upstairs in the realm of beauty and light.

"The dignity of this house depends upon the dignity with which we all go about our appointed tasks," Mr. Hightower was saying.

He warmed to his subject now. His discourses on the dignity of service would put an Oxford don to shame. "Serving without being servile is an art. It uplifts both parties in the exchange."

Toby rolled his eyes, and Eliza clamped a hand over her mouth to keep from giggling.

"Even the kitchen girl…" Mr. Hightower waved a beefy hand in her direction and then gave her a second look that said he'd forgotten her presence until that moment. "Why are you still here, Eliza? Shouldn't you be taking a tray to Miss Bowthorpe?"

"Yes, sir, right away, Mr. Hightower, sir." She dropped a quick curtsy and scurried from the room, tamping down her disappointment. She'd hoped to at least catch a glimpse of David, the first footman, but he was probably still in the parlor seeing to the family's after-dinner drinks.

Toby was all flash and dazzle, and sometimes the backs of Eliza's eyes burned just to look at him, but David Abbot quietly took her breath away. He was a little taller than Toby, and possessed such dark good looks, they'd made him the target of a number of unattached ladies both upstairs and down.

Yet surprisingly enough, David seemed a bit shy. He moved with a careful self-consciousness that said he didn't know how attractive he was. Sometimes, Eliza imagined him in that cavalier's costume, rakish hat askew, long plume bobbing as he gave her a wickedly flirtatious bow.

But David would never put himself forward like that.

He needs to, or Toby will be running the house someday instead of him.

She certainly didn't intend on chopping carrots and feeding wood to the smoky oven for the rest of her life. She didn't want Mrs. Culpepper's job. One fine day, Eliza wanted Mrs. Grahame's silvery chatelaine with all the keys to the locked cupboards on it dangling at *her* waist.

Then wouldn't her mum be proud? Maybe even her father, if anyone could find the man. Eliza had no memory of him at all.

She assumed David must have his sights set on Mr. Hightower's tidy office, which guarded access to the wine cellar and housed the fine silver service. The butler was lord in all but name below stairs. The power of hiring and firing, advancing some or holding others back would be in his hand.

What young man wouldn't aspire to that?

"Hurry up, girl," Mrs. Culpepper said as she pushed Miss Bowthorpe's tray into Eliza's hands. "Ye're holding up my supper, and I'm right sharp set."

Eliza and the cook took their meals in the kitchen with the scullery maid, but after all the dishes were done, she'd be allowed to join the other servants in the common room for cards and games and, if Mr.

Hightower and Mrs. Grahame were not there, a bit of gossip too. She wasn't sure yet how much she should tell of what she'd seen in the gallery.

She didn't think David would like hearing that she'd spied on his lordship.

Then, as if she'd conjured him, there he was on the back stairs, coming down as she was going up.

"Good evening, David." She forced herself not to stammer or waffle on. If the man wanted to talk to her, he should carry the conversation forward.

"Oh. Yes, good evening to you too, Eliza." He was almost past her before he spoke, as if he didn't notice her until the tray made him flatten himself against the wall, so she could pass. A frown drew his brows together, and she wished she knew him well enough to ask what was troubling him.

She climbed a few more steps before she stopped and turned back to face him. "Just so you know, Toby made a cake of himself at the supper table tonight. If you play your cards right, Mr. Hightower will name you Lord Hartley's valet."

"Thank you, Eliza." David shook his head. "I don't know what I'm meant to be, but I don't see myself as a valet."

Eliza was dumbfounded. "A valet is ever so much more important than a footman. Don't you want to move up the ranks?"

"Don't you ever get the sense that you weren't meant for back stairs and cellars?" he asked.

Amazingly enough, she did. Every time she sneaked into the gallery and pored over the paintings or imagined herself floating up into the painted clouds on the ceiling, she strained at the narrow confines of her life as a kitchen maid. "I understand just what you mean."

His smile washed over her. "Good. I was beginning to think I was the only one with such thoughts. I don't know why I said something about that, but you've an openness about you. A fellow might tell you anything."

Oh yes, David, you can tell me anything, and I'll listen with my whole heart.

But she didn't say that. Her tongue was stuck to the roof of her mouth. She just smiled back, hugging the moment she and David had shared close to her chest. It wasn't much, but for the first time, he'd truly noticed her. He'd given her a glimpse of the man behind his handsome face. Her insides had capered about over him at regular intervals. Now she felt giddy as a drunken faerie on a daisy stem.

Light as her heart was, her workload was still burdensome. However, as she trudged up the stairs, the tray didn't seem quite as heavy as before.

Five

When an old woman says what's on her mind, she's considered outrageous yet charming. When a young woman voices her opinions, she's counted outrageous and decidedly not charming. Still, I can't help but admire the lady brave enough to do it.

—Phillippa, the Dowager Marchioness of Somerset

"I SAY, THAT'S A SMART EQUIPAGE." SOPHIE'S MOTHER turned to watch as a coach-and-four rumbled past Barrett House the next afternoon. It slowed slightly, so the occupants could peer back at the Goodnights.

Sophie looked up from her weeding. If the gardens around the old dower house were going to amount to anything, it was clear she and her mother would have to see to it. The Barretts obviously didn't have the coin to put toward its upkeep. Her father had argued for hiring some of the locals to clear out the flower beds, but Sophie wanted something to do.

Besides, ripping into a few cankerwort roots was

good for taking out her frustrations. And Richard Barrett had left her decidedly frustrated.

The young lady in the coach stared at her from the backward-facing seat as it rattled by. She was fashionably blond and pale, with a jaunty little capote fastened on top of her curls. Next to her was a woman in a maid's cap. The lady took in Barrett House in a swift, assessing glance and then turned to speak to the older couple, who were seated on the opposite squab.

"Oh, I know who that must be." Sophie rose, removed her dirty gardening gloves, and dusted the knees of the apron protecting her frock.

"Who?"

"Lord Hartley's first and only original idea." She swiped the back of her hand across her forehead, tilting the brim of her straw bonnet far enough for the sunlight to kiss her nose. "That's the girl he means to marry, I'll be bound."

Her mother blinked in surprise. "But he's meant to marry you, sweet."

"Only if I decide to have him, and that question, I assure you, is quite unresolved."

Even if Lord Hartley did kiss like a god, Sophie didn't much care for him. Any fellow who would let himself be sacrificed on the matrimonial altar solely for the sake of her bloated dowry couldn't have much depth of character.

Or feeling.

"Oh, my dear, the last thing your father and I want is to drag you into an uncomfortable situation."

"Too late." Sophie raised a hand, shading her eyes as she watched the coach round the bend on its way to Somerfield Park. "Being offered to the highest-ranking bachelor as breeding stock counts as uncomfortable, however benign your intentions."

Her mother bristled at that. "You know we have only your best interests at heart. But we were unaware that another young lady is involved with Lord Somerset's heir."

"I gather Lord and Lady Somerset were similarly uninformed, else they wouldn't have been scheming with you and Father."

"We're not scheming. We're...planning. How very tawdry you make it all sound." Her mother gave a frustrated snort. "Who is she?"

"I didn't ask her name."

"How serious is Lord Hartley's attachment to this young lady?"

Sophie shrugged. "He told me he means to wed her. That sounds rather serious, don't you think? But that was before Father and his boundless bank notes arrived. Cheer up, Mother. Lord Hartley may yet be for sale."

Mrs. Goodnight ignored this jab as she paced, her fingers steepled before her in thought. "We must do something, but first we must learn more about this new young lady."

"Never commit the troops until you've reconnoitered, eh, Mother?" Sophie laughed. "You should have been a general."

Her mother was so lost in thought she seemed not to have heard her. "I have it. We'll send a note to invite Lady Somerset and her daughters to tea tomorrow, wording the request in such a way as to include these new arrivals. We should be able to take this mysterious young lady's measure then."

"A letter takes too long." Sophie pulled off her apron and dropped it into the gardening basket. "I'll simply walk up to Somerfield Park and invite them all in person."

"No, Sophie, wait. You must change. Dress your hair. You can't go up there looking like—"

"Like myself?" She was already through the garden gate with a swinging stride. "Mother, this is how I look. If anyone doesn't like it, they can look the other way."

❧

The coach wound through the woods and then burst into the open meadow, which was dotted with far too many sheep for Lady Antonia's comfort. She lifted a scented hanky to her nose.

Her lady's maid, Martha Quimby, sniffed appreciatively. "Just smell that air, my lady."

"Must we?" Antonia asked. The country was so earthy sometimes, all shaggy mutton and sniffle-inducing grass and other appallingly fresh things she couldn't identify. "Why anyone of sense ever leaves London is a mystery to me."

Unless it's to go to Paris.

Then the lane straightened and hundred-year-old oaks lined the way. At the end of the long drive, Somerfield Park beckoned, like a prize waiting to be claimed.

Which it most certainly is, Antonia thought as she craned her neck to view it. *And a worthy prize at that.*

"Well, there's a proper place for Quality to lay their

heads, if I do say so," Quimby said. "Your young man must be swimming in lard, so he must."

"Quimby, please," Lady Pruett admonished. "Speaking of money is so gauche."

Quimby rolled her eyes and sighed. Antonia could practically hear her thinking, *If you don't have it, speaking of money is better than nothing.*

The lady's maid frequently spoke out of turn, but she was also a veritable magpie when it came to collecting information about the *bon ton* through her connections with other servants. She shared these shiny, often scandalous revelations with her employer with dependable frequency. That, combined with her absolute discretion when it came to being tight-lipped about the family she served, made Quimby worth her weight in gold.

And Quimby was right about Somerfield Park. The manor house was a delight to the eyes, symmetrical and ornate, yet not fussy enough in its embellishments to seem ostentatious. The only thing out of place was the large lilac bush at one corner which looked as if someone had taken a hacksaw to it. No matter. Once Antonia was the marchioness, she'd have it taken out completely and replaced by topiary in the French style. After her stay in Paris, she adored all things *français*.

"The first house we passed on the estate looked a bit shabby, but it appears the main house is in fine repair," Lord Pruett said.

"What do we care about the outbuildings, Papa? Hartley invited us to stay at Somerfield Park. With his family."

The distinction was not lost on her. This was not

a house party with dozens of guests. It was simply her family and his.

"You'll be wearing a marchioness's coronet before you know it, my lady," Quimby said. "His lordship can hardly have declared himself more clearly."

"Of course, it would help if the man actually said the words," Antonia muttered.

But that was an oversight easily mended. If she didn't know how to coax Hartley into saying them, she deserved to return to Surrey to live out her life as a dried-up spinster—which she might, if any suitor looked too closely at the canal shares her father intended to offer as her dowry. Of course, a family as old and venerable as the Barretts, with their vast estate and impeccable connections, didn't need her dowry in any case.

Besides, she loved Lord Hartley. She was almost sure of it. Sure enough to believe *Lady* Hartley had a fine ring to it indeed.

❧

Richard usually rode only in the early mornings, but his mother and grandmother had been pestering him about Miss Goodnight with sidelong looks and out-right entreaties all day. He escaped to the stables after luncheon and took Pasha, his favorite Arabian, out for a second punishing ride along the hedgerows. The vigorous activity soothed him. When he stretched out on the horse's back, his breathing falling into rhythm with the pounding hooves, he didn't have to think.

And it hurt to think quite a lot.

Before his mother's letter had caught up to him in

Paris, he'd been master of his own fate. Now his entire life was being mapped out for him by forces beyond his control. He cursed the South Sea volcano, which had had the audacity to disrupt the entire earth's weather, and the *Betsy Ross*, which had the temerity to sink with his family's entire fortune riding in its hold. He blamed his poor father, who probably wouldn't even be aware his son was upset with him for saddling him with responsibility for the estate too soon. Not even the crumbling Barrett House escaped Richard's silent diatribe.

Sometimes, he wished he was more like Seymour, who could give easy vent to his frustration. Lawrence had been known to howl at the moon on occasion, an action he described as highly cathartic and usually accompanied by copious amounts of alcohol.

But Richard bottled up his anger, controlled it, lest it control him. He didn't know any other way. He feared what might happen if he ever did relent and let it all out.

When he reached the top of a rise, he reined Pasha up short and let the gelding catch his breath. He didn't need to take his frustrations out on the horse.

Besides, of all the people and things he was angry with, Richard put himself at the top of the list.

He was devoted to Antonia. Hers was the first face he thought of each morning, the last imagined smile he enjoyed each night. It had been easy to become enamored of her. Since she was the daughter of an earl, they moved in the same circles, and shared similar interests and acquaintances.

But beyond that, there were no awkward silences between them, for which he was profoundly grateful. Antonia filled them with witty banter, which Richard appreciated because conversation had never been his strong suit. Even though he was perfectly at home on a horse or wielding a cricket bat, the thought of facing a roomful of glittering people and being expected to converse left him with damp palms.

It was Antonia's métier. She dazzled everyone each time she entered a room, and some of her reflected glory fell on him when he was with her. He'd been within an ace of proposing to her before the letter came.

But if he loved Antonia, what on earth had possessed him to kiss Sophie Goodnight?

She was rude. Common. And most shocking of all, not a virgin.

Yet when he woke last night with a flush of guilty pleasure and damp sheets, it wasn't Antonia he'd been twisted up with in his wet dream.

Down on the lane below, a young woman burst out of the trees. Arms swinging, her long stride pushed the limits of the hem of her column dress. She was headed for Somerfield Park, and if her determined pace was any indication, she was on a mission.

"Call up the devil and she will come," Richard muttered. He chirruped to the gelding and nudged him down the hill. Perhaps he could head Miss Goodnight off before she reached the manor house. After all, Antonia and her parents were due to arrive sometime today. The last thing he wanted was for Sophie to accost Antonia before he had a chance to speak to her privately and explain the Goodnight's unexpected presence.

"Hullo," he said as he drew even with Sophie. "Where are you going?"

She flicked her gaze up at him and then back to the lane ahead. "I'll give you three guesses, but if you don't manage it in one, I shall have to conclude that you are not as smart as your horse."

He'd finished at the head of all his forms in school, yet she managed to make him feel like an idiot almost every time he opened his mouth around her. Richard dismounted and fell into step beside her. One of them had to be civilized. It appeared it would have to be him.

"Perhaps I should have asked *why* you are going to Somerfield," he amended.

"Don't worry. I'm not planning to measure the parlor for new drapes." She slowed her pace a bit. "Actually, I'm delivering an invitation to your mother and sisters to join us at Barrett House for tea tomorrow."

"Oh. That's…kind."

"You needn't sound so surprised." She stuck out her tongue at him.

For a hot moment, memories of that pointed little tongue tangled up with his had him crowding his trousers.

"I can be kind," she assured him, "when it suits me, of course."

Of course. He tamped down his body's unwanted response to her. The last thing he needed was to feel anything—especially lust—for the unpredictable Miss Goodnight.

"You might save yourself the trip. I suspect my mother and sisters will be unavailable for tea tomorrow." Despite her straw bonnet, the sun had pinked her cheeks. Miss Goodnight didn't seem bothered by it. Richard wouldn't put it past her not to mind sprouting freckles. "We are expecting guests to arrive today, and it would be rude to leave them."

"Oh, yes, your almost fiancée. I'm so looking forward to meeting her," she said, her lips curving upward. "Who is she, by the way?"

"Lady Antonia Pruett, but that's none of your concern."

"Of course, it is. How else shall I help you disentangle yourself from this situation unless I know all the principals in our little comedy?"

"If you think to come between me and Lady Antonia—"

"You mistake me, Richard." She stopped walking and turned to face him. "I don't want to disrupt whatever little agreement you have with this Antonia person."

Antonia would be aghast at Sophie's easy familiarity, referring to her by her Christian name before they'd even been introduced. But Sophie Goodnight was like the tide. There seemed no way to stop her.

"There is no agreement," he admitted. "At least, no formal one."

"And formal is all that counts with your kind, isn't it? At any rate, I want to help you," she said. "I feel certain that between the two of us, we can show our families how very unsuitable we are for each other. It's readily apparent to me. We just have to demonstrate it to them."

Richard frowned. After being openly hunted on the London marriage mart, he wondered why this woman, who because of the cavernous difference in their station should have been delirious over the prospect of a match with him, found him "unsuitable."

"Which will clear your way to be with whomever you wish," she finished.

It wasn't as simple as that. There was still the money, always the money. And though he and Lord Pruett had never discussed the specifics of a dowry for his daughter, Richard was certain his grandmother was right about the earl's gambling habits. Sufficient funds would not be coming from that quarter.

Still, Sophie was being very decent about the whole thing, and Richard told her so.

She glanced up at him, her blue eyes merry this time. "Just because I'm *nouveau riche* doesn't mean I can't occasionally be decent as well. Father will just have to look for another titled lord who's more desperate than you for me to marry."

"I doubt he'll find one more desperate than me" slipped off his tongue before he thought. "Forgive me. I didn't mean to imply that a man must be desperate in order to wed you. That didn't come out right."

"No, but it came out honest. I like that about you, Richard."

So he was unsuitable, but she liked him. Sophie Goodnight was a riddle with feet.

They walked along in silence for a while. The only sounds were the clomps of Pasha's hooves and the creak of his leather tack. Richard didn't feel the need to fill the quiet for once. Surprisingly, it didn't seem uncomfortable. Sophie didn't expect him to be entertaining or clever. There was no burning need to discuss the weather or make small talk.

It felt...companionable.

He was as at ease with her as he was in his own

skin. After dodging debutantes and his determined wooing of Lady Antonia, which he was never certain would go well, it was a novel sensation to be so relaxed with a woman.

Of all the people in his life right now, it was beyond ironic that Sophie Goodnight was the only one who made no demands on him.

"Do you ride?" he asked.

"Like the wind."

"Pity you're not dressed for it, or we'd ride Pasha double back to the house."

"I'm dressed enough," she said, "though these confounded gowns are terribly narrow."

Without waiting for further invitation, she hitched up her skirts, revealing her pantalets to mid-thigh, grasped the pommel, and mounted Pasha unassisted. Her skin was still completely covered, but the fabric of the pantalets was so sheer as to be nearly transparent in the sunlight. The curve of her calf and neatly turned ankle made Richard forget to breathe for a moment.

"I can leave you the stirrups," she said, patting the pillion behind her, "but I prefer to handle the reins myself."

"I'll just bet you do." Richard mounted behind her in one fluid motion. "Why am I not surprised?"

Six

Young women should practice what every carnival huckster knows. Nothing makes an object more desirable than taking it away.

—Phillippa, the Dowager Marchioness of Somerset

THE HORSE CLATTERED UP TO THE ORNATE DOOR OF Somerfield Park. Laughing and flushed with exertion, Lord Hartley and Miss Goodnight, in a shocking display of stocking and undergarment, half tumbled off their mount and handed off the reins to the waiting hostler. Digory Hightower prided himself on being unflappable, but he was sure the dignified expression he tried to maintain had a pinched look about it now.

"Your guests have arrived, your lordship," he said as he took Lord Hartley's slightly battered hat. "They are in the drawing room with Lady Somerset and the dowager. Shall I have David draw you a bath and—"

"In a moment," Lord Hartley said. "I wish to greet them first and introduce Miss Goodnight."

Miss Goodnight looked as if she'd already been introduced to a pigsty. Both young people were flecked with mud from head to toe but, still breathing hard from their ride, seemed indifferent to their state of disarray.

Hightower followed them into the drawing room. He was a stickler about not prying into the affairs of the Family he served, but this introduction promised to be too entertaining to miss.

Lord Hartley greeted his mother and grandmother with kisses on the cheek, then after quite correct addresses to Lord and Lady Pruett, he kissed Lady Antonia's offered hand. He spoke to her so softly Hightower couldn't hear what was said no matter how hard he strained.

"Hart, how on earth did you become so filthy?" his mother finally managed to sputter.

"Oh, that's my fault, your ladyship," Miss Goodnight said, stepping into the room, bold as brass. "I had the reins you see, and I can't resist a jump. Unfortunately, there was a bit of a bog on the other side of the fence, but we muddled through without mishap."

The dowager raised her lorgnette and looked down her long nose at Miss Goodnight. "You must be an accomplished rider, Miss Goodnight, not to have gone tail over teakettle after attempting a jump while riding double." Then her lips quirked a bit in suppressed merriment. "However, as long as you're both unhurt, I suppose no harm done."

"Exactly, your ladyship." Miss Goodnight smiled at the elder Lady Somerset. Mr. Hightower was struck by the change the expression made in her countenance. Sophie went from being a dirty-cheeked chit to a slightly fallen angel, some of heaven's light still radiating from her mischievous face. "My mother always says if a problem can be fixed by a good washing, it's not really much of a problem, is it? Well, Richard, aren't you going to introduce me to your guests?"

Mr. Hightower blinked in surprise at her easy familiarity with the son of the house. A grasping upstart if ever there was one, no matter how much blunt her father had.

"Certainly." Lord Hartley did the honors, presenting Miss Goodnight to Lord and Lady Pruett and Lady Antonia. Hightower couldn't fault his lordship's manners. Lord Hartley was as correct as if he and Miss Goodnight were dressed fit to be presented to the queen.

"Oh, Lady Antonia, I'm so pleased to meet you," Miss Goodnight said, extending a hand which the lady took with limp reluctance. "Richard has told me so much about you."

"Really?" she drawled, her eyes widening at the repeated familiar address. "Strange that Hartley hasn't said a word about you."

"Not so strange really," Miss Goodnight said. "He couldn't very well have, since we only met last evening."

"One doesn't generally ride double with people one has only just met." Lady Antonia's eyes narrowed. "And how is it you two know each other?"

"My parents are acquainted with Lord and Lady Somerset. They've graciously allowed us use of Barrett House."

"Now I know where I've seen you," Lady Antonia said, burying her pert nose in her teacup for a brief moment. Hightower approved of the delicate way she elevated her pinky finger. Here was a lady worthy of the name. "You were gardening like a common drudge when we drove by earlier. I'd have recognized you sooner if not for the mud."

Hightower was less approving of the nastiness of her tone.

Miss Goodnight's smile didn't reach her eyes as she turned to Lady Somerset, the younger. "Our stay at Barrett House is part of the reason I came to Somerfield today."

"So becoming covered with mud alongside my grandson was not your chief aim?" the dowager put in.

"No," Miss Goodnight said with a laugh, "though that was a definite side benefit. I haven't had a ride like that since the tiger hunt in Punjab. Of course, we were on elephants then.

"Elephants!" Lady Antonia put in. "Dear me. How very…exotic."

Miss Goodnight ignored her and continued. "In any case, as a small way to thank Lady Somerset for her hospitality, my mother and I wish to invite all the ladies to tea on the morrow. Do say you'll come."

Mr. Hightower cocked his head. It wasn't the most correct way to invite a marchioness and her family to tea, but it was prettily done. If one didn't look too closely at the mud…

"We'd be delighted, Miss Goodnight," the marchioness said.

"Please, your ladyship, I wish you'd call me Sophie." She turned to Lady Antonia and Lady Pruett. "Of course, you are both included in the invitation. Any friend of Richard's…"

"Thank you, Miss Goodnight. I look forward to meeting your mother," Lady Pruett said. "She must be an extraordinary lady to have raised such...an adventurous daughter."

"Don't hold her to account for me," Miss Goodnight said breezily. "My failings are my own, I assure you."

"We won't have to ride elephants, will we?" Lady Antonia asked with deceptive sweetness.

"Not unless you wish to, but I don't recommend it in any case," Miss Goodnight said. "Very bony spines."

❧

"Thank you kindly for lending us a hand today, Miss Quimby," Aloysius Porter said as he mopped his brow. "It's not often a lady's maid will condescend to serve at tea."

"Not at all," Quimby said as she took an apron from her satchel and donned it. "I'm right happy to do it."

"Well, as you can see, we're in need of help and not just extra hands either," Porter said as he led her through the residence toward the kitchen. "Barrett House isn't set up for a gathering of this size and importance. Counting the dowager and Lady Somerset, Lord Hartley's three sisters, Lady Pruett and her daughter, and Mrs. and Miss Goodnight, there should be nine of them—ten if Lady Ariel brings her governess, which I hope she will, since no one likes uneven numbers."

The parlor was much too small for ten ladies. The dining room would have been cramped as well and was not really the correct venue for tea in any case.

"I tried to make Mrs. Goodnight see the

impracticality of it." But then she simply suggested something even more impractical that made Porter wish they'd muddled along in the small parlor. "'If the house will not support a tea,' she says to me, 'then we'll have it in the garden.' Of all the ideas…"

"Sounds positively American," Quimby said. "From what I've heard, they're always keen on picnics and such. Are the Goodnights colonials by chance?"

"No, indeed not. British through and through. Though I gather they've not spent much time in England. Mr. Goodnight is quite the nabob, they say, and the daughter was born in India, you know, which might account for any number of queer notions."

But queer notions or not, Porter had been busy till late in the night, setting up canvas awnings to shelter the white lawn chaises. Mrs. Beckworth, Barrett House's cook, was in a fine state trying to pull together a tea on such short notice. She threatened mutiny if he couldn't commandeer someone from the big house to help her.

Having Miss Quimby volunteer was a gift from heaven. And such an unexpected gift. It was almost unheard of for a lady's maid to do such a thing, but Porter wasn't one to turn down willing hands. He and Miss Quimby stopped into the kitchen, where trays of dainties were laid out on the long trestle table. He introduced her to Mrs. Beckworth and Eliza, the kitchen girl from Somerfield Park, and Miss Quimby was put promptly to work icing small cakes.

"Between Mrs. Beckworth and Eliza, they've pre-pared enough petit fours and finger sandwiches to feed a small army." Mr. Porter chuckled with nervousness.

"Instead, we'll be serving ten ladies, who are likely to have appetites like birds."

"Real ladies always do." Quimby didn't look up from her cakes.

"Yes, er, quite," he mumbled, feeling rather dismissed. "Well, I'll leave you to it then."

Porter hurried out of the dimness of the kitchen into the blinding sunlight of midmorning to inspect the final preparations. The arrangement of tables still wasn't to his liking, but since the table settings had already been laid, there was no good way to rearrange matters now. He'd settled for two linen-covered card tables with service for four each and one smaller table which would serve two. With any luck, he'd be able to steer Lady Ariel and her governess to that one.

If the governess didn't come, and the party was an uneven nine, he didn't know what he'd do.

It was an impossible task, but Porter was determined to make this tea a success. If he did, perhaps he'd be called up to serve at Somerfield Park, instead of cooling his heels at the frequently empty Barrett House. He wouldn't accept a position of footman, of course. That would be a step backward, even given the difference in the size of the households. But if he could be made underbutler, or even Lord Hartley's valet, that would be something.

Best of all, he'd have a chance to see Mrs. Culpepper every blessed day. And wouldn't that be a fine thing?

೧⁕ৎ

Eliza slanted a sideways glance at Miss Quimby. She was smart, she was, with her fine muslin gown with real lace at the bodice. Eliza had heard that lady's maids got first pick of their mistress's cast-offs, and this was a still a lovely gown, even if it was secondhand. Quimby's drab brown hair had been pulled into a tight bun at her nape, but a few artful curls tumbled onto her forehead and dangled at the sides of her thin face.

With both Lady Pruett and Lady Antonia to tend, when does she find time to curl her own hair?

Quimby's movements were as crisp as her apron as she laid on the icing with an expert hand.

"You've worked in a kitchen before," Eliza said.

"I've done a bit of this and that, it's true. I was a sous chef before I was a lady's maid. But going into service with Lady Pruett offered me a chance to do some traveling and see something of the world," Quimby said with a friendly smile. "What about you, girl? Eliza, is it? Where did you train?"

"Nowhere, miss. At Somerfield, I guess." Eliza shrugged and kept her voice low. She didn't want Mrs. Beckworth to think she was complaining about her lot. Plenty of girls in Somerset-by-the-Sea would trade places with her quick enough. A position at Somerfield Park, even one as lowly as Eliza's, was more precious than jewels when the whole village was scrambling for work. "Don't know how much training it takes to chop carrots, lay fires, and generally make myself scarce whenever anything interesting is happening."

"Well, when you've a chance at something interesting, take it, my girl. That's my motto."

That sounded like sense to Eliza. She'd wanted to see what would happen at this tea, so when Mr. Porter sent up the request for extra help, she was the first, and only, volunteer. A small candle of pride flickered in her chest. She'd been offered a chance and took it.

But why would Miss Quimby want to be here? Eliza asked her.

"After I heard about the state Miss Goodnight was in when she made the invitation for this tea, I simply had to see how it would come off." Miss Quimby raised her brows in censure.

"Oh?" Eliza wasn't allowed upstairs, and the Somerfield staff had been uncharacteristically tight-lipped about anything to do with the Goodnights, so she hadn't heard anything about Miss Sophia's "state." "What was wrong with her, then?"

"What wasn't?" Quimby quietly described Miss Goodnight's disheveled—no, make that positively grubby—appearance in Lady Somerset's oh-so-proper parlor.

Eliza wasn't good enough to be seen in that parlor even if she were dressed in her Sunday best. She stopped listening for a bit while she stewed over the injustice of it. Miss Goodnight was no more a lady than Eliza was, yet because her father had the chinks, she could parade around in the marquess's parlor covered in mud.

"Makes you wonder, don't it?" Miss Quimby finished.

Eliza blinked, realizing she'd missed a bit of the lady's maid's diatribe while she was woolgathering. "Wonder what?"

"It's clear from talking to Mr. Porter that the Goodnights have no idea how things are done prop-erly, else they'd not have tried to throw this party together at the last moment," Quimby said as she finished icing another row of lemon cakes. "They aren't Quality. That's obvious as a wart on the nose. Just what is the connection between the Goodnights and Lord Somerset? Is Mr. Goodnight his lordship's man of business and his womenfolk are somehow getting ahead of themselves with this tea?"

"No, I shouldn't think so," Eliza said. She'd seen Mr. Witherspoon coming and going from the estate quite a lot over the last month or so. He'd been Lord Somerset's man of business for years. Leastwise that's what she'd inferred from overhearing David and Mr. Hightower discuss which room to arrange for the gentleman when Mr. Witherspoon had to stay over.

"Then why are the Goodnights here at all, much less inviting their ladyships to tea?"

"Oh, that's easy," Eliza said, glad to finally have something definite to contribute to the conversation. "Lord Hartley's meant to marry Miss Goodnight."

"Is he? Indeed." Quimby's lips pinched tight in a prim line for a moment. "And her blood no bluer than yours or mine. What do the servants at Somerfield make of Miss Goodnight?"

"We don't discuss his lordship's guests, miss," Eliza said. Quimby's questions were beginning to make the hairs on her arms prickle. It didn't do to ignore a body's arm hair.

"It don't sound like she'll be only a guest for long," Quimby pressed on.

"How should I know?" Eliza said, remembering how it seemed Lord Hartley and Miss Goodnight didn't like each other much in the gallery. At least, not until they started kissing. "I don't think anything's for certain yet."

"Well, I should think not. They're from two different worlds, Lord Hartley and Miss Goodnight. His is an old, established family with a lineage that runs back to the time of the Conqueror. She's a harpy on the catch if ever there was one. It'll never work."

When it was put like that, barring the buckets of money Miss Goodnight's father was said to have, Eliza had to admit that the young woman's station was far closer to hers and Miss Quimby's than his lordship's. Of course, a body couldn't be blamed for trying to better themselves. Eliza hoped to move up the ranks in the servants' hall. Why shouldn't Miss Goodnight yearn to move up in the upstairs world if she could? It gave Eliza a bit of common feelings with her and made her like her a little better—never mind the bit about not being a virgin, of course.

She hoped the tea went off swimmingly for the Goodnights.

"Like oil and water, fish and fowl," Miss Quimby was saying. "You know what they say, 'birds of a feather' and all that."

"I don't put much stock in old sayings because, well…they're old." All this talk of fish and feathers and oily water was giving Eliza a headache. "I figure Lord Hartley will make the right decision and do what's needful when it comes to it."

"Undoubtedly," Quimby said. "Provided Lord and Lady Somerset have the right information about Miss Goodnight to pass on to their son. You know as well as I that them who live below stairs know more of what's really going on than any of the Quality folk we serve."

That was true. No one but Eliza and Lord Hartley

knew about Miss Goodnight's astonishing confession.
She wondered what his parents would make of her not
being a virgin. Buckets of money or not, that sort of
thing might change everything.

"All I'm saying is, you never know when what
you might see and hear could come in useful like,"
Quimby went on in a softer tone.

"Useful?"

"To your employers. You'll be doing them such
a service, and they'll reward you for it. So keep your
ears open."

Eliza twined her fingers together. "What if I'm not
sure I should tell something I hear?"

Quimby shrugged. "Tell me first and then we can
decide together who needs to know it. Will you do
that, Eliza?"

"I'll think about it." Her arm hair was tingling
again. "If I hear anything, that is."

"Eliza, stop your chattering and come help me
with this ham," Mrs. Beckworth said as she waved
her apron before the smoking oven on the opposite
side of the kitchen.

The kitchen girl trotted to obey. Miss Quimby
took the opportunity to sneak a small bottle of syrup
of ipecac from her pocket. With the brush she used to
apply lacquer to her mistress's fingernails, she coated
one of the lemon cakes with the virulent purge-
inducing substance. The result was a perfectly appealing dainty, albeit one slightly shinier than the others.

Which would make it much easier to serve to the
right person when the time came.

Seven

A proper English garden is a delight to the senses...
provided one has removed all the excess fertilizer first.

—Phillippa, the Dowager Marchioness of Somerset

SOPHIE ESCORTED THE ELDER LADY SOMERSET AROUND
the garden, so she could show the dowager what she
and her mother had accomplished since they came to
Barrett House. It wasn't the exotic profusion of plants
they'd presided over in India, but she was proud of the
riot of blooms beginning to unfurl now that most of
the weeds had been pulled.

At her mother's insistence, Sophie wore a cool,
lemon-colored gown of fine silk. Atop her dark hair, a
broad-brimmed straw bonnet with a matching yellow
ribbon was perched. She felt as if she'd stepped from a
fashion plate. Since the marchioness was similarly well
dressed in deep purple, Sophie decided her mother was
right for once. Evidently, tea was a serious business at
Somerfield Park and required serious fashion as well.

"Gardens, not unlike lives, need to be cleared out from time to time." The old woman leaned lightly on her cane as she pontificated on each flower and bush in the now well-groomed space. "While I generally approve of the changes you and your mother have made to the grounds around Barrett House, I must deplore your methods."

The dowager fixed her with a pointed look, and Sophie tried not to giggle when she noticed that a stuffed pigeon was wedged among the blooms festooning the old lady's hat. The bird seemed to have been frozen with the same dour expression and tilt of head as the dowager, both of them united in scolding her.

"If you would be taken for a lady, my dear," Richard's grandmother said, "you simply mustn't grub about in the dirt."

"That supposes I wish to be taken for a lady," Sophie returned tartly. If she were going to be weighed in the balance and found wanting by the dowager, at least it ought to be for being herself. "If ladies aren't allowed to get their hands dirty once in a while, I rather think they can't have much fun."

Lady Somerset gave a decidedly unladylike snort. "We have fun, my dear. But we do it with clean hands. Don't you see? By insisting upon doing the labor yourself, you have robbed others of an opportunity. To put it more biblically, 'To whom much has been given, much is required.' As the daughter of a wealthy man, it is your obligation to provide employment for those less fortunate."

"I had not thought of it like that."

"Well, it's high time to think of it then. When I laid out this garden years ago, I had six full-time gardeners."

"For this small space?"

"For this small space," the dowager repeated. "Not that the size of Barrett House's gardens required that many, of course, but the families of the gardeners did. The Marquessate of Somerset may no longer function as a feudal overlord, but we are still expected to provide a major source of employment for the village folk as well as support for the tenant farmers who work the estate's land."

Sophie hadn't thought about the landed nobility in that light before either. She'd considered them spoiled, puffed up with their own sense of entitlement, and generally a blight on the land they'd inherited. When her father first brought up the subject of marrying Lord Hartley, she'd been livid. She couldn't see why it was so important to her father that his grandchildren bear a *Lord* or *Lady* before their names. What earthly good could it be?

To learn that the dowager viewed her family's land and the people attached to it as a trust, and that the relationship between the Lord Somerset and his people was a mutually beneficial one, was a bit of an eye-opener.

"So you're saying that even aristocrats have their uses."

The elder Lady Somerset had leaned down to smell the hydrangeas. She straightened instantly. "Dear me! You are determined to be objectionable, aren't you?"

"I'm sorry, my lady. Words tend to slip out my mouth before I've fully considered them."

The dowager's lips twitched in what might have been a half smile. "The same has been known to happen to me from time to time." She linked arms with Sophie and continued their stroll. "To be honest, sometimes I consider my words fully and say them anyway, but if you tell anyone I said that, I'll dispute it with my dying breath."

"Your secret is safe with me."

"I say, what's happened to my roses?" She stopped by the front door to Barrett House and peered down at the woody stubs which were all Sophie had left of the runaway bush.

"I pruned them, your ladyship," Sophie admitted.

"Are you sure? It looks more as if you exacted revenge."

There had been no new growth since she had hacked away at it. No tender green leaves unfurling. Not even a bulge in the woody stock that might indicate one was forthcoming.

"Pruning must be done with a light hand, my dear." The dowager cast a gimlet eye at Sophie. "This poor bush looks as if you held a grudge against it."

"I'm afraid I may have gotten carried away," Sophie said. "I had just met your grandson, my lady."

"Indeed. In that case, I suppose we must be grateful the bush was there to bear the brunt of that meeting." Lady Somerset chuckled. "Let that be a lesson to you. Never wield pruning shears when you're unhappy with a man." She raised her lorgnette to study the ruined bush more closely. "You'd only just met Hartley. One can't imagine there was time for you to become acquainted with him well enough to motivate carnage on this level. Why were you unhappy with him, if I may ask?"

Sophie's shoulders drooped a bit. "It wasn't just him. I was unhappy with myself as well." Now was not the time to go into why her parents felt it imperative to spirit her out of India and why her father was so keen to settle her into a wedded state so quickly. "It just seems as if everything is out of my control of late, and I don't like that feeling one bit."

"None of us do, my dear. And though it will likely be of no comfort to you, no one else is in control half as much as they'd like either. Not my son, Lord bless him, stuck in that wheelchair without his wits, poor man. And not my grandson, who is suddenly responsible for a one hundred thousand acre estate and all the lives attached to it."

One hundred thousand acres? She had no idea Somerset was such a huge estate. If its financial difficulties were as dire as her father thought, no wonder Richard was under pressure to wed her for her dowry.

"And of all those who don't have control over their own lives as much as they wish, I must add myself to the list most especially," Lady Somerset said. "A dowager takes her portion from the estate, you see. If the Barrett family is forced to sell, well…let's just say I will not spend my declining years in the comfort to which I've become accustomed."

"I suppose you mean to make me feel guilty enough to accept your grandson."

"Is it working?" She gave Sophie a searching look and then chuckled. "Don't mind me. It's just the ramblings of an old woman. Think nothing of it. No one else does."

"I think that very unlikely." From all appearances, the dowager was still a force to be reckoned with in the

Barrett household. Richard especially seemed solicitous of his grandmother whenever he was near her.

"Don't trouble yourself about the plans others have made for you. Or the roses either, for that matter," Lady Somerset said. "They are like the Barretts—hardy and hard to eradicate. One way or another, the fortunes of Somerset will arise, just as this rosebush no doubt will. Mark my words."

Sophie wished she could give the old woman a hug, but Lady Somerset didn't seem the sort to appreciate such demonstrations of affection. So instead, she linked arms with her again.

"You know, my mother has been encouraging me to hire a lady's maid," Sophie said. "I've been resisting because I'm perfectly capable of dressing myself."

"Then in that case, you need a new modiste, my dear. Your wardrobe is clearly lacking. No lady worthy of the name wears garments she can don unassisted."

Sophie stifled a laugh because she was sure the dowager was dead serious. "Then I shall have to remedy that. Perhaps you can recommend a seamstress and a likely lady's maid."

"My, you are a fast learner, aren't you? No wonder Richard likes you."

"I don't think he does."

"That's because you didn't see his face when he looked at you, my dear."

"Men have admired me before." In Bombay, on the ship returning to England, she'd never been without a coterie of gentlemen sniffing around. Sophie told herself it was her father's money that drew them in. "It didn't mean they liked me particularly."

"Perhaps, but did they admire you covered in mud and smelling of horse? My Richard certainly did."

A warm sensation coursed through her chest, but she immediately tamped it down. No doubt the smell of her father's money overpowered even the earthy scent of mud and horse. Besides, he'd told her point-blank his heart was otherwise engaged.

She glanced across the green lawn at Lady Antonia, looking cool and willowy in a frosty blue gown with a matching bonnet and satiny slippers of the same azure shade. She was holding court with Richard's two oldest sisters and had apparently shared something funny with them. Her laughter was silvery and light, the sound dew drops on flower stems would make if they could. Collected and self-assured, she was every inch a future marchioness.

Whenever Sophie looked at herself in the mirror, she was reminded of the old sow's ear–silk purse adage. Not that she was unattractive, but she'd never have the polish that seemed inbred in someone like Lady Antonia. She'd always put a foot wrong or say something gauche.

Even if she did become a "Lady," she'd feel like a fraud. How could her parents expect her to live such a lie?

Her mother rang a small bell and called the gathering to join her at the tables. For a moment, there was a bit of confusion, since there were ten places and only nine ladies present. Lady Ariel had not brought her governess as expected. Lady Antonia's pursed-lipped expression trumpeted her disapproval over the uneven party.

As if I give a flying fig what Lady Antonia thinks, Sophie told herself sternly. But before she could suggest how to divide the group, so as to leave Lady Antonia at the table for two by herself, the dowager stepped into the fray.

"Now then," the elder Lady Somerset said. "Why don't we have Lady Somerset, Lady Pruett, and Mrs. Goodnight along with Ariel, there's a dear, right here? I'll join my other granddaughters at that table. This way Miss Goodnight and Lady Antonia can become better acquainted at that small one. Come now, everyone. Take your places before the tea gets cold."

Since they'd been sorted out by someone whom nobody wanted to countermand, the group settled in as the dowager dictated. From the corner of her eye, Sophie saw Mr. Porter's shoulders sag in what looked like relief. Then he leaped into action to begin serving the light repast.

Appreciative murmurs went up over the finger sandwiches and fruit compote from her mother's table. Against all expectations, it appeared their tea was going to come off without a single hiccup. Sophie waited until Lady Antonia was seated and then sidled into the chair opposite her.

"Since Lady Somerset has decreed it, it appears we are to be friends," Sophie said. "I should like that. So, tell me: how did you and Richard meet?"

"*Hartley* and I met in Paris." Lady Antonia stressed Richard's title as Sophie poured out for her. The lady raised her teacup halfway to her lips. "At one of Madame Boulanger's salons for poetry readings."

"Oh? Not in London at Almack's?" Sophie filled her cup with the steaming liquid. "From what I hear, that's all the crack when one is in hot pursuit in the marriage mart."

Lady Antonia blinked hard. "Perhaps it's the done thing in Outer Mongolia or wherever it is you came from, but here one does not speak of such things."

"Really?" Sophie added a lump of sugar to her tea and stirred with vigor. "I had no idea Almack's was so sordid."

"It's not," Lady Antonia said, her evenly modulated voice now edged with irritation. "Almack's is the height of respectability."

"Pity. For a moment, it sounded rather interesting."

"Miss Goodnight, are you attempting to be annoying?"

"Please call me Sophie. And no, I wouldn't call it an attempt." She helped herself to the finger sandwiches Mr. Porter offered her, and waited until he had served Lady Antonia and moved on to the table where the dowager and her granddaughters were seated before continuing. "I am simply being myself. If you find that annoying, I fear I can't apologize."

If Lady Antonia had been a porcupine, all her quills would have been standing on end. "Honestly, I don't know what Hartley could possibly see in you."

"Yes, you do. He sees my father's nearly bottomless purse." Sophie sipped her tea. She hadn't expected to have so much fun today. Lady Antonia was terribly easy to provoke. It almost didn't seem fair, so she decided to toss her a bone. "But, cheer up, my lady. I know full well what Richard sees in you."

"What's that?"

"Someone from his world. Someone who will fill a marchioness's shoes without pinching so much as one of her little toes. Someone who fits in. Believe me, he finds that much more appealing than the Goodnight fortune."

At that moment, a pair of riders clattered to a stop

at the garden gate, their horses blown and streaked
with sweat.

"Hello the house," Lawrence Seymour called from
atop a piebald gelding. He waved his hat in the air
as though every feminine head wasn't already turned
his way. "We've just come from an exhausting ride
around Somerset's holdings. Is there any chance a pair
of weary travelers can gain sustenance here?"

"Certainly, Mr. Seymour." Sophie's mother rose
from her place. "There's room for you at the dowager
marchioness's table."

"Ah, my thanks, Mrs. Goodnight," Seymour said as
he dismounted, eyeing Lady Ella and Lady Petra with
a wide grin. "You're aiding and abetting my evil plan
to charm the unmarried Barrett ladies."

"You're a bit young for me, Lawrence," the dowager said, lifting a lace-gloved hand to him as he drew
near, "but I give you leave to try."

Seymour chuckled and kissed her bony knuckles
before settling at her table.

Lord Hartley was still atop his mount, looking as if he
was likely to bolt at any moment. Sophie could almost
pity him if it weren't more fun to watch him struggle.
She just wished he'd remember that they were in this
difficult situation together. Neither of them wanted
this match their parents had devised. If they worked
together, surely they could extricate themselves.

Of course, it would be easier to remember why she
didn't want the betrothal to go forward if he weren't
so striking on horseback. The man might be a bit
awkward in the parlor, but he was a veritable centaur in
his saddle. A little thrill ran over her as she remembered

the way they'd taken that jump together, the wind singing, their thigh muscles moving in concert, his arm around her waist, and his hard chest against her spine…

"Mr. Porter, please find a chair for Lord Hartley at the small table," her mother said, interrupting her increasingly wicked thoughts. "I think there's room, don't you, Sophie?"

"Certainly. Richard, stop fidgeting on your horse and join us. I'm sure Lady Antonia doesn't bite, and I've given it up since we returned to civilized society."

Her mother shot her a dagger glare. Sophie returned a falsely sweet smile to her.

Sophie hitched her chair a quarter of the way around the small table. "You see, Richard. Plenty of room."

Lord Hartley looped the reins around the fence-post and advanced toward them in long strides. He removed his hat to reveal hair darkened with sweat after his punishing ride. His grim expression was that of a man destined for the rack. It occurred to Sophie that pinned between her and the girl he hoped to marry, Richard must feel even more out of place at this garden party than she did.

"I don't mean to intrude, but Seymour was set on stopping," he said once he settled uneasily on the chair Porter provided.

"Nonsense," Lady Antonia said, lighting up like a candle now that he was there. "We were just talking about you."

"And you think that could only be bad for you, don't you? Rivals of the heart sniping away at each other and all," Sophie said softly as she poured him some tea. The guests at the other tables were conversing in normal tones, but she felt the need to keep their conversation a bit more private. "But actually it's good that we're talking, since Lady Antonia and I are not rivals of any sort, much less of the heart. I was about to explain to her that if she finds my behavior objectionable—"

Antonia nearly choked on her tea. "Never did I say such an ill-bred thing."

"Did you not? My mistake. At any rate, I was hoping to convince Lady Antonia that by simply being myself, I will demonstrate how very unsuited you and I are, Richard." Sophie sipped her tea with her pinky properly out, well aware that her behavior—barring that bit about biting earlier—was exemplary. "Then once all parties are satisfied on that point, the deck will be cleared for an appropriate candidate for your affections."

Richard relaxed visibly and smiled as if he meant it. The tight, harried expression left his face, and she realized in a blinding rush just how much pressure was being brought to bear on him from all sides.

And how it made her chest constrict strangely that she was part of his troubles.

If she'd been alone with him when he smiled, she'd have said something to make light of things like, *"Ah, there's the real Richard. You really ought to do that more often."*

"Smile, you mean?" And then he might say, *"I would if you were with me more often."*

And she'd say, *"If I was with you, you'd never wish for—"*

"Sophie has been incredibly decent about the whole thing." Richard's voice yanked her out of her momentary daydream.

"Sophie?" Lady Antonia hissed. "You call her Sophie?"

"He does." Sophie leaned forward to whisper to the lady. "And while we're plotting together to overthrow the powers that be who would leg-shackle Richard to me, perhaps you and I should be on a first name basis as well."

"Really, I don't think—"

"Oh, I suspect you do think, but if thoughts are small, they're easy to overlook. Shall I call you *Tonia* then?" When the lady didn't respond immediately, Sophie went on. "May I point out to you that your other choice is *Ant*?"

～

"Now's your chance, Eliza," Miss Quimby was saying. "Mr. Porter has more than enough on his hands. Help him out a bit, why don't you?"

"I'm not dressed to serve."

"Doesn't matter. Take this." She shoved a china plate into Eliza's hands. A single helping of lemon cake was arranged artfully in the center, drizzled with a little raspberry sauce. It glistened in the dappled shade and the tart aroma made Eliza's mouth water.

"Who should I serve it to?"

"Miss Goodnight, I should think. She'll be looking for more servants here at Barrett House after this party. I overheard her talking with the dowager about it. This'll make her notice you. Play your cards right, and you could be moving up right smartly, girl. Wait a moment." Miss Quimby took off her own crisp apron and tied it quickly around Eliza's waist. "We haven't time to fix a little cap to your head, but your hair looks fine. Just set the plate in front of her, from the left, mind. Serve from the left, clear from the right. And then come back for the next one."

"But there are three at Miss Goodnight's table," Eliza said. "Shouldn't I take enough for all of them at once?"

"And risk dropping one? I should think not. Go on. The sooner you go, the sooner you're back and the whole table will be served in a wink."

Eliza nodded and crossed the expanse of green with the dainty dish in her hand. No one was paying the least attention to her, but her insides jittered in any case. This could be the start of something. She wouldn't be just a kitchen maid anymore. She'd be somebody. She'd—

She was there.

Did she serve from the right or the left? Which had Miss Quimby said? It was like the old adage about whether to feed a cold or starve a cold. For the life of her, she couldn't remember which was correct.

Eliza stepped closer to the table on Miss Goodnight's right.

"That looks good enough to eat." Lord Hartley, who was on the lady's right, took the plate from Eliza when she continued to hesitate. "I worked up quite an appetite riding with Seymour."

"Since we're dining al fresco, I dare you not to wait for a fork," Miss Goodnight said with a laugh. "Or don't fancy lords eat with their fingers?"

"This one does." He picked up the small cake and put the whole thing in his mouth in one bite.

Eight

Between my son decimating the lilacs, Miss Goodnight savaging the roses, and poor Hartley being sick in the hydrangeas, this family will be lucky to have any sort of garden at all this year.

—Phillippa, the Dowager Marchioness of Somerset

"I'M ALL RIGHT," RICHARD PROTESTED. HE COULDN'T remember a time when he felt more ridiculous.

"If you were all right, you wouldn't have been doubled over in the flower bed," Sophie said as she helped him up the stairs of Barrett House. Seymour had positioned himself on Richard's other side and was bearing most of his weight.

Richard turned his head far enough to catch his friend covering his mouth to stifle a laugh. If he weren't as weak as water, he'd cheerfully strangle Seymour. Another wave of nausea washed over him, and it was all he could do to master his stomach.

"Dear God, how long is this staircase?" he groaned.

"Only a bit further, my lord, and we'll have you right as rain in no time." Porter ran ahead to open the door to an unused room. By the time Richard and his bearers entered, the butler had turned back the bed-clothes and then replaced Sophie at Richard's left side.

"Let us get him settled, miss," Porter said, "and then you can tend him if you like while I fetch the doctor."

"No. No doctor." Richard pulled away from them. Eyes closed, he leaned against the wall, massaged his temples, and drew slow, measured breaths. His irritation at being ill was only exceeded by his self-loathing over it.

He was never weak. Seymour, on the other hand, was unnaturally fearful of heights and had once fainted dead away when the tip came off his rapier in a practice match, and he'd accidentally pinked Richard on the forearm. If there was any justice in the world, Seymour would have been the one casting up his accounts on the hydrangeas.

But the world was not just, and Richard was sick once again, though this time he made it to the ewer on the washstand. He wiped his mouth on the towel hanging on the rod beside the stand as Porter deftly took the ewer away.

"I'll just nip down to the parlor and get you a whisky, shall I?" Seymour said as he followed Porter out. "Expect there's a liquor cabinet there somewhere."

Too shaky to remain standing, Richard sank onto the bed, his chin on his chest.

"Can I help with your boots?" came a soft voice.

Oh God. She was still there. He flopped back on the bed and covered his eyes with his forearm. Would Sophie Goodnight never leave him alone?

Richard felt her tug at his feet, and the boots came off, one after the other.

"You don't have to do that," he said.

"Would you rather destroy the linens?" She lifted his legs, and he found himself being arranged and tucked, and too feeble to protest. "They're a bit old but still quite fine. Besides, I rather doubt you can afford to replace them."

"Unless I marry you, you mean."

"Why, of course, Richard." Her tone dripped with sarcasm. "Because every girl longs to wed a man who ruins her tea party by flashing the hash all over the garden."

He glared at her. She had a point, but he wasn't about to admit it.

Sophie dipped a cloth in the pitcher, wrung it out, and folded it into a rectangle. Then she placed it over his forehead. "Did you arrive already foxed?"

"Foxed? No." He hadn't had a thing to drink all day, though the whisky Seymour was fetching to settle his stomach wouldn't come amiss. Still, he'd expected sympathy from her instead of accusations. Where was the womanly concern? "Your bedside manner leaves a lot to be desired."

She arched a brow at him. "I can see why you might have been tempted to drink to excess, since you knew Lady Antonia and I would be in close proximity. That couldn't help but cut up your peace. But I assure you, I have only the best intentions regarding her." She hitched a hip on his bedside and blotted the damp cloth on his cheeks.

It was cool and soothing. A faint whiff of roses

tickled his nose, and he was grateful for his uneasy stomach's sake that she favored such a light scent. His eyes drifted shut.

"I support your choice, no matter how wrong I think Antonia is for you."

His eyes popped open at that. He reached up and grasped her wrist. "Why do you say that?"

"Well, for one thing, she's not here now, is she?"

"And I wouldn't want her here. No man wants a woman to see him so... Damn it, I don't want you here either."

"Damn it," she repeated with a half smile. "Spoken like you mean it too. Dear me. So you can become upset when properly motivated. I'd wondered. You Barretts seem so wretchedly calm at all times."

He wasn't calm on the inside. Half the time, he felt as if he were about to explode. Then it occurred to him that Sophie Goodnight might not limit herself to needling him with her words. "Is that why you dared me to... Did you do something to that cake?"

Her dark brows drew together, and she stood. "Of what are you accusing me?"

"I was perfectly well when I rode up to Barrett House's gate. That cake," he said slowly. "You had something put in that cake, didn't you?"

"How utterly ridiculous."

"Is it? But was it meant for me?" he wondered. "Or did you intend that cake for Antonia?"

"Of all the juvenile, petty, spiteful—"

"Indeed. It was all of those things. How could you?"

She dropped the wet cloth on his face with a splat. "If you get sick again, my lord, you can tend yourself."

Without another word, she flounced from the room, almost barreling into Seymour in her haste. Lawrence juggled the two glasses and a half-full bottle for a moment after Miss Goodnight's jostling, but he managed to hang on to all of them.

"Looks like you handled that well." Seymour poured up a couple fingers of the amber liquid for each of them and offered Richard one of the glasses. "Miss Goodnight couldn't leave fast enough."

"Good riddance." Richard sat up and sipped his whisky gingerly. At least it cut through the sick taste and warmed his assaulted belly.

"Don't look for Lady Antonia to sully her lily-white hands to care for you," Seymour said, drawing a chair close to the bed, turning it around, and straddling it so he could drape his long arms over the back. "As soon as you started retching, she began sidling toward the curricle she came in."

"Good." But part of him did wonder at her lack of concern. "I don't want her to see me like this."

Seymour shrugged. "What about that whole 'in sickness and in health' bit? Antonia might have at least hovered at the door to learn if you're all right."

"I hate to be hovered over." Richard shot him a glare. "In fact, you're doing it right now. I'm all right. I was just… Do you know I think Sophie Goodnight tried to poison me?"

Seymour snorted. "Well, that's an inventive way to break off your understanding."

"We have no understanding."

"My mistake." Seymour knocked back his glass and gave himself a slight shake at the high alcohol content in the single malt liquor. "That'll put hair on your chest. But back to Miss Goodnight. I thought your parents had the details of the betrothal all drawn up."

"They may have, but it would never work between Sophie and me. We can't seem to be in the same room for more than a few minutes without being cross as crabs with each other." Richard shook his head. "She's terribly touchy."

"And can you blame her after the way you've swatted down any talk of a match between you? I feel a mite insulted on her behalf my own self."

"Believe me, she doesn't want the match either."

"With a tip of the imaginary hat to the Bard," Seymour said, suiting his actions to his words, "'The lady doth protest too much, methinks.'"

"What do you mean by that?"

"Just that if you and Miss Goodnight are at loggerheads with each other each time you're alone, it may be because the lady wants to be doing something else with you." Seymour waggled his brows. "Something just as passionate as arguing but with a good bit less clothing involved."

"Is it ever about anything but shagging for you?"

"Not really. But just because you doubt, that doesn't mean I'm wrong. Mark my words. She has the look of a woman who wants...tending, shall we say?"

Memory of Sophie Goodnight's kiss in the gallery rushed back into him with the force of a gale. She was no pale flower. She kissed like a woman who knew and appreciated passion. And she wasn't a virgin. She obviously didn't want to marry him, but he couldn't deny that her body called to his. Maybe Seymour was right.

"Yes indeed. The lady craves a man's attention. If you won't do it," Seymour mused, "maybe I should."

"She'd eat you alive."

"Here's hoping."

"Seriously, Seymour, if you were caught with her, you'd find yourself saddled with an unintended bride for your trouble."

"A man has to marry some time," Seymour said. "An unintended bride with a dowry that would beggar a king. You know, that's not a bad idea. And it would certainly help you out of your unexpected entanglement, my friend. If I were to shag Miss Goodnight six ways from Sunday, you could—"

Seymour didn't get a chance to finish his thought. Richard was out of bed before he knew what he was doing. White-hot rage flared inside him, the onset just as quick as the sickness he'd experienced earlier—and much more virulent. He dragged Seymour by the collar up from his chair and slammed him against the wall, sending the shot glasses flying. Then he pinned his friend to the faded wallpaper with an arm across his windpipe.

"You are not to touch Sophie Goodnight; do you hear me?"

Seymour's mouth moved but no sound came out.

"Well?" Richard demanded.

Lawrence's fingers clawed at his forearm, and he eased up enough for his friend to gasp a breath.

"All right. Won't touch her," he bleated. "Not so much as a pinky."

As quickly as it had flared up, his anger dissipated, and he cursed himself for losing control. Richard staggered back and slumped into the chair.

"You're no fun when you're sick," Seymour said, taking care to remain out of reach. "Actually, you've been no fun since we left Paris. First, you declare your sisters off limits, and now you warn me off Miss Goodnight. While we're rusticating here in Somerset, is there anyone to whom I may direct my attentions without you threatening to strangle me?"

"My grandmother gave you permission to charm her."

"Thanks, friend." Lawrence retrieved the shot glasses, which hadn't shattered thanks to the Turkish carpets spread over the hardwood. "Your generosity overwhelms."

He refilled both and gave Richard another shot. "But you need to ask yourself something."

"What's that?"

"If you don't want Miss Goodnight, why does it bother you that someone else might?"

❦

All Eliza wanted to do was curl up in a ball by the hearth and cry, but she had to keep working. Mr. Porter was in a frantic state and desperate to remove all traces of the spoiled party, so she kept fetching and carrying while Mrs. Goodnight bade her guests farewell at the garden gate. The poor woman was wringing her hands and apologizing for this horrible bumble-broth, but all the fine ladies were making their excuses, prettily and politely but firmly. They were dead set on leaving.

And who could blame them? After Lord Hartley became ill, no one wanted to eat another bite.

Eliza trotted back and forth between the kitchen and the garden. Outside, Mr. Porter was muttering a blue streak as he removed chairs and tore down the tables. Inside, Mrs. Beckworth rattled her pots and made the crystal in the cupboard hum in sympathy as she shrilly declared it wasn't her fault. Her food had never sickened anybody.

Miss Quimby had vanished.

Eliza blinked back tears. If she wept, everyone would wonder why. She hadn't just fallen off the back of the potato wagon. It was plain to anyone with eyes that Lord Hartley had taken sick awfully quick.

It wasn't natural. Which means it was something he ate, no matter what Mrs. Beckworth said. And the only thing he'd eaten was that lovely bit of lemon cake.

Which Eliza had put into his hands herself.

She fought to keep from shaking. Once the Goodnights started thinking about things, they'd realize she was the one who delivered the offending cake. She'd be out on her ear in less time than a than a hare took with his missus.

And then what would she do? Her mum couldn't take her back in again. There were far too many little ones still at home to feed. Without the money Eliza sent home from her wages each week, they'd be pinched even tighter.

Her friend Celia had gone to London looking for work. Celia couldn't write more than her name, but she'd promised to send word once she got herself settled. Only trouble was no one had heard from her again.

It was as if the big city had swallowed her whole.

Trying her luck in London looked to be Eliza's only choice if Mr. Hightower let her go over this.

She'd be dismissed without character too. She'd never get a position in another reputable house without references.

Oh God.

Unable to hold back the tears any longer, she ducked behind the overgrown gorse bush next to the door that led to the kitchen. Eliza finally let herself weep. She tried to stifle her sobs, but a few slipped out in any case. Then she tried to stop crying altogether and only succeeded in giving herself a case of the hiccups. Eliza pulled out a handkerchief and blew her nose loudly.

"If you're finished back there, I'd like to speak with you, if I may."

Lord, it's that Miss Goodnight. Now I'm for it.

Eliza slipped from behind the bush, mindful not to get too close to it on account of the thorns. She dropped a curtsy before Miss Goodnight and then cast her gaze downward. The lady's silk-covered toe was tapping furiously on the grass.

"You were the one who served Lord Hartley, I believe."

"Yes, miss," she said, misery oozing from every pore.

"But I don't think you had anything to do with him becoming ill."

Eliza's gaze shot up at that. Arms folded over her chest, Miss Goodnight fixed her with a penetrating stare.

"No, miss. That I didn't, but if you don't mind my asking, what makes *you* think I didn't?"

"It would be the height of foolishness for you to taint the food and then serve it yourself." Miss Goodnight cocked her head to one side. "And you don't strike me as a fool."

"You either, my lady." Then because she realized that might have seemed impertinent, Eliza ducked her head.

"I'm no lady, but we'll let that go for now. Eliza, is it?" She nodded.

"Who do you think put something in that cake?"

"I don't know. Not for sure." Mr. Porter and Mrs. Beckworth had been at Barrett House for years. They surely wouldn't have done such a thing, no matter what they might think about the unevenness of a possible match between Lord Hartley and Miss Goodnight. And Miss Quimby had been so nice to Eliza it was hard for her to believe she'd done it. Of course, she had made herself scarce after the incident. "I didn't see nothing for certain, and I don't want to get no one into trouble just from my guessing."

Her gaze dropped again. The slipper toe was still tapping. Then it stopped, and Eliza waited for the boom to drop.

"You don't point fingers when it would help you to do so," Miss Goodnight said in a tone that suggested she thought that was a good thing. "Tell me, Eliza. Do you normally work at Somerfield Park?"

"Yes, miss. I work in the kitchen under Mrs. Culpepper. I'm only here today because Mr. Porter asked for volunteers to help out."

Oh, how she wished she hadn't piped up.

Please God, if I get out of this and still have my position, I'll never be puffed up with pride enough to push myself forward again.

"What else can you do besides kitchen work and serving at table, Eliza?"

"Bit of sewing, miss." Eliza's mind raced furiously, thinking of what other qualifications she might have. She'd helped tend all her younger brothers and sisters, but that wouldn't interest Miss Goodnight. Still, she decided to list the things she'd done for her siblings. "Washing, mending, cutting hair—"

"You can do hair?"

"Yes, miss." Any fool with a pair of scissors and a bowl the right size could give a haircut.

"Then I think you'll do nicely."

"Do nicely as what, miss?"

"As my new lady's maid, of course. Lady Somerset the elder tells me I need one, and I think she's right. My father will no doubt wish to discuss your salary requirements, but I'm sure you'll find he's more than fair. Give your notice at Somerfield Park and report back here as soon as you're able."

Eliza narrowly resisted the urge to pinch herself.

"Unless you prefer to work in the kitchen."

"Oh, no, miss, I'll be happy to come work for you. Indeed, I will. Oh, thank you, miss. You won't be sorry, not a bit."

"I've a feeling they'll be sorry at Somerfield Park. It occurs to me that poaching someone else's servant is not really the done thing, and I've stepped on any number of toes by doing so," Miss Goodnight said with a slight frown, and Eliza worried that she'd change her mind. Then she smiled. "Fortunately, I'm not sort who worries about whether something is the done thing or not."

"It if will ease your mind, miss, my sister Theresa can take my place at Somerfield Park. Mr. Hightower will be pleased with her. She's a useful one, she is. Clever with her hands."

"Very well, but don't tell me anymore about her lest I hire her too," Miss Goodnight said. "And pack your bags, Eliza. Apparently I need a new wardrobe, which requires the assistance of a maid to don, so we'll be going to London for a few days."

If Miss Goodnight was getting new dresses, that meant she'd be parting with some of her old ones. As her lady's maid, Eliza would be in line to receive them as part of her pay. Her vision tunneled, and she forced herself to breathe deeply. She'd keep one or two of the plainest ones to wear for church or if she was ever asked to walk out by a young man, but she could sell the fine ones to supplement her regular wages, which she suspected were going to be buckets better than what she made as a kitchen drudge.

Eliza was suddenly rich. Would she ever be able to stop smiling, or would her face be stuck like this forever?

"Off you go now. And, Eliza, after we get to know each other better, I hope you'll feel comfortable telling me who you think put something in Lord Hartley's cake."

She nodded, not trusting her voice, and set off for Somerfield Park at a brisk trot. Eliza still wasn't sure enough to say Miss Quimby had fouled that cake, but as she neared the door to Somerfield's kitchen, she remembered something.

She was supposed to have given that cake to Miss Goodnight.

Nine

Never underestimate the importance of the little things—a well-laid table, the correct mode of address, a coiffure without a hair out of place. There is nothing so satisfying as seeing something done well, even if it borders on excess. However, if one isn't trying to impress others, it is surprising what one can do without.

—Phillippa, the Dowager Marchioness of Somerset

"TELL ME AGAIN WHY I USED UP THE LAST OF MY CREDIT for this demmed luncheon?" Lord Pruett said testily.

"Because, Papa, after the fiasco at Barrett House last week, *Maman* thought it best to act quickly while that disaster was still fresh in everyone's mind."

Antonia adjusted the tasteful centerpiece of deep purple dahlias on the long table under the pergola. She and her mother had been busy supervising the ornamentation of one of the Somerfield Park follies. A number of such sham decorative buildings dotted the grounds—the fake ruins of an abbey, a portion of an Egyptian pyramid, and half a rotunda that echoed a Roman temple. The one Antonia chose for her bacchanalian-themed picnic was designed to look like a Greek theatre.

"By hosting a flawless event," she said, "we will demonstrate to Hartley's family that I belong in their circle."

Her father grumbled a few less than gentlemanly words under his breath. "I'd feel better about the expense if his lordship had declared himself."

So would Antonia. Hartley had been so close to proposing to her in Paris before that fateful letter arrived. He'd given her all the right signals, but he hadn't said the words. She wasn't too concerned though, because despite his illustrious birth and powerful position, Hartley was the quiet sort.

"Still waters run deep," she assured her father. Just because Hartley hadn't proposed, it didn't mean he wasn't smitten with her. "He'll come to it soon, Papa."

"He'd better."

Since the heir to Somerset had been paying court to Antonia, her father's credit had been extended based on the close association with a future marquess. However, if Lord and Lady Somerset were still pressuring Hartley to wed Miss Goodnight, there must be some money issue on the Somerset side no one suspected.

But a family with as much land as the Barretts had surely couldn't be as strapped as that. Of course, Hartley hadn't told her the particulars. Naturally, he wouldn't.

"I thought it would help that Miss Goodnight and her mother had gone to London," her father went on. "But Mr. Goodnight is still at Barrett House with a standing invitation to join the family each evening for supper."

That certainly signaled a wish for a continued relationship

between Hartley and Miss Goodnight for some reason.

"I know, Papa. It is maddening, but I don't see how I can do more." She waved to the first group of guests making their way across the green. Hartley was surrounded by his sisters. Seymour moped behind them with the dowager on his arm. At a distance, a footman was pushing Lord Somerset's wheelchair. Lady Somerset walked sedately beside it, twirling her parasol slowly.

Lord Pruett made a low growling noise in his throat. "I didn't want you to stoop to this idea, and if you tell your mother I suggested this, I'll deny it. But I think you'd better arrange to be caught with Hartley in a compromising position."

"Papa!" She tried to sound shocked, but in truth, she'd been considering it herself. Of course, being caught *in flagrante delicto* could be difficult, since Hartley had been such a blasted gentleman of late.

In Paris, he'd been so ardent. She'd had to fend him off when their stolen kisses threatened to stray into something more. Now, she barely rated a peck on the cheek when he bade her good night.

He was bridling himself so tightly when he was around her. Well, today would be different. Today, he'd relax in her presence again. And with any luck at all, amid the false ruins of classical Greece, her taciturn man would find the words that would seal her future.

ॐ

"Come, Hartley, it'll be fun," Antonia said. "And it's in keeping with our theme. I have it on good authority that hide-and-seek was played in second-century Greece."

"It's also played by every schoolboy in Christendom,"

Richard said as he raised a hand to stop her from tying a blindfold on him.

"I'm game. Still a schoolboy at heart, you know. What are the boundaries?" Seymour asked.

"How about the follies and woods within sight of this one," Antonia said. "And no hiding in pairs."

"Drat!" Seymour said with a waggle of his brows at Lady Ella.

Richard's sister gave an exaggerated sniff and pointedly looked away from Seymour.

Good. Ella was so keen to have her Season once the family's money troubles were resolved, Richard had been afraid she'd start practicing for her come-out by flirting with Lawrence. Fortunately, his reputation as a womanizer preceded him, and when Ella wasn't giving him a cut direct, she was disgusted by Seymour completely.

"You see the way the women in your family abuse me, Hartley," Seymour complained.

"Perhaps it's because we remember the tricks you played on us when we were younger," Petra said dryly. "It's amazing how pigtails dipped in ink and toads in our shoes have inoculated us against your charms."

"But I only did those things to you, Petra," Seymour said. "What's Lady Ella's excuse?"

"Extreme disinterest?" Petra suggested.

"Please, Hartley. You must be it," Antonia pleaded with a roll of her icy, pale eyes. "Never say you'd rather go with the ancients to feed the swans."

The older members of the party along with young Ariel had already set off in the direction of the duck pond, accompanied by the footman pushing Lord Somerset's chair.

"No, I can't say I want to see bird bums in the air."

"If we're taking a vote, I can think of some other bums I'd like to see smiling at the sun," Seymour said. Ella ignored him again, but Petra swatted him with her fan.

"Now look what you've made me do," she complained as she studied the fan. "Some of the lace is detached."

"Pardon me, Lady Petra," Seymour said with exaggerated manners. "I shouldn't have allowed my shoulder to get in the way of your fan."

Richard grinned. His sisters were more than a match for Seymour and didn't require his constant monitoring. He let Antonia blindfold him, her hands cool as they brushed his cheeks.

"Now then, count to one hundred and slowly, mind," Antonia whispered in his ear. Her breath raised a ripple of goose bumps on his neck. "When you find one of us, we must come back here. Last one to be found wins."

"What's the prize?" Seymour asked.

"How about a kiss from whomever the winner chooses?" There was a smile in Antonia's voice. Richard would try to make sure he found her last.

"One!" he thundered. The group set off in a flurry of laughing voices that faded as they moved farther away, their footfalls ever softer on the spring grass.

Richard felt his way along the table and sat in one of the chairs as he continued to count silently.

The afternoon had been idyllic. Antonia was a consummate hostess, making sure everyone was comfortable and having a good time. She was solicitous of his poor father. It had made Richard's chest constrict to see her help his mother feed Lord Somerset, all the while chatting gaily to keep up his mother's spirits. Once, he was almost sure his father had given Antonia a half smile.

So why didn't he defy his parents' wishes and go ahead and propose to her?

Once he gave his word to Antonia, he couldn't take it back without serious damage to his reputation. Somerset would simply have to find another way to muddle through this financial crisis without the Goodnight fortune.

But even though he hadn't seen Sophie for a week, she still plagued his dreams. He'd never considered himself particularly inventive when it came to matters sensual, but the erotic nature of his dreams of late gave the lie to that.

He'd wake with his heart hammering, images of silken limbs and furious kisses fading as he regained full consciousness. Blue eyes languid, her mouth passion-slack, her glorious dark hair spread over his pillow, Sophie Goodnight laid siege to his imagination and battered down his defenses every time his eyes closed.

Seymour, on the other hand, had always been comfortable with the sensual side of his nature. When they were at school together, he regularly led forays over the wall and into town in search of willing tavern girls. But Richard had always been a little embarrassed by the demands of his body and found excuses to bow out of Seymour's occasional prowls. It seemed the height of vulnerability to need someone else so intimately.

And Richard was never comfortable with being vulnerable.

Of course, in his dreams of Sophie, he was in total control, and she responded to his lovemaking the same way she'd kissed him: with heart-stopping abandon. The way she sighed, the way her skin was all soft and giving, the smell of her—sweet roses with a musky undernote of wanting woman…

It struck him suddenly that he'd stopped counting. He had no idea how long he'd sat there with that stupid blindfold on his head. With a muttered curse, he tore it off and looked around.

No one was in sight. All the other hide-and-seek players were no doubt holed up in the follies. But suddenly the faux temples and abbeys seemed beyond ridiculous to him. If only his ancestors had invested the money they wasted on imitation buildings, perhaps Somerset would be solvent now. Besides, after the way his dreams had invaded his thoughts, Richard desperately wanted something real.

He turned away from the sham structures and started walking toward the actual ruins of the old keep that had once been the stronghold of the first marquess of Somerset. The remains of the castle might be tumbling down more with each year, but at least they once had a purpose.

The Somerset follies never would.

*   ❧   *

Richard climbed over the crumbling stone that had been part of the curtain wall and into the remains of a little gothic chapel. There, lit by a shaft of light that spilled in through the open roof, was Sophie Goodnight. She was seated on a heavy plaid blanket spread out over the grass that had reclaimed the sacred space. A drawing pad was propped on her knees, and her soft lead pencil scratched away furiously.

He almost wasn't surprised to find her there. He'd been thinking about his dreams of her so intently it was almost as if he'd conjured her.

Sophie gave no evidence of being aware of his presence yet, so he felt free to study her as intently as she was studying whatever it was she was drawing. She'd removed her bonnet, and her hair had tumbled down in unruly locks over her shoulders. He'd felt those long strands in his dreams, sliding over his palms, gliding over his bare chest as she kissed her way down to torment his groin, thousands of silken fingers caressing his skin.

He wondered if the real-life article would live up to his nocturnal imaginings. She bit her bottom lip in concentration, and he burned to suckle it as well.

What was wrong with him? He was supposed to be in love with Antonia. Could it be he was as randy a rake as Seymour and no more faithful?

He moved a little closer, dislodging a few bricks from their place.

"Hello, Richard," she said without glancing his way.

"How did you know it was me?"

"Anyone else would have announced their presence." She turned to look at him then, her eyes sparking with amusement at his expense. How did she always manage to make him feel a fool? "But not you. You're the sort who likes to reconnoiter before committing to an action."

"Reconnoitering is a type of spying. You make me sound like a miserable Peeping Tom."

"No, just someone who never does anything without deliberation. I like that about you." Sophie turned back to her drawing. "Besides, I'm not naked."

"I beg your pardon." Since she planted the idea in his head, a vision of Sophie Goodnight in nothing but her glorious skin popped up in salacious detail.

"I refer, of course, to the first Peeping Tom. Surely you've heard the legend of Lady Godiva?" Since his tongue had suddenly cleaved to the roof of his mouth, he couldn't form an answer. Undeterred, she went on. "She rode naked through the town to persuade her lordly husband not to tax the poor so heavily. All the townsfolk agreed ahead of time not to look upon her, and they all lived up to their part of the bargain. Except for someone named Tom who couldn't keep his eyes where they belonged."

Richard's imagined Sophie had high full breasts with pert nipples the color of berries. She wouldn't be the sort to cover herself coyly. The Sophie in his dreams always invited him to look on her, as much and wherever he liked. He plopped down on a large, dressed stone to cover his growing erection. "In fairness to Tom, he was sorely tempted."

"So you're saying you were sorely tempted to peep on me?" She flicked her gaze at him, then back to her sketchbook.

"A bit. You're quite lovely, you know," he admitted. "When you're not being sarcastic."

She laughed at that. "Which is pretty much whenever I speak, so I forgive you for resorting to peeping." She bent her head and continued sketching.

While he found her silences comforting, Richard realized he'd also come to enjoy the musical sound of her voice. He cast about for a way to keep her talking. "I didn't think you'd returned from London yet."

"Just this morning."

"The word is that you went in search of a wardrobe that requires assistance to get out of." Why on earth had he said that? The vision of Sophie unclothed had just begun to fade.

"And I found it. This is one of my new dresses."

Richard eyed her thin muslin gown with its raised waist. The trim at the hem was very fine and under-stated. The bodice was cut low enough to show a bit of the hollow between her breasts. But baring the better materials, it didn't seem all that different from the gardening smock she'd been wearing the first time he met her. "It looks like any other dress to me."

"Oh, you silver-tongued devil." Sophie shook her head and presented her back to him, flipping her hair over one shoulder. She unhooked the first few buttons that marched down her spine, but there was another full dozen below that which she couldn't reach. The fabric peeled away on either side to expose the skin between her shoulder blades. Richard bridled himself not to hurry to her side to finish the job. "There. You see? I can't reach all the buttons. Blame your grandmother."

"My grandmother?"

"Yes, she's the one who alerted me to the fact that I need to provide employment for others. Being unable to dress or undress myself means I need help, so I engaged a maid." She lifted her heavy hair off her neck and fanned herself with her sketchbook. A sheen of perspiration showed on the newly exposed skin. "It's so warm today."

"Not as hot as India, I'll warrant."

"No, not as hot as that." She dropped her hair and looked away. "You may as well share my blanket. Otherwise, you'll spoil your trousers on the granite."

"Inexpressibles," he corrected.

She shot him a puzzled look.

"Trousers. Ladies refer to them as 'inexpressibles.'"

"Why?"

"Because most ladies don't want to admit they notice the lower half of a man, I suppose."

"Another reason I'll never be a lady."

Richard settled beside her, wondering if she was objecting to the coyness of proper speech or if she was admitting to enjoying looking at a man's trousers. He rather hoped it was the latter because he filled his out well, if he did say so himself.

He peered over her shoulder at the sketchbook. She'd captured the remaining half wall of the chapel with its gothic arched window openings. "This chapel once used to be quite ornate, I'm told."

"I'm sure it was nothing compared to the ornamentation in Indian temples," she said.

"Tell me about them."

She chuckled. "I think not. I've already shocked you with the story of Godiva. If I describe the sybaritic friezes at the temple in Khajuraho, you'll be hopelessly scandalized."

His interest was definitely piqued. "Somerfield Park is hopelessly mired in correctness. Perhaps I could use a little scandal."

"My word, is the staid Lord Hartley flirting with me?"

"Flirting? Of course not." No, he wasn't. He tried very hard to imagine Antonia's blond loveliness, but her face wouldn't come into focus. "Tell me something else about India then. What did you see in it?"

"That's the amazing thing about the place. It's whatever people wish to see. If you want to find an incredibly rich culture with art and music and myriad tongues, you won't be disappointed. If you want to see impressive scenery, the jungles and the distant Himalayas are amazing. But if you wish to see ignorance and squalor, you will find that as well."

Richard shrugged. "One only has to look as far as Whitechapel to find that."

Her gaze snapped toward him sharply. "Exactly. You'd be surprised how many Englishmen bewail the plight of poor natives when his countrymen wallow in poverty and crime-ridden ghettos."

"Careful. You sound like a reformer."

"Not me. I have enough trouble with my own life. I've no wish to direct anyone else's." She closed the sketchbook before he could get a look at anything else she was drawing.

"That's something I like about you, Sophie." There were plenty of people trying to direct his life at the moment, but the woman next to him was not among them. "You know when not to stick your oar in."

"Someone is pushing you?"

"The line forms at Somerfield Park's front door." He leaned back and stretched his legs in front of him. "But no one puts as much pressure on me as I do myself."

"Then you'd better do what you must to satisfy yourself." Her words made great sense, but he was captivated by the way her little pink tongue peeped from between her lips as she spoke. "After all, you're going to be with you for a long time."

"On the moment, I can think of only one thing that will satisfy me." Richard sat up, reached to cup the back of her head, and leaned in to kiss her.

Ten

While I'm a firm believer in careful planning, the things that happen to us by accident often turn out to be delightfully astonishing.

—Phillippa, the Dowager Marchioness of Somerset

SOPHIE ALMOST JERKED AWAY IN SURPRISE, BUT Richard moved with such deliberate purpose, she was mesmerized. The first time he'd kissed her, it had come in a frenzied rush. It was hard and fast—a kiss that had something to prove. That kiss had been almost a dare, and not one to back down, she'd responded with all the passion of her nature.

This kiss was a leisurely question. He explored her mouth with tenderness. She answered him in kind. She lost herself in the gentle play of lips and tongues, and the sweetness of a shared breath.

"Are you willing to know this part of me?" he murmured between kisses.

"Yes, Richard."

"I won't hurt you." His kiss deepened, turned darker and more beguiling. She'd heard of swimmers being lost to the "rapture of the deep," unwilling to surface even to save themselves. She began to understand them.

"You won't mean to," she gasped.

"You've been hurt before." He claimed her mouth with more insistence.

"Only once." She surrendered to him before remembering she had to keep the upper hand. Her tongue teased him till he groaned into her mouth. Then she tore her lips away long enough to say, "I take care that it will never happen again."

But for the moment, his mouth, his kiss was all there was. Somehow without realizing how they had gotten into that position, Sophie was dimly aware that they were both lying on their sides facing each other on the plaid blanket, and Richard's large hands had found those tiny pearl buttons on the back of her gown. His fingertips brushed her shoulder blades, sending little pixies of pleasure dancing along her exposed skin. He tugged the gown down over her shoulders, pinning her arms to her sides. Sophie wiggled her arms free. She never wanted to feel helpless.

Her breasts were spilling over the top of her stays. The only thing separating them from his touch was the thin linen of her chemise.

Richard kissed down her neck and took the ribbon that held the chemise closed in his teeth. He tugged the knot free. Then he nuzzled the undergarment aside and covered her breast with kisses, his warm breath swirling over her charged skin.

Her nipple ached so she couldn't keep herself from

arching into him. When he finally took it into his mouth, she cried out for the joy of it. She buried her fingers in his hair. She wanted to hold him there forever.

Tugging. Suckling. Nipping.

Everything was heat and wanting and slick wetness. That drumbeat between her legs... Oh yes, she remembered that. She didn't think she'd ever feel that rhythmic ache again, but there it was, even more demanding and powerful.

As long as that is only what it is and not pretending to be something more.

When Richard kissed his way back up to her mouth, he hitched a leg around her and drew her close. There they were—pressed against each other, all their hills and valleys filling each other with such rightness. He rocked against her and a thrill shot through her.

The great and proper Lord Hartley, the man who kept himself in check at all times, wanted her desperately. If she encouraged him only a little, he'd tug up her skirts and rut her like a magnificent beast.

Then he tore his lips from hers, his breathing ragged.

"I can't," he said.

"Yes, you certainly can." His hardness proclaimed his readiness so loudly she could hardly hear anything else. "Though I haven't said you *may*."

"But I shouldn't have let myself... I'm sorry, Sophie."

"There's no need." She wedged a hand between them to lay it on his chest. "You haven't done anything to hurt me. It's been wonderful actually. In fact, I don't know why you stopped."

"You don't understand." Richard rested his forehead against hers, his eyes still closed. Beneath her hand, his heart pounded like a coach and six. "I stopped because I had to while I still could. You haven't said yes. God help me, I didn't even ask, but I can't answer for my actions if we continue, and I don't want that for you. I'm deeply sorry. I shouldn't—"

"Don't apologize. Not for this. We shared a moment, Richard. We were genuine with each other. Do you have any idea how rare that is?"

He opened his eyes and met hers for the space of several heartbeats. His pupils were so wide his usually amber eyes went almost black, deep wells a girl might tumble into and never be able to climb out of. It was too open, that look. Too enticing.

Sophie was relieved when he broke off their gaze and began retying her chemise closed and hitching up her gown. Then he stopped and looked at her face again, a bit of wonder in his eyes, as if he was seeing her for the first time.

"You are…" he whispered, "quite extraordinary."

She sat up and arranged her gown so that she was completely covered once again. "One of a kind, that's me."

He sat up as well and began refastening the row of buttons at her back. "Why must you always do that?"

"Do what?"

"Make light of it when I try to compliment you."

She had to make light of it. If she took a man's pretty words to heart, she'd risk opening herself to hurt. And that was not going to happen.

"Have you been trying to compliment me?" she said as she put her bonnet on and tied the ribbons under her chin. "I hadn't noticed."

"Then I shall have to try harder," Richard said.

"But what I must not do is more of this. Truly, I apologize, Sophie. It's not fair to you."

"Why? I was having a wonderful time. Didn't you enjoy it?"

He blinked at her as if she'd suddenly sprouted a second head. "That's not in question."

"Then I don't see the problem." She rose to her feet and began dusting pine needles and grass seeds off her skirt. "Honestly, Richard, it's not the end of the world. We kissed. We did a bit more than kiss. I liked it. You liked it. No one has been hurt by it."

Richard stood, hands in his pockets. "Antonia would be if she knew."

"Well, she won't hear it from me." Sophie picked up the blanket and began folding it. "But why should she be hurt? Have you proposed to her?"

"No."

"Told her you love her?"

"Not in so many words…"

"Believe me, there are only three that count," she said, bending to retrieve her sketchbook and pencil. "Do you kiss her and a bit more sometimes too?"

"No, it wouldn't be proper."

She arched a brow at him. "But it's all right to do so with me because I'm not proper to begin with."

"Sophie, I didn't mean… I don't think of you like that."

"Never mind. I'm teasing you." She swatted his broad shoulder with the back of her hand. "I know I'm not proper so no harm done. But if we aren't going to do any more kissing, we need to do something else. Will you walk with me, Richard?"

"I'm supposed to be playing hide-and-seek."

"Really? It doesn't sound as if you're enjoying it much."

"I wasn't." He grinned wickedly at her. "Until I found you."

"Yes, but I'm not part of your game."

"No, you're playing one of your own, and I have no idea what the rules are."

"Good." She smiled at him. He was dazzlingly handsome when he frowned a bit in confusion. "That's the way I like it. While we walk, you can find the others as we go. Two birds with one stone."

He took the blanket from her and draped it over one arm while offering her the other. She took it, and he led her through the ruins of the Gothic arch and out of the ancient keep.

"I'll bet this was a beautiful place in its day."

"Beautiful and deadly," Richard agreed. "The Barretts used this castle to hold Somerset for hundreds of years. Pity that force can't hold it now."

"No, now it takes buckets of money to run an estate," Sophie said. "Isn't it amazing that there is nothing the *ton* despises so much as someone who makes his own fortune while they all desperately need some of their own?"

"I'm not after your fortune, Sophie," he said with such earnestness she believed him. "It's insulting, you know. The idea that someone should wed you for your father's purse. You should be enough for anyone."

"Some might argue I'm too much."

"You're doing it again. Can't you just accept that I have formed a good opinion of you?"

She knew she shouldn't let them, but his words sank in and warmed her chest in a way that made her want to retreat. It wouldn't take long before she came to depend on his good opinion. Need it, even. And it wasn't safe to need someone.

Was that why he'd stopped kissing her? She had a hard time believing Richard Barrett would ever not be in complete command of himself.

Did he also have reason not to need anyone?

"You bridle yourself quite severely, Richard. Wound tight as a crossbow, my father would say. Why is that?"

"Because I know what can happen if I don't."

That sounded ominous, but he didn't expand on it. They walked in silence for a few steps, the only sound the swish of their footfalls. The forest floor was carpeted with leaf litter from the previous fall, vining ground cover, and the occasional mushroom. A few spindly trees grew under the dense canopy of the forest, but most of the tree trunks were bare of branches until they spread out in the sunshine far overhead.

"No decent climbing trees here, are there?" Sophie said.

"I guess not."

"Don't you know? Didn't you climb trees when you were a boy?"

"I wasn't at Somerfield Park all that often actually. When I was eight, I was sent to my bachelor uncle's place in London to study Latin and rhetoric and sums with his old tutor. Then it was off to Eton at twelve. After that, I read law at Oxford and then traveled the Continent for a couple of years with Seymour."

"Sounds as if you've had a broad range of experience."

"If we're talking about the last couple of years, yes. I've seen a good bit of the world and liked it." He covered the hand she'd slipped around his elbow with his warm one. "But all in all, my education was pretty much the done thing for someone like me."

"I can't imagine what it must have been like to be away from one's family so much as a child. Were you lonely?"

"If I was, I didn't dare admit it. You've met my family. We Barretts aren't the demonstrative sort. Stiff upper lip and all that, so I doubt I missed much. But public school life was rather like being raised by wolves."

"How so?" she asked.

"'Might makes right' in a setting of all boys, and there was a beastly prefect who had it in for me from the first day. He was a scholarship student."

"What do you mean by that?"

"No title. Not even a 'Sir Somebody' in his lineage. He was a hothead commoner with a sharp mind, a wicked left hook, and a chip on his shoulder. I was the highest-ranking new boy, and to make matters worse, I was small for my age."

She cast him a dubious glance. At a couple inches over six feet, broad shouldered, and narrow hipped, Richard was anything but small now. "You seem to have outgrown your puny stage quite nicely."

He smiled. "Thank God I hit a growth spurt after my thirteenth birthday, but that didn't help me when I was twelve. Samuel Moffat pummeled me every chance he got and encouraged others to do so as well."

"How did the school officials allow such a thing?"

"They didn't know about it. I certainly wasn't

going to tell them. Cry foul to the professors and you're marked for life."

"How long did this go on?"

"Until the start of the Lent half that first year. A new pupil arrived who was even smaller than me, and Moffat transferred his attentions to him immediately. The first time I caught him beating the new boy, something snapped inside me, and I tore into him like a whirlwind."

"Good for you."

"Not so good for Moffat though. He'd only given me bruises up to that point, and he was careful to deliver them where they wouldn't show." Richard shook his head. "I wasn't so fastidious. The rage inside me was so great I fear I might have killed him if the other boy hadn't pulled me off him. As it was, I knocked Moffat's front teeth out."

"Good. The bully deserved it, and I hope his soup strainer serves as a reminder to him not to torment others in the future," she said. "Whatever happened to him?"

"Last I heard Samuel Moffat was a magistrate in Essex with a pronounced lisp and a reputation for hard-nosed sentencing."

"And what about that new boy?"

"Oh, him. He became a layabout and a wastrel," Richard said. "And my best friend. The new boy was Lawrence Seymour."

Sophie laughed. "No wonder you're so close. I'll bet no one bothered either of you after you whaled the tar out of Samuel Moffat."

"No, they didn't."

"Why don't you say that like it's a good thing?"

"I guess because it taught me something about

myself that I'd rather not have learned. I have a temper, Sophie. A violent one, as it turns out. And if I don't control it, someone can get hurt."

"That explains your need to maintain a tight rein on yourself," Sophie said. Perhaps it made sense for his temper, but it didn't account for why he bridled himself when they were kissing. She wondered what he'd be like if he ever let himself lose control.

"Samuel was a bully, it's true, but looking back, I think I understand why," he said. "There he was, a commoner in a crowd of the privileged. He must have felt like an outsider. And no matter how bright he was, he was doomed to the fringes of our society once we all matriculated, and he knew it. While he was at school, at least he could exercise the power he'd been given as prefect and lord it over us all."

"What keen insight you have into the common mind," she said.

"It hasn't helped me understand you one whit." Then he gave himself a slight shake and shook his head. "Not that I think of you as common. To be honest, I don't know what to think of you most of the time. Oh, hang it all, that didn't come out right either. No offense intended."

"None taken." Sophie chuckled. The man was undeniably appealing when he was trying to extricate his foot from his mouth. "But what don't you understand about me? I'm an open book."

"Unlike Moffat, you could move into the ranks of the privileged by marriage, yet you seem pretty seriously opposed to it."

"It's nothing personal, Richard."

"On the contrary"—he stopped walking and she was forced to pause and look up at him—"marriage is nothing if not personal."

"Too many treat it as nothing, then." Sophie did not want to talk about this with him. If she did, the barricade she'd erected around her heart might crack, and she'd be utterly defenseless. Better to hold on to her shield and remain an enigma. "Please, Richard, this is far too serious a topic for such a lovely day. So am I right in assuming that Somerfield Park doesn't feel like home to you since you haven't lived here much?"

"No, you're wrong. Of course it's home." He put a hand to the thick trunk of a ponderous oak. "It's where I belong."

"But not where you've put down roots."

"I'm a Barrett. Believe me, I could not be more deeply attached to this place if I had roots to rival this old fellow." He thumped the trunk with the heel of his hand and moved on. "Now that the marquess is incapacitated, Somerset is my duty."

"And I suppose I'm a duty too. Marrying the money to keep it going, I mean," Sophie said with a sigh. "What a pity you can't come up with another way to fund the place."

Richard eyed the woods speculatively. "Yes. A pity. No, I'm sorry. I don't mean it would be a pity to have to marry yo—"

"Stop that, Richard. Never apologize for speaking your mind with me. We both know what our parents want, and have very wisely joined forces against them." Sophie walked on, forcing him to trot to catch up to her. "Besides, even if you asked me, as you say, I'm in no hurry to join the ranks of the aristocracy. There's no guarantee I'd accept you."

"Really?" he said with a grin. "If it comes to down to it, maybe I'd have to kiss you into submission. You seemed open to suggestion then."

"Suggestion, yes. Submission, no." She pointed to the break in the trees where the folly designed to look like a pyramid could be seen. "Correct me if I'm wrong, but I believe I saw your sister Ella duck behind the obelisk."

"That sounds like a blatant attempt to turn our conversation away from kissing." He caught her hand in his.

"Aren't you the one who said it was something we shouldn't do more of?"

"I say a lot of stupid things."

She smiled at him. Lord, she was lovely with her lips kiss-swollen and her hair tumbling from beneath her bonnet. And that smile... He could die happy if Sophie Goodnight would just keep smiling at him like that.

Then a blur of movement caught the tail of his eye, and he spotted Ella peering over the slanting wall of the Egyptian folly.

"You're right. There's my sister. We'll have to revisit the issue of kisses another day. Time to find my first hider." Richard sprinted toward the Egyptian scene and found Ella crouched beside the pyramid.

"Finally," Ella said as she stood. "I was beginning to think you'd never find me. Am I the winner?"

"No, you're the first one I've found."

"What have you been doing all this—oh! Miss Goodnight, I didn't see you there." Ella's sharp gaze swept over her. "We didn't know you were back from

London. If we had, I'm sure my mother would have insisted Lady Antonia invite you to her picnic."

"And I'm sure Lady Antonia would have been delighted to have me," Sophie said sardonically. "But Mother and I only just returned this morning. I'm sure she would have been too tired for frivolities after the trip."

Ella cast a suspicious eye at the blanket folded over her brother's arm. "So you've been...resting in our woods then?"

"Oh no, I've been sketching." Sophie waved her art book. "Do you draw?"

"Not beyond stick people," Ella admitted.

"Maybe you'd have better luck with architecture. It's just basic lines and angles really. Once you find a fixed point for perspective, it's nearly as predictable as mathematics," Sophie said. "There are some lovely ruins in your woods that want capturing."

"Apparently, that's not all that wants capturing," Ella muttered, then a look of panic crossed her features. "Oh, you said I'm the first you found?"

Richard nodded.

"Then you'd better hurry to the abbey. Seymour was bedeviling me a bit, and after I sent him off with a flea in his ear, he headed that way."

"I should probably try to find Antonia," Richard said, checking his pocket watch. Time had gotten away from him badly while he was tangled up with Sophie on that plaid blanket. "She's our hostess for this little fete, after all."

"You'd do better to find our sister," Ella said meaningfully. "Petra was going to hide in the abbey."

"You're right. I'm off then." He handed the

blanket back to Sophie. Their fingers touched, but he forced himself to pull away. "Thank you for the walk, Miss Goodnight. Why don't you join the party now? Ella will walk you back to the Parthenon."

"I wouldn't want to intrude."

"I insist," he said with the air of a man who had only to speak and it would be done. Sometimes, it was very good to be Lord Hartley, heir to the Somerset marquessate. Then, because it was Sophie Goodnight he was speaking to, he added, "Please."

She flashed that brilliant smile of hers, the one that made him want to climb mountains for her, and nodded.

Richard started to turn away, but she stopped him with a hand to his arm. "I shouldn't worry about your sister if I were you. Petra strikes me as the sensible sort."

He grinned at her. "She's not the one I'm worried about. I'm going to rescue my friend."

Eleven

Of course, I appreciate the value of books in the finishing of a young lady, Petra dear. If one wishes to dine on hearts for breakfast, elevenses, and teatime, learning to walk smoothly enough to balance a book on one's head is a must.

—Phillippa, the Dowager Marchioness of Somerset

PETRA DANGLED HER LEGS FROM HER PERCH ON THE remains of a balcony in the sham ruins of a cloister. Despite her spectacles, she was blessed with fine, even features and truly lovely eyes. The way she leaned, chin on her palm, Lawrence could almost imagine her as Ariadne on the rocks, sighing for her lover Theseus.

Then, of course, Petra had to ruin the effect by speaking.

"Antonia said no hiding in pairs."

"Trust me, Petra, we aren't a pair." He lay back on a large slab of granite that was supposed to be the altar in this folly of an abbey. From this position, he could see quite a way up the narrow column of her gown when she swung her legs just right. If she weren't wearing pantalets, he'd have been treated to occasional glimpses of her knee caps. "In fact, I very much doubt we're even from the same species."

"Really?" She peered waspishly down at him. "Do you consider yourself that much a simian?"

"A what?"

"A simian. A lower species which most nearly mimics humankind. Apes and chimpanzees and such. Honestly, do you never read?"

"Not if I can help it." If Petra didn't favor such severe clothing and left her glasses behind once in a while, she'd be considered a passably pretty girl. He imagined her for a moment in a ball gown with her creamy shoulders bare. She might take the *ton* by storm if only she could be taught not to speak.

"That's your problem then," she rattled on. "You aren't familiar with the work of Lamarck, I suppose."

"La who?"

She sighed. "The brilliant French naturalist and taxonomist."

"Taxonomist, hmm? Well, that's all right. I never hold anyone's religion against them."

"That's not his religion, you cretin. It's his field of study." She gave a low growl of frustration. "Oh, why am I even talking to you?"

"Because I'm the only one here, and if one talks to oneself, one is apt to be considered a bit dotty."

She hooked her legs at the ankles and let them swing back and forth. Her ankles were slim and appealing, he had to admit. There was plenty to like in Hartley's second sister.

"You are absolutely beneath my touch, you know," she said, arching her pale brows in a scathing manner that perfectly aped the worst old dragons of the *ton*.

And plenty not to like about her as well, Lawrence decided.

"I must say it's not very inventive of you to hide in the ruins of an abbey." Lawrence inspected his fingernails for any trace of dirt beneath them and found none. No surprise since one would have to actually do manual labor to accumulate any smut there. "Hartley is certain to look for you here."

"And why, pray tell, is that?"

"Because nunneries are where women who don't much like men go."

She looked pointedly away from him. "I like men just fine, thank you very much. It's with you I take umbrage, but since you've already admitted to being less than a man, I think we've discovered the problem."

"Ouch." He put a hand to his chest to signal a direct hit. "You've certainly got a set of claws on you, my kitten."

"I'm not your kitten. I'm not your...anything."

Brown eyes snapping, her color high—when she was riled, Petra might actually be a diamond of the first water. *If only there was a way to strike her dumb.*

"By that same token," she said, "Hartley might very well expect *you* to be skulking here."

"Skulking? I'll have you know I never skulk. I saunter. I stroll. I've even been known to meander when the occasion calls for it, but I never skulk." He was tempted to rise and demonstrate the various means of locomotion, but that would mean he'd lose the chance to see lacey pantalets fluttering in the non-existent breeze. "But for argument's sake, why would your brother expect to find me here?"

"Because you're the sort who thinks he's irresistibly attractive enough to cause a riot in a nunnery." She stuck out her tongue pettishly.

"My dear girl, what have you been reading? The memoirs of Don Juan?"

She blushed to the roots of her mouse-brown hair. He'd hit her little secret bang on.

"So your taste in literature runs to the scandalous, does it, m'dear? How very interesting," Lawrence said. "Remind me to send you my copy of *Tom Jones*. I've highlighted all the delicious parts."

"That's a horrible thing to say to a lady." Petra crossed her arms, the gesture subtly accenting her nicely rounded bodice. "Do you know what I think?"

"I certainly do. You think I can't see up your dress from here."

Her eyes went wide as an owlet's and she tucked her legs up under her. "You beast."

"Now you've got it. You know what I am, fair maiden. Not a simian, whatever that may be, but a beast." He rose and gave her a mocking bow. "I trust you'll never forget it."

The sound of boots scuffing paving stones came from the entrance of the abbey.

"Well, this is a pleasant surprise, I must say," Hartley said, beaming over catching Lawrence bowing to his sister. "I can't tell you how refreshing it is to see the two of you getting along for once."

"Note the date. I doubt the moment will be repeated. Good day, Lady Petra." Lawrence turned on his heel and started to leave. *God save me from educated women.* Bluestockings were worse than the plague.

"Honestly, Hartley," he heard Petra say as he went, "I don't know why you're still friends with such a bounder."

Sometimes Lawrence wondered the same thing.

He and Hartley were cut from very different bolts of cloth. While Richard stood to inherit a vast, if impoverished, estate, Lawrence was a second son. Once his father passed and his imperious older brother became the earl, Lawrence's more than adequate current allowance would dry up like Egypt after the Nile recedes. He'd have to make his own way in the world then.

But while Hartley would be planning for that eventuality already, Lawrence tucked it away in a far corner of his mind, to be dealt with only when it became necessary. Life was too uncertain to worry about things before they happened.

He didn't used to be that way. When he and Hartley first met, Lawrence was a studious little fart trying to make good and earn his father's approval. He and Richard had teamed up right away in school, and even now, there was no one else to whom he might speak with seriousness.

But some things he wouldn't even talk to Hartley about. Even in his own mind, he wouldn't name the disaster that had upended his life. He shoved every unwelcome memory of it aside as if it carried the pox.

Since that horrible day, he'd made no plans. He drifted like a piece of flotsam. He let the empty march of years wash over him. One place was as good as another. He filled his life with hedonism when he could, frivolity if that was all that was available.

But while he could control his waking thoughts, sometimes Tabitha still stole into his dreams.

Lawrence lengthened his stride, determined to put all sober thoughts behind him. Ella was waiting under the pergola in the Greek folly with Sophie Goodnight beside her. To his surprise, Antonia was there as well.

"I thought you were still in hiding, milady," he said as he came up on the three of them.

"I gave up on being found and made my way back to the base," Antonia said, the tight set of her lips the only visible evidence of her displeasure, but Lawrence could feel it emanating from her in scalding waves. He wouldn't trade places with Hartley for worlds. "Has Hartley found Petra yet?"

"They're right behind me." As if on cue, the pair sauntered out of the ruins of the abbey and headed toward the Parthenon.

"Well, that's it for this game then," Antonia said.

"Guess that makes you the winner since you have yet to be officially found," Lawrence said. He cupped his hands and shouted to his friend. "Hurry up, Hartley. Lady Antonia is ready to claim the winner's prize."

"What is the prize?" Miss Goodnight asked.

"The winner claims a kiss from whomever she chooses," Antonia said, her eyes glittering dangerously. "But there's no need for Hartley to hurry. I choose you, Seymour."

"I'm honored." He reached for her hand.

"No, not on my knuckles, silly," she said, stepping

close so that he had to take her into his arms or risk
an awkward situation with her standing near enough
for her breasts to brush his chest. She glanced toward
Hartley who was approaching and waited until he was
able to take everything happening in quite handily.
"Make it a good one."

"Never let it be said that Lawrence Seymour
doesn't come to the aid of a damsel in distress."

"I'm not in distress."

"You will be."

If there was one thing Lawrence knew, it was how
to kiss a woman so her knees turned to water. He
dipped Antonia. The occasion seemed to require that
sort of overblown play-acting. Then he covered her
mouth with his and brought all his sensual prowess
to bear. She was stiff at first, as he expected, but after
a moment her lips softened. Then her whole body
seemed to melt. If they'd been in a broom closet
somewhere, he could have had his way with her
after a few more minutes of this. She'd be begging
him for it.

Of course, he wouldn't, since Antonia was all but
spoken for. But the woman certainly didn't kiss him
like she was spoken for. She was probably trying to
make Hartley sorry he dallied so long in the woods
without finding her. Perhaps she hoped to goad
Hartley into speaking up and proposing in a fit of
envy. Antonia was using him, Lawrence was certain.

Sometimes, it wasn't at all unpleasant to be used.

A loud, throat-clearing sound broke the mood.

Lawrence released Antonia's mouth and stood her
back upright. Then he turned and looked not into his

friend's disapproving face, but Hartley's second sister's.

Petra harrumphed deep in her throat again.

"Lady Antonia was just claiming her prize," Lawrence said, kicking himself for feeling the need to explain matters to her.

"Is that what it was?" Petra said peevishly. "It looked to me as if you were examining her teeth."

Hartley, by contrast, didn't seem the least concerned as he looked around at the group. "Everyone back now? Good. The game's over, and I hope never to play hide-and-seek again."

"Perhaps you'd change your tune if you'd been picked to give me my prize," Antonia said, running her ring finger along her lower lip.

"Probably," he said with a noncommittal shrug.

Lawrence could have boxed his ears. If Hartley didn't respond with even a speck of jealousy, Antonia would be forced to escalate this new game. While he didn't mind playing with a delectable lady like Antonia, he didn't want to come between Hartley and his chosen one. His friend had been so hotly devoted to Antonia when they were in Paris.

Now he seemed decidedly lukewarm.

The flicker of a glance passed between Hartley and Miss Goodnight. It was brief, but there was a definite shift in the undercurrent crackling between the pair. Lawrence scented the change as clearly as a hound scents a hare in the thicket. What had started as mutual disdain had definitely graduated to something warmer. He needed to get Hartley away from all these hens to find out what had happened between him and this girl.

But before he could suggest he and Hartley should

repair to the nearest watering hole to discuss matters, a long, thin wail rent the air.

"What on earth is that?" Miss Goodnight said.

"Whatever it is, it's coming from the duck pond." Hartley was off at a bound, knees and elbows pumping. The ladies followed him at a trot, as quickly as the confines of their column dresses would allow.

"Saved by the shriek, old son," Lawrence said as he brought up the rear. Between Hartley not finding Antonia at all, his tepid reaction to Lawrence kissing the lady, and the moment that sizzled between Richard and Miss Goodnight, there'd been all the makings for someone to pitch a wicked fit with his friend Richard in the center of it.

Until the timely scream, of course. The shrill cry came again.

"Some blokes have all the luck."

Twelve

Spare me your "O, what a tangled web we weave" nonsense. If a certain young man could simply be relied upon to do as the family wishes, there wouldn't have been any need for deception in the first place.

—Phillippa, the Dowager Marchioness of Somerset

RICHARD FOUND HIS GRANDMOTHER PACING THE SHORE of the duck pond, her cane's pewter tip digging into the soft ground. Lord and Lady Pruett seemed frozen in horror at the water's edge. The dock that had once jutted into the pond to give visitors a place to sit and fish, or tug off their shoes and socks and dangle their feet in the water was now submerged beneath the murky surface.

"Where's Ariel?" Richard demanded as he hopped one-legged, pulling off his boots in preparation for going in after whoever was still in the pond. The water where the dock had been churned furiously. An arm flailed on the surface then disappeared ominously. Someone, maybe several someones, was struggling under there.

"It's not Ariel, dear." His grandmother waved a dismissive hand, and Richard surmised the shrieks had come from Lady Pruett. Gran was as calm as the swans on the far side of the pond who hadn't let the human activity on this side disrupt their stately procession. "Your little sister and her governess returned to the house some time ago. One can only feed ducks for so long, you know. So tiresome. All that infernal quacking."

"Then who—"

His father's head broke the surface, followed by David, the footman who'd lately been pressed into service as Richard's valet. Then the marquess seemed to find his footing and rose with a lily pad dripping from his left ear. With his wife sputtering in his arms, he waded toward the shore. David followed, dragging the sodden wheelchair whose spokes were chinked with dark mud.

"Oh my," Richard's grandmother said with a shaky chuckle. "It's a miracle."

"A miracle, my foot." Richard narrowed his eyes at his father. "How long has he been able to walk?"

"Come now, Richard," the dowager hissed. "Is that any way to act when your parents might have drowned?"

"I happen to know the water is only about four feet deep at the end of the dock. The likelihood of them drowning was slim." Richard yanked his boots back on. His grandmother studiously refrained from meeting his gaze as the wet members of the party trudged out of the water. "Slimmer, I'd imagine, than my chances of getting the truth of what's really going on from anyone."

"Hush, boy. Not before your guests."

Before Richard could wangle any more information

from his grandmother, Sophie, his sisters, and Antonia
came running toward them, babbling like a gaggle
of geese. Ella and Petra threw their arms around the
father, excited over his incredible cure.

"Stand back, girls," the marquess said, as he deposited
his wife into the wheelchair. David knelt to swipe out
the mud between the wheels' spokes with his gloved
hands. The footman's crushed velvet livery would never
be the same. "Your mother has had quite a fright."

"She's not the only one," Gran muttered.

Petra and Ella now crowded around their mother,
smoothing her wet hair and crooning protestations
of thankfulness for their parents' deliverance. Lady
Antonia was complaining to whoever would listen
that her picnic was utterly ruined. Only Sophie
seemed to have the sense to do something helpful.
She draped her plaid blanket over his mother's lap and
tucked it around her before she began to shiver.

"Will someone please tell me what happened
here?" Richard demanded.

"Lord Somerset seemed to want to venture out on
the dock. He indicated with a hand motion or two
that the footman was to take him, and of course, Lady
Somerset went with him," Lord Pruett explained. "I
fear the dock proved a bit rickety and wouldn't support their combined weight."

It was evidence of yet more deferred maintenance
on the Somerset property. Richard had to do something and soon, or eventually all the improvements to
the estate would be as useless as the follies.

"If you'll excuse us, Lady Antonia, I believe we
must end the festivities for today," Lord Somerset said

without the slightest slurring of his words or any other indication that, until now, he'd been mute for weeks. "My wife requires rest."

"And I require some explanations," Richard said quietly.

"Oh no, the party's been ruined." Antonia's perfectly shaped brows drew upward and together in distress. "I'd hoped to set up butts and host an archery competition once we all came together again."

"Oh, I daresay anything involving sharp pointy objects would be counterproductive at the moment, my dear," the dowager said.

"Another day perhaps," Lord Somerset said as he turned, pushing his wife in the chair, for a change, back toward Somerfield Park. David squelched after them, his big feet leaving muddy prints as they went. The dowager made good her escape, leaning on the footman's arm.

They weren't getting away that easily. Richard followed for a few steps, and once they were out of earshot of the others, he grasped his father's arm. "Today, sir. You will give me an accounting for this subterfuge of yours."

The marquess frowned but nodded. "Wait for me in the library."

Richard returned to the rest of the party where his sisters were taking leave of the Pruetts, still so delirious over their father's recovery they gave short shrift to praising the picnic's virtues. Lady Antonia's bacchanalian-themed party was officially over.

Sophie patted Antonia on the shoulder. "Cheer up, Tonia. No hostess can foresee all outcomes when she plans an event. My tea had a near poisoning, your picnic a near drowning—these things can happen to anyone."

Antonia's mouth worked furiously, but whatever she was thinking, she was too well-bred to say.

"Miss Goodnight, you're closer to Somerfield Park than Barrett House," Richard said. "Why don't you walk there with us, and we'll send the coach round to take you home?"

"How kind of you, Hartley," Antonia said, claiming Richard's arm before he could offer it to Sophie. "Always thinking of others whether they have any business being here or not."

Richard jerked his gaze to Antonia sharply. She must be terribly overwrought over her party breaking up so disastrously. He'd never heard anything remotely ungracious drop from her lovely lips before this.

Seymour stepped up to Sophie to play the gallant with another of his mocking bows. "If you please, Miss Goodnight, I'd be happy to escort you. Seems to me it's high time you and I got to know each other better."

Sophie took his arm, and the pair started off in the direction of Somerfield Park, chatting like old friends.

Richard watched them go, knowing Seymour meant nothing by it. He was game for flirting with any available female. But for some reason, seeing Sophie on his friend's arm bothered Richard far more than when Lawrence had fastened his lips on Antonia's.

❧

Contrary to Sophie's expectations, Lawrence Seymour could be a witty and pleasant companion. He regaled her with tales of his and Richard's exploits on the Continent, and whether by design or simply because it was true, he made himself look the scoundrel in the stories.

She was also surprised that Seymour was so well acquainted with the contents of Lord Somerset's expansive library. She'd heard that the marquess collected a number of books which featured art prints. Seymour was able to confirm that his lordship's shelves were well stocked.

"There was a lecturer on the ship in which we traveled from India who specialized in female artists. I'm quite interested in learning more about one called Artemisia Gentileschi," Sophie said.

"The name doesn't seem familiar."

"I'm not surprised. She was an Italian Baroque painter and a rather obscure one at that."

"Well, the Somerset library, rather like all country manors, majors in obscurity, so I don't doubt you'll find something."

"Good," she said. "I'd rather not return to Barrett House until I've had a chance to look. The library there is restricted to gardening tomes and a rather exhausting history of the Peloponnesian Wars."

"You mean 'exhaustive,' don't you?"

"Clearly, you haven't tried to read it."

Laughing, he led her over the meadow and up to the grand front entrance. Then he escorted her through the parlors and corridors to the library in the southeast corner of the great house.

"One has to negotiate a bit of a labyrinth to find the library, but here we are, Miss Goodnight," Seymour said as he opened the door for her. "You know, I believe you're a good influence on us."

That was something she'd never been accused of before. "Really? How's that?"

"Ordinarily, English country society is about as exciting as watching bread molder. Since you've been here, we've had no end of unexpected developments."

"If I've upset the natural order of things…well, I suppose I should apologize."

"Don't," Seymour advised. "However, for what it's worth, Hartley is a fool not to snap you up."

She grinned up at him. "Ah, but that assumes I'm available for the snapping. Don't let my parents' machinations fool you into thinking I agree with them."

"Hard to get, eh?" He laid his finger aside his nose in the time-honored gesture of collusion. "Well played."

"I'm not playing," she protested.

"Of course you are. We all are. If you're versed in obscure Baroque painters, you're surely familiar with the Bard. 'Life's but a walking shadow, a poor *player*, that struts and frets his hour upon the stage, and then is heard no more.'"

"'It is a tale told by an idiot, full of sound and fury, signifying nothing,'" she finished for him.

"Touché. I am an idiot most of the time."

"I sincerely doubt that." Sophie wondered why Seymour seemed to delight in giving people reasons to underestimate him. Then she remembered how he'd kept Richard from doing more damage to the bully who'd tormented them both when they were young. There was character in Lawrence Seymour, however much he tried to hide it. "Richard is fortunate to have you as a friend."

"I hope you'll count me yours as well," Seymour

said. "Well, I'm off. This is the time of day when Petra
and Ella usually ride, and I don't think I've bedeviled
Hartley's sisters enough for one day yet."

He turned and sauntered down the hall, hands in his
pockets, whistling as he went.

Sophie went into the library, and it nearly took her
breath away. The ceiling soared twenty feet. A spiral
staircase in the corner led to a wrought-iron balcony
ringing the room at the upper level. Not only were the
shelves full to bursting with leather-covered volumes,
there was a string of cushioned alcoves with tall, Palladian
windows filling the room with light. Red leather wing
chairs flanked a marble fireplace and a cabinet labeled
"maps" stood opposite a massive burled oak desk.

"This library is a little slice of heaven," she said with
a sigh of contentment. "Maybe I *should* try to become
the next marchioness."

❧

Questions bombarded Richard with every step down
the polished marble hall. Why had his parents, and
even his beloved grandmother, perpetrated such a
cruel ruse? He doubted his sisters were in on the
deception. Their joy over their father's supposed
miracle seemed genuine enough.

Why did Lord Somerset feel he had to resort to
such lengths to bend Richard to his will?

His father would probably argue that Richard was
stubborn, and he was. He knew this about himself, but
he wasn't irresponsible. If the Somerset marquessate
was in trouble, Richard wasn't about to let it fall apart
if he could help it.

He just disagreed with his father about how he should go about reversing the family fortunes. At first, he'd recoiled from wedding Sophie Goodnight and her bloated dowry because of his attachment to Antonia. He wasn't the faithless sort, and he felt he owed Antonia his allegiance. Now he rejected the scheme because it wasn't fair to Sophie herself. She didn't deserve to be the human embodiment of a financial endowment to Somerset.

She deserved to be loved for herself.

The thought surprised him when it first surfaced, but once it formed, it took instant root. Such ideas were dangerous, he knew. The fact that he considered Sophie's happiness meant he no longer saw her as merely a block to his own.

He'd been ready to pledge his undying devotion to Antonia in Paris. Now, even if the infernal money debacle hadn't raised its ugly head, he wasn't so sure of his feelings toward her. Antonia was still the same polished young lady, the same confident daughter of privilege who fit neatly into the beau monde and would help him fit in too.

Only now, he wasn't sure he even wanted that world. Richard feared he'd become changeable as a weathercock.

It didn't help matters any when he opened the door to the library and found the source of his dilemma there, in all her disheveled glory. She lounged in one of the alcoves, her slippers discarded so she could prop her stock-inged feet on the cushions, a book balanced on her bent knees. After an afternoon of tramping in the fresh air and sunshine, most women would scurry off to their boudoirs to repair the damage of too much wind and exertion.

Not Sophie. She'd removed her bonnet, revealing her tumbled-down mass of hair. The fact that the hem of her gown had a grass stain visible from across the room obviously troubled her not at all. She was so intent on her book, she didn't seem to notice that he'd entered.

Until she spoke without looking up. "Hullo, Richard."

"How did you know it was me?"

"Magic," she said with a wink.

He arched a skeptical brow at her.

"And excellent peripheral vision," she conceded. "What has you so captivated there?"

"Your father has a book about a Baroque painter in whom I've developed an interest. There are some very fine prints here."

"Oh?" He strode across the space and peered over her shoulder. The print that filled the entire page of the oversized folio was clearly the work of a master. The dramatic use of light and dark was reminiscent of Michelangelo. The color palette was as sophisticated and vibrant as Titian's, but the subject matter was disturbing, to say the least. "What on earth is that?"

"*Judith Slaying Holofernes*," Sophie said calmly, "by Artemisia Gentileschi. Realistically rendered, don't you think?"

"Never having seen a beheading, I can't say."

"I doubt Miss Gentileschi ever did either, but art is more about the possible than the probable, isn't it? I've rarely seen such passion in a canvas."

"That's one way of putting it." Richard cocked his head to get a better angle on the scene, but any way he looked at it, the painting was still a writhing mass of fury. "Who was the artist angry with?"

"Why would you say such a thing? Men have been painting horrific things for centuries, and no one ever asks if they were angry."

She had a point.

Then her shoulders slumped a bit. "Actually, Artemisia was angry with someone. Her art teacher, Tassi."

"Remind me never to do whatever it was he did."

"You wouldn't," she said, closing the book with a snap. "Artemisia was young and innocent when she came under his tutelage. Tassi violated her. When he refused to marry her, she fought to bring him to trial, and during the course of it, *she* was tortured with thumbscrews to try to make her recant her testimony. He was finally ordered to serve a year in prison, but the sentence was never imposed. He wasn't incarcerated for a single day."

"Well, that explains her choice of subject matter, a woman's revenge," Richard said, though he wondered why the disturbing image held such fascination for Sophia.

Had she been similarly violated? It might explain her odd way of looking at things. And her cryptic remark, *What makes you think I'm a virgin?*

But before he could think of a way to ask such about such an indelicate topic, she changed the subject on him.

"So Lord Somerset is in full possession of his wits and his mobility once more," she said as she toed on her slippers and returned the art book to its place on the shelves. "Remarkable recovery."

"Isn't it?"

"I'd imagine it takes some of the pressure off you."

"Not really." He stared out the window, over the

seat she'd just vacated. The Somerset woods stretched
in the distance for hundreds, probably thousands, of
acres up and down the distant coastline. "Actually, I
have an idea that might do the trick though."

He told her about his newly formed plans. In addition to the massive oaks, the woods were filled with
maples, alders, spruce, and sycamores. The lumber had
to be worth something, and if properly husbanded, it
was a resource that could be replenished.

"That's brilliant, Richard," she said, her blue eyes
sparkling with approval. "And think of all the jobs
you'll provide for the local people."

He hadn't thought about that. His only goal had
been to bring Somerset back to solvency, but she was
right. In harvesting the Somerset woods, he'd have to
employ hundreds of men from the village. The notion
opened up several new avenues of thought.

"We could build a mill here on the property,"
he said. "Finished lumber will fetch more than raw
timber and provide jobs for even more people."

"Careful." She grinned at him. "You'll be accused
of thinking like a tradesman."

"I'm thinking like a man who has to paddle fast to
keep his head above water."

Her smile faded only a little. "If your plan works,
you won't need my dowry to keep Somerset afloat."

"No, I don't suppose I will." He took her hand
and pressed it between his. Her fingers were slender
and her skin smooth—such fragile-seeming hands
for a young woman who was anything but. "When
the time comes that a man asks for your hand, he
shouldn't seek more than that."

"Oh, I rather hope if I were to ever marry, my husband would want more of me than my hand."

"Never doubt it." His body roused to her innuendo almost immediately, and for a moment he imagined her cool palm on the hottest part of him. It almost made him forget what he'd meant to say, but then he recovered himself. "I simply meant that you alone, without your father's burgeoning purse, ought to be enough for any man."

"Just keep repeating that and you may find you believe it."

He shook his head. "You're still doing it. Like a champion cricketer, you bat away every compliment I bowl toward you."

She looked down, her dark lashes laying in a sooty crescent on her cheeks. He ached to place a kiss on each of her eyelids, to taste that tender skin.

He realized she felt herself undeserving of his compliments, and he wondered why. But before he could ask her what had happened to make her reject kindness, or move to kiss her as he wanted to do so badly it was almost a sickness, his father burst into the library.

"I believe I'll ask Mr. Hightower to arrange that coach for me to return to Barrett House." Sophie tugged her hand free, made her good-byes to his father, and skittered out of the room without a backward glance.

Though he wasn't ready for her to leave, he could have almost kissed her. Again. If he was going to accuse his father of lying to him, he didn't want any witnesses.

Thirteen

*In every pride, there comes a time when the young
lion beards the old one in his own den. However, lest
the young male get too cocky, let him remember that
the magnificently maned fellow is nothing more than a
figurehead. It is the lionesses who hold the real power.*

—Phillippa, the Dowager Marchioness of Somerset

"SIR, IT GIVES ME NO PLEASURE TO SAY THIS, BUT WHAT
the blazes were you thinking to perpetrate such a
fraud?" Richard started softly but crescendoed to a
blistering snarl. "And on your own son, no less."

No one spoke to the marquess like that. His face a
mask of outrage, Lord Somerset drew himself up to his
full height. It only served to accentuate the fact that
Richard now topped his father by a couple inches.
There was a good deal more silver at his lordship's
temples than he remembered, and creases of worry had
set up a picket line around his eyes.

"Are you speaking of the son who hadn't deigned

to show his face here in so many years his youngest sister couldn't recall what he looked like?" Lord Somerset thundered.

"That's not fair. You knew where I was. Have I ever failed to answer a summons?"

"Not since… Well, wasn't there that time when… Oh, hang it all, Hartley." His father seemed to crumple into himself a bit. "It was your grandmother's idea. And you know how she gets when there's a bee in her bonnet. Woe betide all who wander into her path."

"Why did she think it necessary?"

"It hardly signifies now, but she claimed it would help you see your duty more clearly."

"I've never failed you," Richard said through clenched teeth. He'd slaved through his years at Oxford, though his father had never acknowledged his stellar academic accomplishments. They were no more than what was expected, after all.

"She seemed to think Seymour's devil-may-care attitude might have rubbed off on you. I'm sorry for my part in it." The marquess strode to the liquor cabinet and poured a whisky neat each for himself and Richard. "The thing is, the women in this family, and by that I mean mostly your grandmother, are afraid, Son."

He accepted the drink from his father.

"The prestige of the family is everything to her. She senses it slipping away," Lord Somerset said.

Richard couldn't believe his beloved grandmother was the author of this mendacity. "If Gran does feel herself diminished by our present circumstances, she still doesn't seem a jot less imperious."

His father snorted. "She wouldn't. But to be fair, she knew you'd be difficult about accepting the way we've found to fix matters."

"Anyone who can't be manipulated into bowing to her will is now considered difficult?"

"My lady mother rightly claimed that you wouldn't feel the full weight of ownership of the problem unless I was…unavailable. And I daresay she's right." His lordship sank wearily into one of the wing chairs. "You can't imagine the burden of the marquessate until it falls onto your shoulders. It has the weight of history, Son."

Richard's father knocked back half his whisky and then went on speaking. "Our lineage stretches back to the Conqueror. There have been Barretts here since the first Domesday Book was compiled in 1086. The family name was Barat then. We may have started off French, but we've made this corner of England ours." The marquess finished off his drink, hard and fast, not savoring the twenty-five-year-old Scotch in the least. Alcoholic fog could feel like absolution at times, Richard knew, but he didn't think his father deserved any. "Damn, it galls me to be the one who failed."

At this candid admission, Richard's chest constricted in sympathy for his father's misery. He sat down in the wing chair opposite the marquess. "I wouldn't say you failed, sir. I would rather say you've had bad luck. But for a South Sea volcano and a disaster at sea, Somerset would have been right as rain."

"Well, thank you for that, Hartley. But in truth, we've been in decline for a number of years. And I've been in decline. My memory is still as full of holes as a moth-eaten cloak. Our financial bad luck, as you call it, is simply the final nail in the coffin." His father dragged a hand over his face. "I believe I saw Miss Goodnight's hand in yours when I first entered the library. Am I to see this as proof that you're now amenable to the match?"

Since he wasn't really sure of the answer himself, Richard posed his own question. "What would you say if I told you I have an idea that will answer Somerset's financial woes?"

"Go on."

Remembering the light dancing in Sophie's eyes when he first suggested it, Richard launched into an enthusiastic description of his plan to harvest the estate's forest. He capped his proposal by telling his father about building a lumber mill to provide employment for Somerset-on-the-Sea's struggling families.

"Sell the wood?" his father said when Richard finally paused for a breath. "Where will we have the hunt next fall? You know I invite key members of the House of Lords to shoot partridge and pheasant each year."

"Perhaps you could invite them to see what might be done to improve an estate's financial outlook and uplift a village's economy at the same time."

"But…you'll be engaging in *trade*." His father spat out the word as if it soured his tongue.

"Yes, *we* would." Might as well get the old lion used to the idea that he too would be tarred with the tradesman's brush.

"I forbid it."

"How is this different from investing in that doomed whaling vessel?"

"That wasn't engaging in trade. It was speculation. Somerset's assets were being soundly—"

"Lost off the coast of Nova Scotia," Richard finished for him. "I will allow that your investment was a smidge more sensible than gambling it away at White's, but the money's still gone all the same."

Lord Somerset glared at him. "Now see here. If you sell the forest, it's…well, it's drastic. It's as low as selling the household silver. It announces to the entire world how dire our predicament is."

"Do you think they won't know soon enough in any case?"

His father threw up his hands. "You may as well petition the House of Lords for permission to chop up the estate and sell it off piecemeal."

"If we don't do something soon, that's exactly what we'll be reduced to."

"And that's precisely why you must marry Miss Goodnight as her father and I have agreed," Lord Somerset said triumphantly, as if certain he'd trapped Richard with the only logical conclusion.

"Sir, I can't tell you how repugnant that idea is."

"Repugnant? What's the matter with you? She's certainly pretty enough."

"Miss Goodnight's not the problem. The whole idea is." Richard stood and leaned on the mantelpiece. "You would sell us both for thirty pieces of silver."

"Oh, trust me, Son. Miss Goodnight's dowry is worth considerably more than that."

"I don't care if it's enough to pay off the Prince Regent's personal debts," Richard said. "Don't you see you have reduced both of us to mere commodities? Sophie is part and parcel in a trade, of no more consequence than an extra bag of wheat tossed in to sweeten the deal. You demean her in the exchange."

"So you do care about the girl?"

"That's not at issue," Richard argued. "Doesn't it bother you that in this bargain, I may as well be a cicisbeo?" He thought certain his father would object to him being no better than a kept man. He thought wrong.

"A cicisbeo with generations of noble blood running in his veins," the marquess countered. "You'll hardly be the first wellborn young man to take a bride who's beneath him in consideration for financial gain."

"Sophie is not beneath me." In fact, he'd never met a woman he felt was so far above him. He was in awe of her each time he reached for her.

"The daughter of a nabob? Of course she's beneath you. If not for this present emergency, the whole Goodnight family would be so far beneath our touch…" His father caught himself before he said more against the young woman he expected Richard to marry and laughed. "You are heir to the marquessate of Somerset. There are damned few in this country who aren't beneath you."

"Then I wish I was anything but your heir, sir." Richard started for the door.

"Now just a moment, you insolent pup." His father leaped to his feet. "We're not finished here."

"Yes, Father, we are," Richard rounded on him. "You played your part too well, you see. Mr. Witherspoon was hesitant to do anything on behalf of the estate on my orders without proper documentation,

so he went to Dr. Partridge, and between the two of
them, they had you declared *non compos mentis*. I
signed the papers the night I returned home. You are
no longer in control of this estate. I am."

"A formality. Once I tell Witherspoon to tear up
those worthless papers—"

"He can't. They've already been submitted to the
court. It would take a lawsuit to reverse the finding
and you, Father, have no funds with which to pros-
ecute one," Richard said. "Unless you wish to sell
Mother's jewelry, of course."

"You're going to regret this." Cold fury burned in
his father's eyes.

"I regret many things, your lordship, but not this."
He didn't flinch under his father's unyielding stare.
"I will harvest and sell off the estate's wood, but I'll
replant as I go, so the next generation of Barretts will
still have the asset. I'll build the mill and hire the
villagers. I'll save Somerfield Park because I believe
it's worth saving. But I'll do it my way, not as part
of some scheme you and Mr. Goodnight have con-
cocted." Richard stalked to the door and paused with
his hand on the crystal knob. "I do feel the weight of
the estate. I feel it every moment of every day. It's
mine now, in all but title. And there's not a damned
thing you can do about it, sir."

❧

Sophie knew it was incredibly bad form to listen at
keyholes, but the temptation was so great. Besides, she
rarely resisted temptation, even when it was not.

Richard was easy to hear through the small aperture.

He spoke about his plans for the forest with confidence and clarity. He wasn't going to raze the whole thing, he argued. After he hired a forestry expert, they'd put together a rotating schedule for cutting that allowed for regrowth and wouldn't disturb the wildlife more than necessary. Her idea about the mill to create more jobs had already been folded seamlessly into his projections.

She was so proud of him for wanting to provide relief, not only for his immediate family, but for all the families of the village and surrounding farmsteads who were dependent upon the estate. But even as laudable as that goal was, she knew there was another reason a small, glowing lump of something delightful was building in her chest.

The man had *listened* to her.

He'd taken her idea and promoted it as if it were his own. He didn't try to change the subject, or pat her on the head and assert that women didn't know anything about commerce.

Richard accepted her idea and was eager to implement it.

Men had always been keen to get their hands on her father's money. More than a few wanted their hands up her skirt. Only Richard had seemed interested in what buzzed around between her ears.

Perhaps her father hadn't done so badly when he tried to orchestrate a marriage between her and Richard.

Then the conversation on the other side of the door took a turn toward their arranged match. She heard Richard say clearly, "Sir, I can't tell you how repugnant that idea is."

Her breath hissed over her teeth. Sophie recoiled from

the keyhole as if it were an adder poised to strike. She clapped a hand over her mouth and ran from the library.

Repugnant.

Was she repugnant when they were entwined on her plaid blanket in the ruins of the old castle? It hadn't seemed so at the time, but now she knew, from his own lips, what he really thought of her.

That glowing lump in her chest began to ache so badly she found it hard to breathe.

She took a couple of wrong turns in the great house, but she wasn't about to ring any of the bell pulls she fled past to summon help or a coach to take her home. The last thing she needed was for anyone to see her like this.

When she finally found the foyer and massive front doors, she flung them open and escaped into the coming twilight. Sophie swiped her eyes angrily as she strode down the tree-lined lane toward Barrett House.

How dare that man make her weep!

She didn't care what he thought. She didn't care what any man thought of her. She ought to have been more careful though. She knew what could come of trusting, of letting a man become important to her, of opening herself to the possibility of closeness.

It always led to betrayal.

It would be dark by the time she reached Barrett House, but she didn't care. Somehow, she had to convince her parents to leave this place. She'd never ride in a Somerset conveyance again, never darken the door of Somerfield Park.

And, please God, never set eyes on Richard "high and mighty Lord Hartley" Barrett ever, ever again.

Fourteen

When one has lived as long as I, one realizes that the ultimate enemy is not the passage of years. It is the change those years bring.

—Phillippa, the Dowager Marchioness of Somerset

"I HAD TO STEP LIVELY TO CONVINCE MRS. GRAHAME to let me walk out this evening, since it's not my half day," Sarah babbled as she and Eliza settled at the small table in the kitchen of the Hound and Hare. "But I finished my work early and promised I'd tell Mrs. G all about your trip to London when I get back."

Fortunately, Eliza hadn't needed to beg for time away from her duties. Miss Goodnight proved a very liberal employer and encouraged Eliza to meet her friend in the village. Sarah had always been pleasant toward her, even when Eliza was nothing but a kitchen maid. Now that Eliza had leaped over several rungs of the below stairs ladder and was a full-fledged lady's maid, Sarah seemed eager to cement their friendship. She was the one who'd suggested they meet in the kitchen of the village inn, where her cousin Mabel served as cook.

Mabel set down a tea tray before them, ordered Sarah to pour out and turned back to the big pot of stew bubbling over the brick-built range. At this time of evening, if a body didn't want dark ale and a hearty bowl, he shouldn't visit the inn. The menu at the Hound and Hare never varied, except for the type of meat in the stew. This night, the pot gave off a decidedly muttonish smell. "You must have had such an exciting time," Mabel gushed. "Oh, tell us just everything while I finish with this stew."

"There's far too much to tell over one cup of tea." Besides, Eliza decided Sarah and Mabel didn't want to hear how dirty, smelly, crowded, and noisy London was. Of course, it was nicer in Mayfair, where the Goodnights' new town house was located, but even though she and her employer rode in an elegant coach everywhere they went, traveling through the more dicey quarters on their way to St. Paul's had left a sour impression. "The servants at the Goodnights' town house were a jolly group, but there weren't as many of them as you'd expect."

"We don't want to hear about below stairs folk, silly." Sarah eyed Eliza's secondhand gown with unabashed envy. "I hear Miss Goodnight had a new wardrobe made. Tell about the trip to the modiste."

Eliza launched into a description of the reams of beautiful silks and laces from which her mistress could choose. She'd never seen anything so fine as the fashion plates they had pored over. The modiste had helped her mistress pick just the right pattern to

go with each fabric and the oh-so-fashionable trim-
mings and furbelows to add in order to please Miss
Goodnight's mother. Then the seamstress somehow
managed to keep the lines of the gowns clean enough
to satisfy Miss Goodnight's desire for simplicity. Eliza
could talk for hours about the cunning little hats and
darling slippers made to match. They left London with
two new outfits complete with matching spencers and
pelisses, but the rest of Miss Goodnight's wardrobe
would take weeks to deliver. Eliza's throat was getting
dry when Mabel brought more water for another cup
of tea along with a plate of gingerbread biscuits.

Eliza didn't want Mabel to get into trouble for
filching some of the inn's biscuits and wondered if
she should leave some payment for her when their
evening of gossip was done. She didn't need to fret
over spending the coin. Miss Goodnight was generous
beyond her wildest imaginings.

Eliza only wished she was a better lady's maid.
She could definitely care for her mistress's wardrobe,
keeping her hems clean and her boots polished to a
spit shine. She was a deft hand at helping her employer
dress and choose the right accessories for each outfit.

But Eliza was hopeless with hair. Try as she might,
she couldn't seem to pin Miss Goodnight's dark tresses
well enough to keep them from coming down. While
she was in London, she tried to pry a few tricks from
the lady's maid in the house next door, but the woman
was tight-lipped about her trade.

*Poor Miss Goodnight will just have to make do with my
fumblings till I get the hang of it.*

Fortunately for Eliza, her employer seemed

indifferent about her hair, so they rubbed along together very well indeed.

While Sarah munched on a biscuit, Eliza took the opportunity to change the topic from herself. "So how is everyone at Somerfield Park?"

Sarah knew she meant the below stairs folk. However stellar her rise, Eliza wouldn't be bold enough to ask after the marquess and his family.

"Everyone's fine, but there have been a few changes. Your sister Theresa is working in your stead now, though Mrs. Culpepper threatens to box her ears at least once a day. Theresa gets distracted, you see," Sarah said. "Actually, don't tell her you heard this from me, but she's a terrible flirt."

"Theresa?"

Sarah nodded. "Anything in trousers. The stable lads are all but at war over her."

"What has Mrs. Grahame done about it?"

"Nothing. Theresa's clever enough not to be caught flirting when she's about." Sarah's nostrils flared slightly, indicating she was quite miffed about the whole thing. "Even Toby seems quite taken with your little sister."

"I suppose she's really not so little anymore, is she?" The last time Eliza had made the trip back home, she'd spent most of her half day off trying to give her mother a rest from the demands of her smallest siblings. Eliza was the eldest of six, so the Dovecote household was a study in chaos at the best of times. However, now that she thought about it, she hadn't seen Theresa in several months.

"I know you've come into some of Miss Goodnight's old clothes. If you have any to spare, you might give your sister a bigger blouse or two. She's fair busting out of the ones she has. Mrs. Culpepper is forever telling her to mind her buttons."

With a chest almost as flat as a boy's, Sarah would never have to be warned of that.

"I'll see to it," Eliza said, promising herself she'd give Theresa a stern talking to. A girl in service had to be mindful of her reputation or she'd lose her position quicker than she could spit. Eliza took another sip of tea and asked after the only person she really wanted to hear about. "How's David?"

"We have to call him Mr. Abbot now. He's been promoted to valet," Sarah said. "He's taking care of Lord Hartley, though what with things the way they are, Mr. Hightower can't hire anyone to replace him in the dining room, so he's still serving as footman too. Never complains, though. As quiet as ever. Secrets, that one has. I've always said so."

"Really? What sort of secrets?"

"Well, he doesn't seem to have any family hereabouts. He isn't even from this village. He's from Brighton. So how did he ever land in Somerset as his lordship's bootblack boy in the first place?"

Eliza felt a twinge of disloyalty over gossiping about David, but she'd bear it if only she could learn more about him. "Must have been recommended by one of his lordship's friends, I suppose."

"I suppose. Drucilla's been here a long time, you know, and she remembers when he first came. Said he was a good enough worker during the day. Willing and eager to please. But the poor little blighter cried at night for the first month. Guess his mother had just died before he came to Somerset."

"Oh, that is sad." To be so alone and so young in a strange place. Her heart ached for the bereaved little boy.

"Must not have had any kin to go to, so I guess Lord Somerset did him a kindness by taking him on," Sarah said as she helped herself to a third biscuit. "Who knows where he'd have landed elsewise?"

Eliza had an inkling. One of the worst things she'd seen in London was all the masterless young boys roaming the streets. Ragged and hungry, they lived, or more often died, by their wits. She didn't think a child who was all alone in the world would fare any better in Brighton.

The back door to the kitchen opened and the fresh breath of night spilled in along with David Abbot.

"Well, speak of the devil." Sarah waved to him.

Eliza's heart did an odd little flip. She hoped that sort of thing didn't show on a body's face. The last thing she needed was for David to know she went all wobbly inside whenever he was near.

"'Evening, Sarah," he said as he removed his hat and smiled at the cook. Then he fastened his gaze on Eliza. "Miss Dovecote."

Now that Eliza was a lady's maid, folk were supposed to call her by her last name, with or without the "Miss" in front of it. She'd always been just plain Eliza before, but she'd finally earned the right to use the surname she was born with. The practice was a sign of respect everyone said. David's voice was so deep and rumbly it made her shiver just to have the sound roll over her. And on the few occasions when he'd said her name, well, even her goose bumps had goose bumps.

"Call me Eliza, please."

"I will, then." He smiled down at her. "But only if you won't insist on calling me Mr. Abbot."

"Of course not, David." Then her head, which was usually full to bursting with thoughts she dared not give voice to, went suddenly blank. She longed for something witty to spill out of her mouth, to dazzle him with her worldliness since she'd been to London and back. Instead, all she could do was stammer, "What are you doing here?"

"I heard you and Sarah were in the village and thought I'd walk you both home when you're ready."

Since Barrett House was nearer to the village than Somerfield Park, he'd be walking much farther with just Sarah. Thinking about it made Eliza feel as if her stays were laced too tight. "Will you…have a biscuit?"

"I believe I will. Hard to resist gingerbread." His dark-eyed gaze swept over her, and she was so glad she'd decided to wear the blue gown she'd inherited from her mistress. It was a bit much for the kitchen of the Hound and Hare, what with the real satin trim and the furbelow at the hem, but she could stand feeling a bit overdressed when David Abbot looked at her like that.

"Thank you kindly, Eliza."

And as he sat down beside her and helped himself to the last biscuit, there they were, right on cue.

Goose bumps on her goose bumps.

Back when he was a footman and she was merely the kitchen girl, she had no right to feel all fluttery about David Abbot. But now, they were on an even footing. It wouldn't be at all out of the question for a valet to ask a lady's maid to walk out with him some fine evening.

"Wake up, silly," Sarah's voice interrupted her musings. Eliza gave a little yelp as her friend's toe connected with her shin under the table. "He asked you about London."

"London, oh, yes. I—"

"She had ever so lovely a time," Sarah cut in again. Then she regaled him with Eliza's tales of the visit to the modiste, even doing Eliza's imitation of how mushy the modiste sounded what with all those pins between her lips.

Eliza didn't mind. For some reason, she couldn't unstick her tongue from the roof of her mouth. Besides, Sarah told it better than she did.

"Oh, I say." Sarah leaned to peer around David's broad shoulders when the door from the kitchen to the inn's common room swung open. "I can scarce believe my eyes. As I live and breathe, it's Miss Constance Bowthorpe out and about."

Eliza had often delivered meal trays to Lady Ariel's governess in her chamber. Other than that, she'd scarcely seen her outside the schoolroom in Somerfield Park and never in the village, unless it was on her way to and from church on Sundays. And even then, Miss Bowthorpe always walked alone.

A serving girl breezed in for more bowls of stew. Eliza peered at the governess through the swinging door. "Who's the gentleman she's sitting with?"

"He's no gentleman or I'm much mistook," Sarah said as she went and held the door open, the better to spy on the governess and her companion. "Not with those shiny elbows. That jacket's late for the rag pile."

Miss Bowthorpe shook her head. Then she leaned

toward the fellow. The man leaned in as well, his mouth moving furiously. "Thick as thieves, aren't they?"

"I'd sooner believe there was larceny afoot than that Miss Bowthorpe has a beau," Sarah said with a sniff.

"Well, now you've piqued my curiosity with your gossip, ladies." David stood and glanced through the open door. Then he frowned and stared without bothering to hide it.

"Do you know him, David?" Eliza asked.

"Yes. At least I know the name he gave me once." As he glared at the fellow, his fingers curled into fists, and he strode the door's threshold. "Thaddeus Clack," he shouted across the common room

When the man looked up and met David's gaze, the whites showed all the way around his eyes. He scrambled to his feet and fled, throwing the few empty chairs to the floor behind him as he went.

Without a word of farewell, David bolted after him.

Fifteen

There are secrets we keep with trembling because we know, if they come to light, we will never be the same. Then there are secrets so deep they cannot be uttered. Those we keep because we don't even know they exist.

—Phillippa, the Dowager Marchioness of Somerset

DAVID DODGED THE IRREGULARLY SPACED TABLES AND thrown-down chairs. He elbowed his way through the crowded room, nearly coming to blows with one burly customer who'd had a few pints too many. But he finally burst into the soft night in time to see Clack tearing down High Street and ducking into a narrow lane.

David stretched into a mile-eating stride and careened into the lane just as his quarry realized it dead-ended into a man-high wall that surrounded the village smith's shop. Clack doubled back and tried to duck under David's outstretched arm.

He managed to escape David's grasp but couldn't evade his out-thrust foot. Clack stumbled and fell headlong onto the graveled lane. David pinned him to the ground with a knee to his spine and firm grips on both the man's wrists.

⁓

"Well, that was rude," Sarah said, her gaze following the footman-turned-valet across the room and out the door.

"And not like David at all." Eliza wanted more than anything to tear out of the Hound and Hare's kitchen and go after him, but if they were going to do that, she and Sarah should have gone immediately. Now, it would seem…intrusive.

If he'd wanted their company, David would have told them to come.

Still, she didn't like the look of that fellow David had called out. And what was Miss Bowthorpe doing with him?

As if Eliza had summoned her, the governess rose from her table and headed their way.

"Good evening, Miss Dovecote, Sarah," she said, her posture so erect Eliza suspected she'd frozen that way and would never thaw no matter how warm she got. "Did either of you chance to hear the name Mr. Abbot called the gentleman who was seated at my table?"

"Clack, miss," Sarah piped up. "Thaddeus Clack."

"Dear me. That's not the name he gave to me." Miss Bowthorpe drew her lips together in a censorious line. "He insinuated himself into a conversation with me, claiming to have known my dear, departed niece." She lifted her chin, accentuating her height, which was quite tall for a woman, and gave herself a little shake. "Let that be a lesson to you, ladies. Never speak to one to whom you have not been properly introduced. Good evening."

"Wait a moment, Miss Bowthorpe." This was the most the woman had ever said to Eliza, even when she used to deliver Miss Bowthorpe's meals on a tray. Eliza burned with curiosity to know more about the recluse. If she could draw the governess out about this niece she seemed to care for so much, Eliza might be able to understand her better. "Would you care to join us? The biscuits are gone, but we've tea enough to share here in the kitchen."

"Thank you, no," Miss Bowthorpe said with a sniff. It was her way of reminding them that, as Lady Ariel's governess, she was far above lesser servants. "I trust you'll be discreet about this unfortunate event."

With that, she turned on her heel and marched out.

❦

"Yow! What d'you think you're you doing?" Thaddeus Clack managed to grunt out. "I never did you no harm."

"Maybe not me, but you are the man who nearly killed the marquess," David growled, wishing he had a bit of twine in his pocket to bind the fellow's hands. He settled for raising Clack roughly to his feet and twisting one arm behind him. The fellow yelped, but David wasn't in a mood to be merciful. He frog-marched him back down the dark narrow lane.

"Where are you taking me?"

"To the magistrate."

"You stupid oaf! Don't you know what I could do for you?" Thaddeus Clack dug in his heels, forcing David to half lift him in order to push him forward.

It was quite a scuffle. Under his threadbare jacket, Clack had the tough, stringy musculature of a former pugilist. And judging from the way he kept trying to butt David with the back of his head, Thaddeus Clack didn't feel himself bound by the rules of the ring. "You don't want to be bothering the magistrate with the likes of me."

"Oh yes, I do." David wrenched the man's arm a little higher. If he didn't quit struggling, he was likely to break it. "I hope you're in the mood for a change of scenery, because once the court gets through with you, you'll be lucky if all they do is transport you to New South Wales."

"Think about it, guv. All I have to do is say you helped me throw his lordship off the roof, and you'll be joining me on that boat to Australia."

"But that's not true and you know it." David tossed him up against the brick wall of the village dry goods shop. The fellow's eyes rolled a bit and he staggered, but then he righted himself and peered up at David from under a set of wiry brows.

"Who's to say you're not in on the scheme? You did let me into Somerfield Park, din't you? And you showed me the way up to where his lordship was."

Hang it all, the man was right. "Only because Lord Somerset ordered me to bring you up to the roof terrace."

"And that's a bit of a facer, ain't it? I'll wager he never met with anyone else on Somerfield Park's roof afore. Shows he din't want me seen by anyone else, don't it?"

"Why did you try to kill him?" David grasped the man by his grimy lapels.

"I never did! I were only there to talk with him

quiet-like, but he's the one what started the fisticuffs. Then it were him or me, guv. Ask his lordship and see if he don't say so."

It was inconceivable that the marquess of Somerset would even know this man, let alone throw punches at him and try to throw him off the roof. Still, David was surprised at the time, when his lordship didn't choose to meet with Clack in one of the public rooms of the great house. Instead, he had ordered David to bring the man discreetly up to the roof, after he heard the two-word message Clack had given him.

Rosewood Chapel.

"I wouldn't presume to ask his lordship about what happened," David said. "Besides, he still doesn't have any memory of that day."

"Well, ain't that convenient? Look here, Son, I don't mean you any harm, but——"

And that was the last David heard. From behind him, someone whacked a solid blow to his skull, and he winked out like a snuffed candle.

❧

"Christ a'mighty, Constance, you've half killed him." Thaddeus leaned over the fallen young man and felt for a pulse at his neck. To his relief, it was thready but still there. *Good.* He'd do a lot for this woman, but he wasn't ready to swing for her. "What the hell do you carry in that thing?"

"My mother always taught us to walk softly and carry a big rock." Miss Bowthorpe reached into her reticule and drew out a goodly sized stone, worn smooth by the river. Then her eyes widened with concern. "I only meant to put his lights out for a bit. He's not really dead, is he?"

"No, but he'll have a whopper of a headache when he wakes up." Thaddeus scratched his nearly bald pate. "I've been having a bit of a think. You've got the proof. Why don't we just tell everyone and be done with it?"

"Kindly refrain from trying to think, Mr. Clack. You'll strain your brains, something with which you are not much gifted in the first place." Miss Bowthorpe stowed the rock back in her reticule. "If the truth comes out, we have no clue whether any gratitude in the form of coin would come our way. Likely not, since this is a very inconvenient sort of truth for everyone involved. It upsets things that folk thought were long settled. However, the violence with which his lordship responded to your visit means he'll be more than willing to be generous in order to keep the secret."

"I take your point."

"And for the right price, we'll be happy to keep the dirty little skeleton in the cupboard," Constance said as she straightened the severe little capote she had tied to her head. "This is the sort of well that never runs dry. We can dip into it as often as we need, for as long as we need, into the future, *ad infinitum*."

Thaddeus nodded. Constance always did have a corner on the thinking market. Them fancy Latin sayings might not mean a thing to him, but she sure sounded intelligent when she said them.

"It won't do for us to be seen together after this fracas," she went on. "As it is, I came up with an innocuous excuse for why we were sitting together."

Thaddeus didn't know what innocuous meant, but it didn't sound like she was paying him a compliment.

"You must leave Somerset-on-the-Sea tonight," she said with a firm nod.

"Now see here. I been part and parcel of this little game since the beginning. If you think you can cut me out now that we're about to—"

"No one's cutting anyone," she said, swinging her reticule back and forth in a manner that might have seemed threatening if Thaddeus and she weren't partners. "You don't have to go far. Crimble will do. You can stay at the inn there, and I'll send word when you're needed."

The village of Crimble was about fifteen miles away. In Somerset-on-the-Sea, the air was fresh with an occasional ocean breeze, but Crimble sat on the edge of a salt marsh that stank like shite on a shingle when the tide was out.

"Well, I won't have trouble finding an empty room, that's for damn certain," Thaddeus said as he nudged the fallen man with the toe of his boot. The footman didn't stir, but he was breathing regular.

"Be certain to take your room under a different name. *Thaddeus Clack* was heard by everyone in the Hound and Hare."

"No frettin' on that score. Clack ain't my real name in any case. Guess a change o' scenery won't come amiss. I don't expect I'd be allowed back into Somerset Park, even if this fellow isn't the one who answers the door."

"No, you won't be. But never fear. Now that his lordship's wits have returned, I have another plan."

She patted Thaddeus's cheek with her gloved palm. "Just you leave everything to me."

&

Eliza fidgeted with her teacup for a few more minutes, but then she could stand no more. "Don't you think we ought to see if David caught up to that fellow?"

"If he did, it's the other man I pity. David seemed pretty upset with him, and David's twice Mr. Clack's size and half his age."

That was a bit of an exaggeration, but David did look like the sort who could handle himself.

"Still, it's a mystery." Eliza drummed her fingers along the side of her cup and turned it in its saucer this way and that. "And I can't bear not knowing something once a question begins niggling my brain."

"All right," Sarah said as she stood. "If only to keep you from wearing a groove in that saucer."

The girls thanked Mabel for letting them meet in her kitchen and left the Hound and Hare, but once they reached the street, it was too dark to see anyone. The only light came from the inn, spilling from the window in a broad slab onto the cobbled street. Eliza looked up and down High Street, but not a soul was in sight.

"In London, householders are required to light a lantern by their door, so it won't be so dark," she said.

"In London, they have the coin to waste on oil evidently," Sarah said with a sniff.

The soft night breeze seemed to carry a moan to Eliza's ear. She cocked her head, willing the sound to come again. When it did, she set off down the street, heedless of whether Sarah followed or not.

She might have barreled right past the narrow lane if another groan hadn't stopped her. Her eyes had sharpened in the dark, so she could make out a crumpled form in the middle of the lane.

"David," she cried and ran toward the prone figure. Heedless of her fine, new secondhand gown, Eliza dropped to her knees and cradled his head in her lap. There was something sticky and wet on his temple. The metallic tang of blood wafted up to her.

"Lud, it's David," Sarah said as she skidded to a stop beside them. "How did that happen? I wonder where that Mr. Clack got off—"

"Quick, Sarah, we haven't time to waste. You must go for Dr. Partridge and bring him here at once."

Sarah seemed to sprout wings as she tore back in down the lane. Eliza pawed through her reticule for her lace handkerchief, which truly was new and was probably the finest thing she'd ever owned in all her living life. She might never get the blood out, but if it would comfort David, she'd be content to have it stained. She pressed the Brussels lace to his temple.

David mumbled a few words. Eliza didn't understand most of them, but two stood out.

"Rosewood Chapel," he muttered.

"No," she said fiercely. "There'll be no talk of churches or chapels or anything else connected with funerals, do you hear me?"

Then because she figured she might never have the chance again, she palmed his cheeks and lowered her lips to his.

It wasn't a kiss. Not really. Just the brush of her mouth on his, but it made her agony all the more sharp-edged. This was not the way she'd imagined the first kiss she'd share with David Abbot would be.

Not at all.

"Wake up, David," she whispered. "Please. You have to wake up, so someday you can kiss me for real."

Sixteen

A word, once spoken, can never be recalled. But it doesn't hover in the air like the Sword of Damocles. A blade slices too cleanly to be compared to the devastation a word can cause. A wound from a sword may scar, but it will likely heal. A word doesn't play so fairly. Once a harsh word is loosed, it burrows deep, like a worm into an apple, to gnaw upon the heart of the hearer.

—Phillippa, the Dowager Marchioness of Somerset

"Looks as if the rosebush is trying to make a recovery."

Sophie straightened from her weeding around the new tendrils curling from the plant's woody stalks and turned toward the sound of his voice. She knew it was Richard, knew seeing his damnably handsome face would be a fresh lance to her insides. She couldn't help herself. It had been over a week since she'd seen him last, but despite what she'd promised herself about being remote and untouchable, she craved the sight of Richard Barrett more than she craved her next breath.

Even if it hurt, seeing him was so much better than not.

She was no better than a moth that beats itself to death on a glass lamp chimney trying to get at the flame.

Richard was just beyond the gate of Barrett House, mounted on a bay stallion and holding the lead reins of a chestnut mare. He removed his hat, and his hair was dark with sweat after his brisk ride. When he leaned on the pommel with his knowing gaze sweeping over her, she could almost imagine he was a centaur come calling, powerful, untamed, and undeniably male.

Repugnant, she reminded herself. *He might want to dally with me, but he finds the notion of marrying me repugnant.*

"Roses are more resilient than their delicate fragrance might suggest," she said, careful not to let any of the flutters she felt creep into her tone. *And so am I.*

She'd never expected their relationship to warm as quickly as it had. After that first kiss in the gallery, they'd been allies against their parents' machinations. Then they'd had that surprisingly naughty interlude on her blanket in the castle ruins. She still woke with a blush of pleasure when snippets of that memory found its way into her dreams. Against her will, she'd admired Richard. She'd been impressed by his desire to find a way to save Somerfield Park and the people who depended upon it, without forcing the pair of them into a marriage neither of them reputedly wanted.

But not wanting to wed because they were total strangers and she would not be bullied into it was entirely different from finding the notion repugnant.

However, she couldn't let him see that everything had changed between them. If she did, he might demand an explanation, and she would never admit to eavesdropping.

"It's a beautiful morning," he said. "Would you like to ride with me, Sophie?"

"You've brought no groom to protect my reputation, and I employ none here."

"Do you think you need protection from me?"

"No." That was a lie. The way her insides cavorted about meant she was definitely in danger, but she wasn't concerned about her reputation. It was already spotty enough that an unchaperoned ride would be the least of her worries. She was more concerned that she couldn't control the way her stomach fluttered at the sight of him. "Doesn't Lady Antonia ride?"

"As a matter of fact, no. She's rather afraid of horses, actually. I've tried to coax her out of it, but she's adamant."

"That's because she doesn't realize that for all their size, horses are very silly creatures, and a nice biddable mount would let her control it."

He nodded. "Maybe that's why you're not afraid of anything. You never met anyone or anything you couldn't control."

Except you.

She wished he was right and she could control him. Obviously, his family couldn't. Even her father's bottomless purse didn't bring him to heel. But if she held his strings, she'd make Richard Barrett beg. She'd make him repent in sackcloth and ashes, wishing he'd never said such a hateful thing. She'd make him fall helplessly in love with her and then stomp his heart to bits. She'd—

No, she wouldn't.

If she could control the man, there'd be no joy, no truth in having him care about her if it were forced. That was one of her main objections to her father's plan to buy a titled husband for her—as if all the wealth of the gorgeous East could buy a heart.

And Richard was wrong about something else. There was something of which she was very afraid.

She feared no one ever would really care for her. So long as she had her father's money hanging about her neck, she'd never know for certain. Never know if a man wanted her just for herself.

"Well, what about it?" he said. "Are you game for a ride, Sophie?"

"Give me a few minutes to change." She walked sedately to the front door and disappeared inside. Then once the latch clicked behind her, she bolted up the stairs to her room, taking the steps two at a time. She fully intended on making him wait, but the more time she could give Eliza with her hair, the better. The girl seriously needed the practice.

❧

Richard dismounted and looped both sets of reins around the iron gate in front of Barrett House. The chimney bricks might still need repointing, but the garden had improved out of all knowing under Mrs. Goodnight's and Sophie's care. The roses weren't out of the woods after the scalping Sophie had given them, but even they showed promise.

As did nearly all his plans. He still wasn't sure it was wise to come calling on Sophie, but there wasn't anyone else he'd rather discuss them with than her. Antonia's eyes glazed over if he started explaining what he'd learned about the timber market and how best to implement his scheme to build a working lumber mill at Somerfield Park. He didn't want to bore her.

But Sophie wouldn't be bored. After all, this was partly her idea. She'd be excited to hear about his progress.

Then she stepped out the door of the house and all thoughts of timber contracts and construction deadlines flew right out of his head. Dressed in a peacock blue riding habit that hugged her figure to her hips before spreading in a broad skirt, she fairly took his breath away. Then she walked toward him, the gentle sway in her step a mesmerizing motion that left him slightly light-headed.

Why was it I resisted a match with her again? Oh, yes. Antonia, he thought guiltily. He wished he was more like Seymour. His friend transferred his affection from one lady to the next as easily as he changed his socks. And nearly as often.

But Richard was not that sort of man.

Or was Sophie Goodnight turning him into that sort?

He laced his fingers together and bent over, offering to help her mount. She breezed past him. Lifting her skirt in a dazzling display of ankle and pantalets, she put her neatly shod foot into the stirrup and hoisted herself into the sidesaddle in one fluid motion. Once she hooked her right knee around the upper pommel and her left thigh under the leaping head, she arranged her skirts modestly.

But the damage was done. After that flagrant display, he could imagine all of her in long-legged detail.

Of course, he hadn't actually seen more than a couple inches of bare skin between the top of her half boots and the lacy edge of her pantalets, but he could picture the rest. The curve of her calves, her lean thighs, and then the pantalets would end in an open crotch. Seymour frequently blessed the modiste who came up with that conveniently enticing bit of feminine frippery. Richard grew hard imagining the softness of her tender folds and—

"Well, are we going to ride or do you intend to stare like a halfwit all morning?" Her blunt words shook him out of his waking dream.

Lord, she was lovely, but her tongue was sharp as a lash. His cock settled enough to allow him to mount without discomfort.

"I thought we'd ride to the eastern border today. There's a trail on the bluffs overlooking the sea."

"Lead on," she said. "I have no place else to be."

Then, before he could chafe under her seeming indifference, she surprised him by asking after his father.

"His lordship is quite recovered physically," Richard said. "Though he continues to have no memory of the events that led to his falling off the roof."

"Perhaps that's just as well. I wouldn't want to remember that either. Must have been the shock of the pond water that brought him back the use of his limbs and tongue."

Richard wasn't about to tell her that his father had been shamming his debility as a way to coerce him. She'd only be more insulted by the knowledge that he resisted marrying her even with that level of skullduggery behind the plan. As they started into the village, it occurred to him that she hadn't smiled once. He was coming to need those smiles of hers more than he wanted to admit. "Mother says you missed supper at Somerfield Park all week. I trust you haven't been ill."

"No, just not in the mood for company."

Had she wondered why he hadn't come to see her sooner? Had she even known he was gone? She'd been in his thoughts while he was London, and not only when he was working on the mill project. Traces of Sophie came to him unbidden in a soft whiff of roses or the sight of a dark-haired woman on the other side of the street. He'd thought, perhaps if he saw less of her, she'd fade in his consciousness as an unwelcome dream from which he was fortunate to awake. But far from expunging her from his mind, she'd become even more firmly ingrained.

She was like a tune that played over and over in his head.

Of course, if she kept up this brooding silence, it might drown out that song.

"I was in London all week," he said.

"I know." She slanted him a quick glance and then looked away. "Eliza let slip some of the servants' gossip from the 'big house' about Lord Hartley going to Town. Pity you didn't take your valet with you. You might have saved him from a nasty knock on the head. How is Mr. Abbot, by the way?"

No other lady of his acquaintance would ask after the health of a servant. "He's fine. A glancing blow, Dr. Partridge says, or it might have been a different story. Abbot is recovering nicely, but it was quite a surprise for us all."

"As I heard tell, only poor Mr. Abbot was the one who was surprised."

"I mean we were stunned that something like this could happen in Somerset-on-the-Sea." He drew a deep breath of the sea-washed air. It was a scent he'd always associate with home. "In London, yes. There are plenty of unsavory places there, but Abbot was accosted in a lane off High Street, for pity's sake."

"People are the same wherever they are. The place has little to do with it. Obviously, whoever struck down your valet would be an unsavory person no matter where he was."

"I suppose you're right."

She rolled her eyes at him. "I usually am."

He decided not to challenge her on that when she added a wisp of a smile.

"My maid was a bit fuzzy on some of the details. Do you know why Mr. Abbot was attacked?" Sophie asked.

"It seems he recognized a fellow in the Hound and Hare as the same man who was with my father the day he fell off the roof," Richard said. "Naturally, the felon is no longer in the village, but Mr. Abbot was able to give us a name, and we've engaged a Runner to locate him. He'll be brought to justice."

"For what he did to Mr. Abbot or to your father?"

"Both," Richard said firmly. "And before you get onto your republican high horse, yes, I'd have seen the man was tracked down even if he'd only accosted my servant."

"Good, though how you guessed my political bent when women aren't even allowed the vote is beyond me," she said. "Back to your London trip. The word below stairs is that you were meeting your man of business about some ingenious plan to take care of what they call 'the troubles.'"

"I don't know about the ingenious part, but they seem surprisingly well informed."

"You're too modest, Richard. I think your forestry idea is brilliant." Her words warmed a part of his heart he hadn't realized was cold. "But don't reproach your servants for telling tales. Did you think to keep secrets in a great house like Somerfield Park?"

"No, but I do expect a bit more discretion from the help."

"Can you blame them?" Sophie said. "They're worried, so they piece together what information they can and talk about it amongst themselves. Is that so bad? It's not as if they were making speeches about it in the common room at the inn."

"I suppose not." Still, his father would be livid if he discovered the servants were even aware of the family's present difficulties.

"After all, the financial health of the estate affects them too." When they reached the edge of town, Sophie broke into a comfortable trot. "Probably more than it does you."

That wasn't fair. He was shouldering the burden of the welfare of every soul attached to the estate. No one was more affected than he.

"Well, Richard, I hope you don't start lopping heads and giving people the sack over a few indiscreet—"

"Now just a moment. I never said anything about letting anyone go," he interrupted. "I'm not some sort of medieval tyrant, you know."

"No, I'll grant you that. You'd never do something you found...*repugnant.*"

His gaze cut to her sharply. She said the word with such venom she obviously meant something more than face value by it. But before he could ask her what, she changed the subject.

"Are you going to tell me how it went in London?" she asked then, her tone turned testy. "Or do you subscribe to the notion that women should be kept in ignorance about monetary issues as if we were mushrooms and needed only darkness and dung to thrive?"

"Any man who thinks of mushrooms when he looks at you needs spectacles."

"No, when a man sees me, he sees the Goodnight fortune."

"Not all men," he said.

She reined her mare to a stop. "I stand corrected. You're right. You have never seemed in awe of my father's money. No amount of it will make you do something you find *repugnant.* You can take great pride in the fact that you cannot be bought."

But nothing in her tone or the frown that accompanied it remotely suggested she thought he had anything of which to be proud.

Seventeen

Despite my age, I do remember what it felt like to be young. There's something quite terrible about how desperately important everything was then. It's a bit of a relief to discover with age that only a few things are truly essential. The trick, of course, is to discover what those things are.

—Phillippa, the Dowager Marchioness of Somerset

SOPHIE WAS PRICKLY AS A HEDGEHOG WITH ITS SPINES out, but just when he expected to be speared by them, she drew them back in.

"Don't mind me, Richard," she said, looking pointedly away as the vehemence drained from her. "I'm feeling…out of sorts and taking it out on you."

Somehow, he'd done something to upset her, but for the life of him, he couldn't imagine what. Still, he was grateful her irritation had fizzled out. He wasn't about to ask why.

"That's all right," he said, trying to make light of

her pettishness. "Someday I'm sure I'll deserve your
ire, and you can let it slide then since you've whipped
me a bit unnecessarily today."

She gave a little laugh that sounded suspiciously like
a cross between a "hmph" and a snort.

"Very well. You have one deferred tongue lashing
on deposit with the Bank of Sophie. Withdraw it when
you will. Now, tell me the outcome of your trip to
London, or I'll believe you do think me a mushroom."

This was safer ground. He could report success
all around. "Of course, a venture like this requires
a good deal of capital."

Which he would have had instantly if he'd only
agreed to wed Sophie Goodnight, but it felt so much
better to do this on his own without her father's bottomless purse. Richard was heir to a proud title. He'd keep it
proud with the effort of his mind and his own two hands.

"I found an investor willing to take on the project at
a reasonable rate of return," he said. "Mr. Witherspoon
located a man with forestry experience whom we'll
bring on as our foreman. He assures me we'll be able to
repay the investor with the initial cutting. The placard
announcing the local opportunity for employment will
go up in the village next week, and the first trees will
be felled a few days after that. Building the mill will
take much longer and employ more men."

"That's wonderful, Richard. Truly," she said,
her blue eyes warmer than he'd ever seen them. "It
will mean so much to the families who get work, to
the whole community really. With wages in their
pockets, they'll buy more goods at the shops. The
store owners will then take on more help. Those

people in turn have more money to spend and so on. Everyone wins."

He shook his head in wonderment. "I guess I shouldn't be surprised by your grasp of economics."

"Why?" she said, suddenly remote and wary again. "Because my father is a mere tradesman?"

"No, because you always see things differently. In my experience, most women don't think about things as you do." As far as he could tell, Antonia and his sisters' grasp of economics reached no farther than the cost of their next gown, if they considered it at all. Except for Petra, of course. She had an unwomanly way of wading into masculine subjects at every turn. "I doubt my mother or sisters even have an opinion on trade, except maybe to condemn it."

"To be fair, your family only condemns it because they know your stooping to trade will tar them with lack of respectability as well."

"Now you're playing the devil's advocate. Would they rather live in threadbare gentility?"

"Men may thumb their noses at the rules, but women are always held to them with ruthlessness. I'm not saying it's fair. Lord knows it's not. But that's the way the world is."

Somehow, he had the feeling she wasn't talking about engaging in trade any longer.

"If you don't know what the women in your life think about important things," Sophie said, "perhaps it's because you've never asked them."

Now that he considered it, he and Antonia hadn't ever really discussed anything of substance. He had no idea of her views on politics or religion. He didn't even know her taste in music beyond whether a piece warranted a gavotte or a quadrille.

Since he and Antonia had met at a salon which featured poetry reading, he might have expected to discuss literature with her. But once the poets finished their recitation, his conversations with Antonia generally devolved into typical non-topics, amusing anecdotes of mutual acquaintances and remarks about the weather meant to substitute for clever repartee. She was very skilled at making time spent in her company pleasing, but in the end, it was as insubstantial as a soap bubble.

"You're right, Sophie," he said slowly. "I haven't asked a lady what she thinks about more serious things."

"Which is why you feel comfortable speaking with me about them, since I'm categorically *not* a lady."

"I didn't mean that." Hang it all, why did she constantly goad him into verbal missteps?

"It's all right. I appreciate you treating me as if you thought I had a brain. On second thought, it might shock the well-bred women in your life to be drawn into such unfamiliar conversational waters. I'm sure you'd never want to do anything so *repugnant*."

There it was again. That word with a barb attached to it. Clearly whatever had upset her was still swirling about it.

He might need that tongue lashing reprieve he'd banked sooner rather than later.

The meadow stretched ahead of them, green and freshly dotted with vibrant yellow patches of rapeseed. Sophie urged her mount into a canter across it. Richard followed, enjoying the rise and fall of her bum in the sidesaddle. Halfway across the space, she lost her bonnet. In a bit of horsemanship he wished she'd seen, he leaned down far enough to one side in order to snatch the straw capote before it hit the ground. By the time they reached the woods on the far side of the meadow, her hair was tumbling down in dark waves.

Good. He liked seeing it that way, but he handed the bonnet back to her in any case.

"Thank you," she said as she fixed it over her windblown hair and tied the ribbons beneath her chin in a jaunty bow. "Mother is forever after me not to go without a bonnet lest I freckle, but I can't seem to keep one on my head."

"I think you'd look fine with a freckle or two."

"That shows how little you know. Above all else, my parents long to make a lady of me. Freckles, Mother says, belong on a milkmaid."

"There are worse sins than having a few freckles."

"Amen. But since I've already committed most of those, I must indulge my parents in the small matter of freckles."

His imagination ran rampant. Thoughts of Sophie and sin all twined up together made his body rouse once more. If this kept up, he could set his watch by how often he had erections in Miss Goodnight's presence.

"The trail by the sea is a bit narrow and slopes steeply enough to make riding dangerous," he said as he dismounted in a smooth motion. "We'll hobble the horses and go on foot."

"Hmmm, I decided my reputation was safe with you so long as we were on horseback. On foot…"

"It's been my experience that no matter what you

do, your reputation is fine so long as no one knows what you're actually doing. It's the things you're *seen* doing that make a difference." He slid off his horse's back, crossed over to her, and lifted his hands, offering to help her dismount.

She slanted a sideways gaze down at him. "I ought to say 'Get thee behind me, Satan.'"

"I assure you I'm not that bad."

Her lips twitched in an attempt not to smile. "A minor minion of the Prince of Darkness?"

"Well, maybe worse than that," he admitted. "A minor minion makes me sound like an imp."

"A demon then," she decided. "Skilled at temptation and ruin."

"Temptation, maybe. But no one's ruining anyone today if I can help it." He took her gloved hand. "Come, Sophie. Trust me, the view is spectacular."

"Very well. Lead me into temptation, O Dark One."

Most men would take that as a challenge, but Sophie wasn't most women. If the past was any predictor of the future, Richard would be the one tempted beyond bearing. He'd never been less than correct in his behavior toward Antonia, but something about Sophie made him want to throw convention out the window.

It wasn't that he respected her less than Antonia. There was just something raw and feral that sprang to life inside him whenever Sophie was around. It was like uncaging a tiger, taking him for a walk, and expecting him to stay on the leash.

When he helped her down, the tiger in him growled his approval at the narrow span of her waist under his hands. The beast almost purred when she slipped one of her hands in the crook of his elbow and let him lead her through the brush to the path that skirted the headland.

"Oh my!" She dropped his arm and hurried close to the edge. Richard always stayed a step or two back from the steep drop to the breakers below, but Sophie obviously suffered no fear of heights. The cliffs weren't nearly as tall as the ones at Dover, but the land fell away sharply in jagged columns, to dip its granite toes in the foaming water. Sophie spread her arms wide as if she'd hug the entire vista and fold it into herself. "This was worth the trip."

"It's not so long a ride actually."

"No, I mean the trip back from India. This view is amazing, Richard. Wild and ungovernable and unspeakably lovely."

Just like her.

The wind caught her bonnet and blew it back off her head. The ribbons under her chin loosened but didn't give way, so the capote dangled down her back. She didn't bother to fix it. Instead, she lifted her hand to shield her eyes and continued to gaze out over the purling blue water.

"You miss India, don't you?"

Her quick, sad smile confirmed it.

"You miss someone who's still there," Richard guessed again. The tiger inside him tensed, lashing its body with its own tail.

"I don't know where he is," she said with a small shake of her head. "And I certainly didn't know who he *was*. Not really. But you're wrong. I don't miss him. I miss the *idea* of him."

She sank to the crisp grass, drew her knees up under her skirts, and folded her arms across them. Any other young lady might have succumbed to a fit of vapors after making such a strange admission, but Sophie just continued to gaze into the distance where the grayish-blue water met the soft, summerish sky.

Richard settled beside her, burning with curiosity. "How do you miss the *idea* of someone?"

She cut her gaze to him for a blink and then back to the horizon. "Didn't you ever imagine the girl you'd someday love?"

"No. If I dreamed up a perfect woman, I'd risk being disappointed when a real one came along later."

She shrugged. "You're ever so much wiser than I then. Perhaps it's a female failing, but from the time I was very young, I imagined the man I'd someday love. I even dreamed of him some times."

"Let me guess. He was tall, dark, and handsome."

"Yes, I imagined him as very fine to look upon, but that's hardly a crime. Can you honestly tell me men don't examine a lady's figure first and her character a distant second?

Richard raised his hands in mock surrender. "Guilty."

But he didn't feel the least guilty when he looked at her. What man wouldn't notice Sophie's striking beauty and be fascinated by her? Until she unleashed that acerbic tongue of hers, of course.

"Well, give me a little credit for not being totally shallow," she went on. "I imagined him inside as well as out. My dream man was honest and trustworthy, brave and selfless."

"You were in love with a myth."

"It didn't seem like a myth when I first met Lieutenant Julian Parrish. He was my walking dream." Her eyes took on a hazy quality. Richard suddenly hated this Julian Parrish with a burning passion. "We met by accident. One day I was shopping in the bazaar, minding my own business, when a mad fakir started stirring up hotheads against the *Angrezi*. That's us, by the way. I know it shocks people to learn the English aren't universally loved and hailed as saviors bearing the gifts of civilization wherever we roam, but we're not."

"You don't have to tell me. I've spent time in France. Hatred for us there runs deep."

"And both ways, but that's a topic for another day. In any case, on this particular day, my *ayah* urged me to leave the bazaar, but I didn't listen to her. I had no idea I was in danger. I'd lived in India all my life. I didn't think of myself as the foreign devil the fakir railed against. However, my white face seemed to prove otherwise."

Sophie plucked a grass stem and began tearing it into ever smaller strips. "A mob isn't a group of people, you know. It's one entity, one throbbing heart. A beast with a thousand arms and legs, and only one thought—to lash out in violence. I'd have been killed if Julian hadn't ridden into the swirling mass of shouting men with his sword flailing on both sides. He snatched me up, plopped me behind him on his saddle, and I clung to him as we rode for our lives."

"After an experience like that, it would only be natural for you to become infatuated with him," Richard said grudgingly. "Don't reproach yourself. Of course, you were impressed with the man after that."

"I wasn't infatuated. I was in love, completely and hopelessly. You see, I *recognized* him. He was the embodiment of all I'd imagined. For years, when I'd peered up at the moon and wished, it was Julian Parrish I was longing for. I just didn't know his name until that day."

Richard's gut clenched. "So what happened?"

She looked down.

"No, forget I asked." Besides, every time she said the man's name, Richard's insides burned as if a knife were twisting into him. "You don't have to tell me."

"But I've already told you."

He frowned in puzzlement.

"The first night we met I told you I was no virgin. Of course, at the time I thought it would discourage you from the match our parents were planning. I didn't realize then that you had already purposed in your heart to resist their machinations," she said as she removed her riding gloves and folded them on her lap. "You wouldn't have had to know of my disgrace, but I couldn't see keeping it from you. It didn't seem fair."

"What's not fair is that the man took advantage of you."

"Nevertheless, like Coleridge's ancient mariner, I arise each morning sadder but wiser, Richard."

The temper he worked so hard to control simmered inside him. He wished Julian Parrish were readily available for him to pound into a bloody pulp. Seymour wouldn't be able to pull him off this time. "I would happily pummel Lieutenant Parrish for you."

"And part of me would like to see it, but it wasn't all Julian's fault. You know how I am. When I set my sights on something, I'm difficult to turn. I thought I'd met the One, so I made every effort to see him after that," she said. "Bombay may be a large city, but the English world within it is small enough. It was a simple matter to befriend the daughter of a general, and I suddenly found myself invited to all the military balls."

"Women pride themselves on the art of the cut direct, but a man can dissuade a woman from pursuing him as well."

"Spoken like a veteran of Almack's."

"You have no idea. An eligible man is no more than a trophy to the matrons and debutantes that hunt there. I learned to step lively."

She laughed. "Well, Julian was not skilled in evasive maneuvers. In truth, he didn't try all that hard. Of course, the fact that my parents disapproved of him made him all the more attractive. When you're not quite eighteen, love is relentless and all consuming. If it's forbidden, so much the better."

"So your father had his sights on a titled husband for you even then?"

"No, that came later. After I learned Julian was already someone's husband."

"The cad." Richard swallowed back the more vulgar names for the man that threatened to choke him. Anger boiled in him. He couldn't very well beat Julian Parrish senseless as he wished, but Richard had resources to locate him. He was just about to promise he'd find out where the man was, and if he was still in uniform, Richard would bring the full weight of the Somerset marquessate to bear on seeing him cashiered and ruined.

Then a single tear rolled down Sophie's cheek.

Anything he said would only hurt her more, so he clamped his lips tight.

"His wife lived in Surrey. They had two young children, so she refused to accompany him on his tour in the East. He never spoke to anyone about her, so there was no way I could have known I was acting as... as some sort of vile temptress," she said. "But I was."

"Don't blame yourself, Sophie. The man made use of your youth and inexperience."

"Surely you know me well enough by now to realize I could never be that innocent," she said with a self-deprecating roll of her exquisite eyes. "I know I should be mortified admitting these things to you, but if there's nothing else between you and me, at least there's been honesty, and I would keep that."

Richard reached over and took her hand, pressing it between his. "Honesty is a rare thing."

"As rare as an adventurous virgin, it seems," she said wryly. "Do you know what I regret most of all? It's not the loss of my virginity."

"What is it then?"

"I regret the loss of that dream man. I'll never find him now."

"Maybe that's not such a bad thing. No mortal could live up to your imaginings, Sophie. Now that you've lost those illusions, perhaps a flesh-and-blood fellow has a fighting chance."

"None of them want a chance with me, fighting or otherwise. They're all too quick to form an attachment to my dowry to give me a second thought." She gently tugged her hand free, stretched her legs out before her, and leaned back on her elbows. Tipping her chin, she tilted her face to the sun and closed her eyes. "Now you know my secret. It's time for you to share yours."

"I have none."

"Of course, you do. Men are expected to have a certain level of carnal experience. No man can kiss like you do and claim to have been a monk." She slanted a catlike gaze at him. "How did you lose your innocence?"

Eighteen

Quite often something is deemed scandalous simply because no one has had the courage to try it before—or admit to it if they did.

—Phillippa, the Dowager Marchioness of Somerset

RICHARD SWALLOWED HARD. "I'M NO JUDGE, BUT I think this may well be the most scandalous conversation ever carried on between a gentleman and a lady in the history of Somerset."

"Oh, come, Richard." She gave his shoulder a playful slap. "You can't have lived that sheltered a life. Didn't you say you'd been to Paris?"

"Yes, but—"

"No buts. I've heard what goes on in the City of Light, and it doesn't involve much spiritual contemplation," she said. "I shared mine. Will you have me believe you possess less courage than I?"

"This has nothing to do with courage. It has to do with delicacy."

"You didn't complain of indelicacy when I was confessing," she pointed out.

"That's because I was too busy being affronted on your behalf." He shook his head. "This is not at all the done thing."

"Nothing between us since we kissed in the gallery has been the done thing, and you know it." She abandoned the view of the sea to skewer him with a sharp-eyed gaze. "Our relationship, such as it is, transcends the manufactured constructs of being polite or well-bred."

"Why do you think that is?"

She lifted one shoulder in a shrug. "I don't know. I only know I can tell you anything, and while I may shock you, you haven't called me a monster yet. I trust you not to call out the villagers to hunt me down with torches and pitchforks. Even if you do find me *repugnant* on some level."

"What? Where on earth did you get that addle-pated notion?"

"Oh." She drew her legs back up under her skirt and seemed to curl into herself, not meeting his gaze. "Never mind."

"I do mind. You've used that word repeatedly, and I want to know why."

Her fingers curled into fists at her side. "If you must know, I've done something of which I'm not very proud."

After admitting so coolly how she lost her virginity, he was surprised she'd be reticent about admitting anything to him.

"What was it?"

"That day your father regained his wits and the use of his legs, I listened at the door of the library while the two of you…had things out. He was still determined that you should marry me, and you said you found the notion repugnant." She stared determinedly out to sea. "Not that I blame you. I know what I am and so do you—common and damaged."

"Don't be a birdwit. I think no such thing." He took one of her hands and uncurled the clenched fingers so he could twine his with them. "I find you absolutely *uncommon*. I've never met anyone like you, Sophie."

"It's hard to refute the evidence of my own ears."

"I resent being spied upon, but if you're going to do it, at least have the goodness to hear the whole conversation before you run away with a single piece of it." He lifted her hand to his mouth and brushed his lips over her knuckles. "What I found repugnant was the notion that anyone should expect to marry you simply for your father's wealth. You are quite enough, all by yourself."

Her brows lifted slightly in surprise. "Oh."

Then because he realized suddenly that his words had begun to have the ring of a declaration, he decided to flout convention and tell her about his first time with a woman. It was also the best way he could think of to pull back from this matrimonial cliff.

"Her name was Maddie Wharton."

"I beg your pardon?"

"My first time. You wanted to know, so I'll tell you. Her name was Maddie, and she was an upstairs maid at Seymour's family home." Richard's voice had still been unsure which octave to settle into that summer, but his body had changed completely. He'd learned to "beat the bishop" as well as any of the other boys at school when he was off by himself. However, the first time he saw Maddie, he feared he might spend on the spot. "It was the summer of my fourteenth year. I was spending a couple of weeks with Lawrence and his family before the Michaelmas term began."

Sophie frowned at him but didn't withdraw her hand. "I can't believe you're the sort to despoil the help, Richard. Even someone else's help."

"Who said I was the one doing the despoiling?" He traced lazy circles over the thin skin at her wrist. "Maddie was about five years my senior. Not so old, but she knew perfectly well what she was doing."

Maddie would slide past him in a corridor, brushing her breasts against him in a seemingly accidental way. The buttons on her shirt were always straining to burst, setting Richard's imagination humming. If she brought something to him, she'd lean low enough he could see down her neckline, to the shadowy hollow between her breasts.

He had nocturnal emissions so often that first week, he washed out his undergarments in his bedroom ewer and was embarrassed for the Seymour maids to make his bed.

Once Maddie happened to graze her hand over the front of his trousers. She tossed him a sly look, licked her luscious bottom lip, and said, "My word, Lord Hartley! You really are a man fully grown."

But Richard decided he couldn't tell Sophie that. It would seem boastful.

"When Maddie slipped into my room and appeared by my bedside in naught but her wrapper one night, I almost wasn't surprised."

Sophie stretched her legs out once again. "And now I suppose this is the point at which I'm supposed to say, it wasn't your fault, dear Richard."

"Well, it wasn't."

"You tried to absolve me of my guilt over the affair with Julian, but it won't work. I made my own choice, devil take the hindermost. It sounds like you did too."

"Will you at least allow that I was sorely tempted?"

"Yes, I'll give you that. And this Maddie person was terrible to prey on such a green boy."

He hadn't felt green. When Maddie was sighing under him, he'd felt like a man. She taught him things. Secret things she liked, astounding things she could make him feel. He took to love play like an otter on the riverbank.

"I didn't think she was terrible," he said. "I thought I was in love."

Sophie snorted. "You mean part of you was in love. You didn't know a thing about her character except that she was adept at seducing boys."

"An attribute for which I did not fault her at the time. Besides, a fourteen-year-old boy can't distinguish between what his body wants and what his heart tells him. As far as I knew, I'd discovered why poets wrote bad verse. I'd never felt anything quite so intense. It had to be love. I was tormented every waking moment, wondering where she was, when I'd see her next."

They made games of quick joinings in semipublic places. He rutted Maddie with her spine pressed against the wall under the stairwell. Seymour's mother and her Society for the Improvement of Morals in the Lower Classes were having tea in the parlor while Maddie sucked his cock behind the door of the music room just down the hall. That particular time, he'd bitten his fist to keep from crying out and left teeth marks so deep, he had to feign sickness so he could have a tray sent to his room instead of appearing at the dining table.

"I have a feeling this affair did not end well," Sophie said, breaking into his randy memories. "Did you go off to school and break her heart?"

"No. I caught her in the stable with one of the grooms." Maddie had been on her knees before the fellow, doing the same heart-stopping things she'd done to Richard.

"And so I suppose you went to Seymour's parents and had her sacked."

"No. I couldn't do that. I loved her. Or thought I did. So I did what all sufferers of unrequited love do. I plunged into the depths of despair over her," Richard said with a shake of his head. "Only a fourteen-year-old boy can enjoy misery quite that thoroughly. However, my need for self-flagellation was satisfied in less than a month."

Sophie laughed. "Boys don't have a corner on the market for self-indulgent pity. Seventeen-year-old girls can beat that drum just as loudly. Whatever happened to Maddie then? Never say she still slips into your bedchamber each time you visit Seymour's family?"

He shook his head. "The next time I went home with Seymour for a brief visit, I learned she and that groom had run off together and were living in sin in Cornwall. My education in matters of the heart was complete. You see, I too am sadder but wiser."

"Yes but as I said earlier, woman are held to the

rules ever so much more forcefully than men. Your youthful indiscretions are winked at. Mine would be enough to doom me forever if they were known."

He reached over and cupped her chin to turn her to face him. "I'd never betray your trust."

"I didn't tell you I wasn't a virgin that first night because I trusted you. I didn't you know then. I just wanted out of our parents' arrangement, and shocking you seemed the best way to make sure you found me...repugnant."

"How very flattering."

"I'm sorry. It's no reflection on you." She palmed his cheek for a moment, her touch cool and comfortable. "It's me. I'm such a hoyden. Always have been. I'd settle for obscure spinsterhood if only I didn't have the weight of Father's expectations on my shoulders."

Richard was vaguely disappointed by her wish for spinsterhood. Evidently, Lt. Parrish had stolen more than her maidenhead. He'd made off with her dreams. "So Mr. Goodnight still wants a titled grandchild?"

"Lud, yes. It's all he talks about. When he talks. He spends most of the time working on his memoirs. Father seems to think the world wants to know how to make a fortune."

"He wouldn't be wrong."

"Well, when he stops scritching away in his study, he's hinting about the need to see his grandson before he dies." Tears trembled on her lashes. "The last time he had a recurrence of his fevers, we thought we'd lost him. Each time it strikes him, he's left weaker."

"I don't know if there's a cure for your father's illness, but there is a remedy for our situation, you know," he said as he untied the bow under her chin so her bonnet slid down her back. "We could relent and bow to our parents' wishes."

"And lie to ourselves? You don't love me." She went perfectly still as he ran his hand over her tousled head and followed a long curl to its end down the middle of her back.

"You belong with someone like Lady Antonia," she whispered.

Richard continued to stroke her hair. It was wild and unruly and beautiful. Like her.

"Someone who knows how to behave properly and be a help to you in Polite Society," she added.

She gave a little shiver when his fingertips brushed the side of her neck. Richard was certain she wasn't cold.

"And I certainly don't love you," she pronounced.

"I'm that unlovable?"

"Certainly." But she didn't look away. If anything, she leaned toward him by the smallest of measures. "For one thing, you're entirely too stubborn."

"Without doubt." He moved closer by finger widths.

"And you have a temper." Her mouth went kiss-ably slack.

"A violent one," he agreed. "But you'll never be in danger from it."

Her eyes went soft and dark as her pupils widened. Then they fluttered closed as he stroked her cheek. "If I had any sense, I'd flee from you as fast as I could."

"And yet you're still here."

Her eyes opened again, only a thin edge of indigo around her pupils. "Guess I haven't any sense."

"That is my great good fortune."

"No, I'm the one with the fortune, and don't you forget it."

"I can't see a single pence of it," Richard said. "All I see is you."

Then he kissed her.

Nineteen

How much simpler life would be if young people simply did as their elders asked without question. Surely they realize we have their best interests at heart. Most of the time.

—Phillippa, the Dowager Marchioness of Somerset

SHE KISSED HIM BACK. SOON IT WASN'T ABOUT WHO was kissing whom. There was no question about who was in control.

Neither of them.

Richard knew he ought to hold back, but he couldn't. Sophie was too inviting. Too welcoming. Too...herself.

They sank back together on the soft grass, never breaking off their kiss. Her mouth was a whole world, a new and uncharted country. He explored it with relish.

She returned the favor, biting his lower lip in teasing nips.

At first Richard thought he might try some of the old

tricks Maddie had taught him, but then, when his kiss with Sophie deepened, all thought of the object of his calf-love fled from his mind. It was as if he was that green boy again and had never kissed anyone but Sophie.

No one had ever experienced this heart-stopping exchange of breath, this exchange of souls. It was entirely new. He and Sophie were making it up as they went along.

When she touched him, it burned clear to his bone, but it was a healing fire. She wiped all memory of past dalliances from his mind. He was coming to her with all the fervent urgency of a lovesick lad but with the depth of feeling of a grown man.

He wanted all of her—good and bad. There was nothing about her he would change. Not her sharp tongue certainly. It was all twined up with his. Not her acerbic wit. They were of the same mind, at least at this moment.

She was his. His very heart. His Sophie.

But when she moaned into his mouth, he remembered that a man had taken from her before. Richard was determined to give.

This dalliance would be about her, he decided. His cock rioted, but he was a stubborn man and he was about to prove it. He'd give her pleasure without expecting it in return.

He stroked. He kissed. He undid the silver frogs that fastened the front of her blue riding jacket with studied slowness. He teased her breasts with glancing strokes that had her arching into his hand.

All the while he made love to her mouth in slow thrusts.

He ran his fingertips over the top of her chemise.

With each pass, he slipped farther beneath the lace trim to tease her taut nipples. They were barely peeping above the boned stays, but it was enough. He undid a couple of the hook and eyes, and peeled back the stays so her breasts were bared to the sun. He would torment them until she begged him for release.

But Sophie wasn't the sort to beg. She grasped him by the ears and moved him down to her breasts.

∽

"Oh, yes. Just like that," she murmured when he latched on to her aching nipple and sucked. She knew she ought to be working to remove his jacket, to focus on giving him pleasure, but joy was singing in her head so loudly she could scarcely think of anything. Besides, whenever she tried to disrobe him, he gently pushed her hands aside.

"Just be, love," he murmured. "Just be."

So instead of doing, she was free to feel.

Sophie could simply put herself into his strong, capable hands. She was a bundle of needs desperately seeking to be released, a handful of kindling ready to burst into flames. She ached—a good kind of ache— in so many places, but Richard was working to ease them all.

Her breasts had sent a fiery message to her belly. Warmth and heaviness and a slow pounding settled between her thighs.

Richard was saying things into her neck as he kissed his way back up. Delicious things like "so beautiful" and "oh God" and her name. Over and over again, he said her name as if it tasted like honey on his tongue.

Julian had never done that. Perhaps he'd been afraid he'd say the wrong name at an unguarded moment.

Then Richard suckled her earlobe and all thought of Julian fled. He might never have existed at all. Or maybe he was only a bad dream, one she never need revisit again.

Richard's hand fumbled under her voluminous skirt. He found her knee and shot up her thigh.

Oh Lord. She ought to stop him. A good girl would. A girl like Antonia would never have let things get this far. She felt a twinge of guilt, thinking about Antonia. She'd never known about Julian's wife until it was too late. Richard had told her about Antonia almost immediately.

She was a Jezebel after all, a temptress who stole men from other women.

But if he was so besotted with Antonia, why was he kissing her?

Careful, Sophie. That's how light skirts reason so they can sleep at night.

Then Richard's mouth was at her breast again, and there was no more thinking after that. Her knees parted as his hand continued to slide up her leg. He fingered the tops of her pantalets. Then he brushed his palm over her hot, secret center, not staying nearly long enough.

She whimpered.

"Hush, love. It'll be all right. I'll make it all right."

She wanted him to touch her *there* so badly, but he seemed to be taking pains to skirt that part of her.

Men were like that. She had ached for Julian to touch her there too, but he never did. Not with his hand. She'd wanted it so much, but she wouldn't beg.

Besides, she was ashamed of that wanting.

She'd had a very English governess in Bombay

when she was about fourteen. Her mother wanted to make sure she knew how to behave properly, so Mrs. Pritchard, who came with a flawless list of references as long as her arm, was engaged to "civilize" Sophie. Along with instruction on which fork to use, Mrs. Pritchard had drummed into her head that a specific part of her was shameful. She even made Sophie wear scratchy wool gloves to bed, lest she be tempted to touch herself.

As soon as Sophie's mother discovered this component of her daughter's education, she sacked Mrs. Pritchard and hired a native *ayah*.

"There are worse things than using the wrong fork," Mrs. Goodnight had said.

But the damage was done.

Sophie was still afraid that very needy part of her that so wanted to be touched wasn't worthy of it.

What if Richard was repelled by her? Something hurt inside her chest at the thought. Then it hurt worse at the idea that he wouldn't *want* to touch her.

Then, wonder of wonders, he did touch her.

Gently. With reverence, almost. He cupped that part of her and held her hot little self in his hand.

She squeezed her eyes shut to hold back the tears. Then his hand began to move, and she let them flow. They were tears of joy, of wonderment, and of such relief.

Everything went warm and liquid. His blessed fingers slid between her soft folds. Just when she thought she couldn't hold another drop of wanting, he found a spot that unleashed such a flood of sensations, she gasped at the shock of it.

Pleasure radiated through every bit of her. Then he

returned to that spot and stroked it until she thought she'd go wild.

She'd thought herself so very worldly. So un-virginal. She'd been the other woman, after all.

She'd never experienced anything like this.

Then the pleasure turned sharp-edged. The wanting was back with a vengeance. She moved her hips. She moaned. She was wound so tightly she was sure something inside her was near to breaking. She hadn't wanted to plead, but the word danced on her tongue.

"Please."

"Come to me, Sophie," Richard urged.

And then something inside her did break. It was rather like the recoil of a shotgun, except bliss ricocheted through her instead of bird shot. Her limbs bucked as pleasure spread from the source of her release. She cried out. Nothing intelligible, of course. She couldn't form a coherent thought, let alone a word. She turned into him, hooking a leg around his legs, her hands feverishly seeking the buttons over his hips that would drop the front of his trousers.

He pulled back slightly. "No, Sophie. I won't demand anything from you. I want to give. Not take. Besides, when I take you completely, it'll be in a proper feather bed with silken sheets." His hand continued to draw out her release for another few moments.

When her body finally settled, Richard was still holding her, still looking down at her.

"Part of me wants to wipe that smug grin off your handsome face," she said. The other part wanted to half worship the man.

"Don't I have something to feel smug about?"

Whatever it was he'd done to her, it was the most extraordinary thing she'd ever experienced. "I won't say that wasn't…"

"Breathtaking?"

"Yes," she admitted.

"Heart pounding?" He laid his head between her breasts, his warm breath feathering over them.

Her chest was still pounding. "You know it was."

He rose up to look into her eyes. "Loving?"

The word snatched her breath away. "Who said anything about love?"

"I just did."

"So are you trying to say you love me?"

"I'm not trying." He pulled his hand from under her skirt, leaving her feeling strangely bereft. Then he smoothed down the fabric. "I'm saying it…" He paused as if the seriousness of his words had finally hit him. "It may well be possible that I love you, yes."

"My word, what a declaration. It may be possible that you love me." She sat up, tucked her breasts back into her stays, and refastened the hooks and eyes, smarting at his underwhelming statement. Why couldn't he simply say he loved her with no qualifications? He'd taken her to the heights. Now he was tossing her off a precipice. "Careful, Lord Hartley. You'll turn my head."

"Stop it, Sophie. I'm serious."

"So am I. A girl has to pace herself with you. First, I'm repugnant—"

"No more of that." He put his fingers to her lips to silence her. "We thoroughly debunked that myth."

"I suppose we did," she admitted, wishing the

warm glow they shared hadn't faded so quickly. "But that doesn't change the fact that I'm never quite sure where we are with each other. We bare our souls, and you make me feel…"

"What?"

Her cheeks heated. She despised girls who colored up at every little thing, but now she couldn't help doing it. Of course, this was not such a little thing. "You made me feel things I've never felt before."

"Really?" The smug grin was back. "Your Lieutenant Parrish was a total rotter then."

She shot a dagger glare at him. "I would appreciate it if you refrain from mentioning him. Ever. Again."

"I'll try." He plucked a bit of grass from her hair.

"Because if you do keep casting him in my teeth, I shall never speak to you. Ever. Again," Sophie promised.

The grin disappeared. "Then I consign him to oblivion. Consider He-who-shall-remain-nameless eternally forgotten. May I take it that Maddie Wharton is similarly relegated to the flames of forgetfulness?"

"Yes. Yours, as well as mine, if you please," she said as she fastened the last frog on her riding coat. "If I catch you smiling over nothing, I don't want to have to wonder about the source of it."

"Fair enough. But I promise you, if you catch me smiling over nothing, I'll be thinking of you." He captured her for another quick kiss. "Now, shall we tell our families about our change of heart?"

She blinked slowly at him, hoping he would make an unequivocal declaration. Love with no limits. Love with no conditions. Simply love. "What change of heart?"

"You'll marry me now, surely."

Sophie shifted uncertainly. His "may well be possible" sort of love didn't inspire her confidence. "With
Lady Antonia still in residence at Somerfield Park, I
think an announcement of any sort is premature. And
a bit unfeeling. She had expectations when you invited
her and her family to visit."

"You're right. I'm being selfish, and I don't wish
to be unkind to her. Very well." He stood and pulled
her to feet. "I shall speak to Antonia as soon as I return
home. She and her family will be gone by tomorrow."
He grasped her waist and tugged her close. "And you
and your family will move out of Barrett House and
take up quarters in the guest wing at Somerfield Park
until the banns have been read."

"What? No special license? Father will be dis-
mayed." She sheltered behind flippancy to hide her
disappointment that Richard was all details but no
declaration. How could a man who made her body
sing for the pure joy of sensation be so taciturn about
his own feelings? She put on her bonnet and failed
miserably at tucking her hair back up under it. "He
always says that everyone who is anyone is wed by
special license these days."

"Those things cost the earth." Richard tied the
bonnet ribbons beneath her chin, obviously not caring
how disheveled she looked. "Remember, my dear,
you'll be wedding a title, not a fortune."

"That's right. You're the one who would be wedding a fortune." How had he missed that she hadn't
really accepted his awkward proposal?

His smile faded. "I don't want your father's money,
Sophie."

"You wouldn't have a choice."

"We always have choices. Haven't we proved that this very day?"

He was right. Nothing had happened between them without both of them wanting it. That did bode well for a marriage. She imagined accepting his suit. If they presented a united front, surely they'd be able to turn her father away from showering them with all his wealth. Henry Goodnight would still probably insist their wedding be the grandest occasion ever witnessed in Somerset and would likely send them on a honeymoon that would beggar the royal family. But Sophie thought she could temper his generosity enough to save Richard's pride.

"We can talk terms later," she said. "For now, we only have to let our families know that we have decided to tolerate each other."

"Oh, I think you do far more than tolerate me."

That was an understatement. She adored him. He'd shown her that she was precious—all of her. For the first time since she realized she'd been duped by Julian Parrish, she felt worthy of love. Though he hadn't really said the words, Richard Barrett's eyes shone with it. Perhaps that look would be enough till he found those words. But until he did, Sophie couldn't admit that she loved him so much her insides ached with it.

"Yes, I more than tolerate you, Lord Hartley. In fact, I think you'll do quite nicely as a permanent adornment to my arm."

"I'll take that as an acceptance of my suit."

He bent to kiss her with gentleness this time. With

the unhurried leisure of one who expected to kiss her every day for the rest of her life.

When he released her lips, she palmed both of his cheeks. "When we do marry, Richard, you will be the most exciting adventure of my life."

"From one who's ridden an elephant, that's high praise."

Twenty

It's not often I find anything to commend in the Scottish race—all those infernal bagpipes and ridiculous kilts and general boisterousness. Quite unsettling. But I must say that Robert Burns fellow was right when he penned the bit about how the best laid plans oftimes "gang agley."

—Phillippa, the Dowager Countess of Somerset

"HARTLEY, DEAR, I'M SO GLAD YOU'RE HOME," his mother said when Richard strode into the parlor. He'd expected to find his family sedately taking their afternoon tea. Instead, his mother was composing lists, and his sisters were busily addressing envelopes. Reams of paper were scattered over the low tea table. His father and Lord Pruett had evidently fled in the face of such feminine industry. "Just wait till you hear. Lady Antonia has had a wonderful idea."

Antonia clutched a small portfolio crammed with loose papers to her impeccably stylish bodice. "I was concerned that we were lingering so long in the

country. It's interfering with Lady Ella's Season, and that hardly seems fair."

"You see, Hart," Ella said with a sniff, "at last, *someone* is thinking about me."

It had been a bone of contention that he wouldn't spare any of the funds he'd just secured for the forestry project to foot the bill for Ella to lark off to London and join the husband hunt. If all went well, he promised her a new wardrobe and a whirlwind of fashionable outings next year, but he couldn't in good conscience waste his seed money on fripperies now.

He probably should have thought of different words to describe Ella's longed-for Season when he explained matters to his mother and sisters. His refusal to bend to feminine pressure had not won him any allies at home.

"What are you scheming now?" he demanded.

He directed his question to Ella, but it was Antonia who flinched as though he'd slapped her. "It's not a scheme," Antonia said. "It's just a little house party with a ball thrown in. If Ella cannot go to London, London must come to her."

He dragged a hand over his face. "May I speak with you in private, Mother?"

Antonia looked stricken as she turned to go. "We thought you'd be pleased."

He felt low as boot leather for his harsh tone, especially since he was honor bound to wound her even more in a very short time. "After I speak with Mother, I wonder if I could have a word with you, Lady Antonia...also in private."

A smile lit her face, knowing glances passed from

woman to woman around the room, and he realized he'd erred badly. That was just the sort of thing a man might say when he wished to take a girl off by herself so he could propose.

"Certainly," Antonia said. "I'll wait for you in the garden by the fountain."

Lud, the most romantic spot in the garden. But there was nothing else for it. That would have to do.

Once Antonia and his sisters filed out of the parlor, his mother patted the cushion beside her on the settee. "Come, Hartley, and rest yourself. You look positively drained after that ride. Really, you'd ought to limit such outings to once a day. As I always tell your father, a man—"

"Mother, how could you have encouraged the idea of a house party when you know the delicate situation of our finances? We'll need to take on extra help for all the guests. Mountains more food. Musicians. Decorators. You know we haven't the funds for such an extravagance."

"But I'm certain your new venture will succeed," she said soothingly. "Your father has expressed his disapproval over your plan for Somerset's woods, but honestly, trees grow back, and I'm sure you'll save enough wilderness on the estate for your father to have his hunt each year. In any case, I have confidence in you, Hart."

"Thank you, Mother, but house parties can't be paid for with confidence. Merchants require cash."

"That's just it. We don't need to have the money now. Everything will be done on credit." Lady Somerset gestured eloquently. Richard sometimes wondered whether his mother would be struck dumb if someone tied her hands. "We'll simply delay payment. Within half a year, maybe a bit more, you'll be able to pay for the party and ball Antonia is helping us plan.

"I don't wish to use credit for this."

"But it's how things are done."

"It's not how I wish them to be done, and at the moment, my wishes hold sway. Or hasn't Father told you?"

Lady Somerset's lips drew into a disapproving moue. "He has. And it really was too bad of you and Mr. Witherspoon to go behind your father's back to have him declared *non compos*...to have him declared unfit."

As if it wasn't too bad of his parents to deceive him into thinking his father had been gravely and permanently injured. But Richard didn't want to fight an old battle when he hadn't won the new one yet. "If we fail to pay in timely fashion, what happens to the poor tradesman we owe? Does he have credit to draw upon in order to stay afloat?"

"Spoken like a tradesman," she said, narrowing her eyes at him.

"Not you too, Mother. By the way, speaking of tradesmen, Mr. Goodnight and his family will be moving from Barrett House up to Somerfield Park tomorrow."

"Why?"

"I thought you wanted me to marry the Goodnight heiress. If she's in residence, it will make the job of courting her that much easier." He tried not to smile, but courting Sophie sounded like the best job in the world. He'd have to be careful not to let it consume him while he was getting the forestry venture under way.

"But...if all goes well with your plans for the

woods, you don't need to marry Sophie Goodnight," his mother said.

"What?"

"We assumed that was why you're so adamant about dabbling in trade." She leaned forward and straightened a pile of completed invitations on the tea table into a neat stack. She'd organize his life just as easily if he let her. "I know you had your heart set on Antonia, dear, and now you can have her."

Richard sighed. "What if I don't want her?"

"Bite your tongue, Hart," his mother said with vehemence. "Don't you see? Now we *need* you to marry someone like Antonia."

"I know I'll regret asking, but for heaven's sake, why?"

"To take away the taint of trade, of course," she said. "You insist on solving the estate's problems by slogging away in business, as if you were a grubby clerk trying to make good. It's not at all the sort of thing a marquess in the making does. A match with Lady Antonia will temper your…eccentric leanings in the minds of others. Lord and Lady Pruett are good *ton*, an old family with impeccable connections. People will overlook your trafficking in matters better left to the lower classes if you have someone like Antonia by your side."

"I don't much care what people think," Richard said. "The *ton* blows with the wind. Who knows what their collective small minds will pronounce proper from one day to the next?"

"Hartley, we are not talking about how to wear your cravat. We are speaking of the future mother of your children, the future prestige of the title and estate. If you cause Somerset to be awash in dirty trade money with your forestry scheme, you simply must make certain the bloodlines of the marquessate at least remain pure."

"You weren't at all concerned about Sophie's bloodlines when she came wrapped in her father's dirty trade money."

"Sophie," his mother repeated in a sour tone. "That familiar, are you?"

Mother, you have no idea. But he couldn't say that, so he tackled her other fallacious point. "Money gotten by honest work cannot be dirty."

"You can espouse whatever political views you want once you take your seat in the House of Lords." She skewered him with an accusing glare. "I assume you haven't caused your father to be unseated there too."

He shook his head. "If England can have a mad king, a lord without his wits is no impediment to the state."

"Good. However, back to the topic at hand, you need to take a responsible position here at home," she said. "If you don't care what people think of you, at least consider the plight of your sisters. With Lady Antonia at your side, dear Ella, Petra, and Ariel won't be tarred so badly with the stench of trade."

"Stench of…" He snorted in exasperation and rose to go. "That's more melodrama than one sees on Drury Lane."

His mother grasped his wrist. "I assure you, it is not. It was a kindness that Antonia thought of the house party and ball before word of your tree business gets around. Once it's out, Ella's acceptability will be severely diminished. She'll have no chance of being approved to purchase an Almack's voucher."

"She won't be missing much."

"A man's assessment if ever there was one. You scoff, Hartley, but remember, a woman's best hope in this world is the protection of a good man. Would you deny your sisters their chances for happiness?"

She had him and he knew it. He adored his sisters. But it didn't mean he was going to give up Sophie. He'd just have to work up to it a bit more gradually.

However, he couldn't let Antonia continue in her expectations for one more day. "I will consider what you've said, Mother."

That was safe, polite yet noncommittal. Perhaps he did belong in the House of Lords.

"If you'll excuse me," he said, "I believe Antonia is waiting for me in the garden."

His mother's face crinkled into a satisfied smile. "Of course, dear. I'm sure you'll do what's best."

Richard was sure of no such thing, but he would do what he must. He strode to the door and stopped with his hand on the knob. "The Goodnights will still be moving up to Somerfield Park tomorrow. I plan to engage some brick masons to repoint the chimney and another crew to repair the roof on Barrett House, so they can't stay there."

"Hartley," his mother chided, "if you can spend money on that sort of thing, how could you in good conscience complain about hosting a little house party?"

Sometimes, a man needed to acknowledge when he was beaten, Richard decided. He'd settle for a compromise. The house party would go forward. His understanding with Antonia would not.

"The Goodnights were your guests to begin with," he told his mother. "See that you make them welcome."

He made good his escape before she could utter another word.

&

When she heard the crunch of his boots on the gravel path, Antonia stopped pacing and arranged herself in an artful pose on the edge of the fountain. She peered into the basin as if she were a female Narcissus, fascinated by her own reflection. She didn't look up even when the crunching stopped and she knew he could see her. Instead, she trailed a hand in the water and sighed.

Very romantic. Hartley couldn't help but be moved. He'd be on his knees before her in just a few moments, and for the rest of his married life, he'd hold this placid image of her in his imagination.

And wonder how he'd been so deceived.

"My lady."

She turned toward him then, flashing a practiced smile. Then she quickly let it fade and assumed a mild expression. Oh, how she wished he'd get the formalities out of the way and she could proceed to planning the betrothal and wedding. She didn't know how much longer she could maintain this façade of docile amiability. All she knew was that once she was in line to be the next marchioness, her husband would discover she was not the mild mouse he took her for.

Antonia intended to be the new tastemaker of the *ton*, and the marquessate of Somerset was the perfect platform from which to embark upon her reign. She would give the most dazzling parties, patronize the most stylish artists, and set the tone in fashion for decades to come.

And if Lord Hartley wanted peace at home, he'd quickly come to heel with her plans.

"How I love this fountain, Hartley," Antonia said, patting the spot on the granite next to her. "Your mother told me it was designed in Paris and moved in pieces to Somerfield Park during the reign of the Sun King. It certainly speaks of all things *français*, doesn't it?" She willed herself to blush. "We have such lovely memories of Paris, you and I."

He looked away suddenly, and something inside her checked. It was entirely possible he wasn't there to propose. She had to improvise quickly, before he said something that couldn't be unsaid.

"Have a seat," she urged. "You look tired. I know this whole business with…well, business is wearing on you."

"On the contrary, it invigorates me," he said as he sat beside her. "Launching the timber venture is consuming, but I haven't been this excited about a project for a long while."

She decided to let that pass. He'd been plenty excited about her at one time. He might be enamored of the process of making money now, but all she needed to do was make sure she'd be in a position to spend it later.

"I hope you're not still upset about the house party," Antonia said meekly. "I'd never have suggested it if I'd thought you'd object."

"No, it's all right," he said dully. "It was good of you to figure out a way to help Ella. She's been chafing at the bit to get to London. This is a fair compromise. I've told Mother to go ahead with your plans."

"Oh, I'm so glad and so very glad you think it fair. Your happiness is of the utmost importance to me."

He sighed and took one of her hands between his. It was not the grip of an ardent suitor. If she'd wondered before, she was certain of it now. He was about to let her down.

"And because your happiness is all I care about," she went on before he could speak, "I want you to know that I don't hold you to anything you said to me when we were in Paris."

The best way to enslave a man was to free him. It would make him wonder why he wanted to get away.

"But I didn't—"

"Come, Hartley, you may not have made a declaration then, but we both know what dance that particular tune called for. It's why you brought me here, but I see now that you are much too involved with your new project to worry yourself about me right now."

Well, that was inspired if Antonia did say so herself. Much better to blame his lack of interest in her on his new scheme than on that vulgar mushroom of an heiress Sophie Goodnight. Plus, it cast Antonia in the Madonna-like light of being so understanding she'd excuse his lack of attentiveness without needing an apology from him for it. That would be useful later. What wife needed that much attention from a husband anyway?

His purse, yes. His person, not so much.

"After the ball, perhaps you'll be more settled," she suggested as she gently withdrew her hand from his.

"Antonia, it's not—"

She put her fingertips to his lips. "Hush, dear. You don't have to explain. I understand perfectly.

And don't fret that I'll feel neglected while you…
work." She tried very hard not to color the word
with the revulsion she felt, but if the new Somerset
timber company funded her future, she wasn't about
to denigrate it. Not now at any rate. "Because I'll be
busy too. Your mother and I will have our hands full
planning the party and ball. There are so many things
to do, but I won't bore you with them."

She rose to her feet and he followed suit. Gentlemen
were so easy to manipulate. They were conditioned
from boyhood to protect the fair sex from unpleasantness, especially if that unpleasantness was coming from
themselves. Hartley would bless her for arranging matters so he didn't have to say baldly what was so clearly
dancing on his tongue.

"Thank you for allowing your mother and me this
chance to get to know each other better," she said.
"She's a lovely woman."

"She's a peach," he said in a tone that suggested he
thought otherwise.

Impulsively, Antonia stood on tiptoe and kissed his
cheek. "You'll be so pleased with the party, I promise." Then she headed back down the path.

Don't call me back. Don't call me back.

If he didn't say the words now, he'd not have another
chance to say them. Antonia would make sure of that.

She'd also make sure, one way or another, that
she'd be betrothed to Richard Barrett, Lord Hartley,
by the end of the ball.

Twenty-one

Sometimes, the most important things in life are decided between one step and the next. The bewildering thing is that one is never quite certain during which two steps this remarkable occurrence might happen.

—Phillippa, the Dowager Marchioness of Somerset

"MISS DOVECOTE."

Eliza's chest constricted at the rumbling sound of that voice. She turned to see David Abbot trotting down the lane after her and her friends.

"I suppose you want us to walk on," Drucilla said snappishly to Eliza. "I might have expected it. The lady's maid and the valet surely won't deign to stroll with the likes of us."

"Oh, go on with you," Sarah said to the older woman. "Just because you haven't a fellow wanting to walk you home from church, that's no call to be nasty to one who has. We'll see you at the house later, Dovecote."

Sarah only called her Eliza now when no one

else was around. Even though they were friends, the traditions of the below stairs folk must be maintained with as much rigidity as the manners of the quality folk upstairs. It was a matter of dignity all around, Mr. Hightower always said.

Sarah wrapped her arm around Drucilla's elbow and fairly dragged her along. Eliza waited for David to catch up. She loved watching him run, his long-legged strides eating up the distance between them.

"Mr. Abbot," she said with a grin when he stopped in front of her. Sometimes her cheeks hurt from smiling so much when he was with her, but she couldn't help it.

"Do you think you could remember to call me David when it's just we two?"

She forced the smile from her face. "I think you should be Mr. Abbot to me for a while, since you let me get halfway back to Somerfield Park before you caught up with me."

One of the loveliest things about Miss Goodnight and her family moving into guest rooms in the big house was the fact that Eliza was once more under the same roof as David. Her cozy chamber—and now that she was a lady's maid, she rated one all to herself!—was just down the long corridor from his, on the fourth floor.

She'd always admired David, but it was different now. The feeling seemed to be mutual. He noticed her and sought her out. Eliza didn't want to think it was only because she'd been elevated so quickly to her new position. She wanted to believe that the brief time she'd been away from Somerfield Park with the Goodnights had made him miss her and realize what she meant to him.

Instead of grinning like an idiot, which was what she really felt like doing whenever David was about, she cocked a brow at him. Her mistress said it was good to keep a man guessing. After all, he needed *something* to think about. Why shouldn't it be puzzling over the woman in his life?

"Don't be put out, Eliza."

"Nonsense, if I were put out, it would mean I care about you."

He smiled at that, and Eliza kicked herself. She'd almost admitted her feelings. That would never do. The man should always make the first declaration.

At least, that's what Miss Goodnight said.

Of course, the lady wasn't doing so well in matters of the heart herself at the moment. She hadn't said in so many words, but Eliza knew it was a bone of contention with Miss Goodnight that Lady Antonia and her family were still in residence at the big house. But Sophie Goodnight's advice still had a sound ring to it. It was a matter of self-respect. Eliza wouldn't gush that she loved David beyond the lot of mortals till he said he loved her first.

"Don't you want to know why I was late to walk you home?" David asked.

"Don't know why I should. It's not as if we have a standing arrangement." In fact, he'd only walked her home from church once before. She turned from him and headed down the lane. When David fell into step with her, his long legs slowing their pace for her comfort, she decided her mistress's advice about men was brilliant. Now that Eliza wasn't mooning about over David, he was starting to moon over her.

"All right," he said. "Let's plan on walking out together after church from now on."

"Are you asking me or telling me?" Eliza said with deceptive sweetness.

He thrust his hands into his trouser pockets. It was an endearing gesture. She took it to mean she'd won this round. "Asking."

"Very well. You may walk me home from church next Sunday. We'll let it be something I decide from one week to the next," Eliza said, tickled that she'd be able to share this little exchange with her mistress later while she worked on Miss Goodnight's hair. If she couldn't produce a coiffure that lasted for an entire evening yet, at least Eliza could supply amusing gossip. "Now that that's settled," she went on, "why were you late?"

"I had to ask the vicar something," David said. "It was about what that fellow Thaddeus Clack said that made his lordship admit him to Somerfield Park in the first place."

"What was that?"

"Rosewood Chapel. At first, I thought it might be some sort of code. You know, something that only Lord Somerset would understand, but it makes more sense that it's an actual place. So I asked the vicar had he ever heard of it."

"Had he?" She peered up at him, trying not to let him see how he still fair took her breath away. Though his coloring was darker, David was every bit as fine to look upon as Lord Hartley—and far more approachable.

"Yes. Turns out, it's not far from here. Only a little farther down the coast from Crimble in a village called Brambleton."

"Oh! My mother's sister lives in Brambleton." She

wished she were learned enough to offer to write a letter asking about the chapel. But then, her aunt wouldn't be able to read one in any case. Besides, Eliza's days were full enough without the distraction of being able to read and write. There was always a hem to mend or lace to reattach to some part of Miss Goodnight's wardrobe.

Her mistress was deucedly hard on her clothing. Eliza still hadn't managed to get the grass stains out of her riding habit. Her mistress must have taken quite a tumble, but she hadn't complained of a fall.

Of course, that particular day, Miss Goodnight had ridden out with Lord Hartley. Eliza drew her own conclusions. The less said about that the better, she decided.

"You know how to read," she said to David. "I've seen you poring over his lordship's used newspapers in the common room often enough."

"The marquess insisted upon it when I first came to live and work at Somerfield Park. So Mr. Hightower saw to my education. I had to spit shine shoes till he could see his reflection in them *and* learn to read and do sums in order to please him."

"And now we're both doing well for ourselves," Eliza said contentedly. "I always knew you'd be chosen to be Lord Hartley's valet."

David shrugged. "Lord Hartley's easy enough to serve."

"But you don't seem happy. Whyever not?"

"I don't know. It's not something I can put my finger on. I just have the sense that I'm not doing what I ought with my life. There's a piece missing."

It's me! Eliza almost sang out, but she bit her lip to keep from it. Still, if only he'd think a moment, he'd realize she was his missing piece. A man needed a woman to steady him and settle him down. She slipped her hand into the crook of his elbow to give him a hint. "What do you think it might be that you're missing?"

He shook his head. "I haven't a clue."

Eliza nearly growled in frustration. Why were men so puddingheaded sometimes?

"But back to Rosewood Chapel," he said. "I need to go there for myself and see what connection there might be between that place and his lordship."

"How will you get to Brambleton?" London was farther away, but it was an easier trip than traveling into the country if a body didn't have a conveyance or a horse to call his own. Every other day, a coach ran from Somerset-on-the-Sea to the great city, but not much serviced the hinterlands.

"I'll take the mail coach as far as Crimble, but then I'll have to walk. Brambleton is too small to have any regular coach routes."

A flash of brilliance struck her. "I could ask Miss Goodnight if I may borrow her equipage and driver to visit my aunt in Brambleton. I'm pretty sure she'd let me because, after the London trip, she told me I might take a couple of days for myself if I liked." She squeezed his arm. "You could come with me."

"I don't want to put you in a difficult spot. It wouldn't be proper for us to travel together."

"No, it wouldn't, but only if anyone knew about it," Eliza reasoned. "Go ahead and take the mail coach to

Crimble. If you start walking after that and my coach happens to stop and pick you up along the way to Brambleton, who would be the wiser?"

"I wouldn't want you to risk your reputation on my account."

Her reputation was the least of her concerns. The idea of being alone in a swaying coach with David left her slightly light-headed. She gave a soft chuckle to show him she was making light of the situation.

"Are you trying to warn me that you have improper thoughts about me, David?"

He stopped walking and met her gaze without a hint of amusement. His dark eyes burned. "Yes."

It was only one word, but it sent a ripple of goose bumps over her whole body.

Her mouth went suddenly dry. She'd hoped for just such a crack in his reserve. Now a whole world of possibilities opened before her. But David wasn't the sort of man to rush headlong into them. After all, he'd managed to limit a declaration of his feelings for her to a single word, for pity's sake.

"Let me worry about my reputation." She could count on David to do right by her, whatever happened. She gave him her brightest smile and started walking again, pulling him along, because if she continued to look into his eyes, she'd be tempted to stand on tiptoe and kiss him then and there, in front of God and everybody. And that would never do.

She'd brushed her mouth over his as he lay unconscious in the lane near the Hound and Hare. If there was another kiss between them, he'd have to start it. Eliza had no doubt she could finish it.

"Besides, you might need my help finding what you seek once you get to the chapel," Eliza continued.

"Fancy yourself a Bow Street Runner, do you?"

"I've been known to unravel a mystery or two," she said. *After all, I intend to unravel you, David Abbot. Indeed I do.*

❧

Sophie ripped the page from her sketch pad and crumpled it into a ball. No matter what she did, she couldn't seem to get the perspective on the statue of Eros right. The fickle god of love defied her efforts to capture him in foolscap and charcoal. Viewed from her place of concealment on a stone bench sheltered by an ivy-covered trellis, the statue in Somerfield Park's garden was turned three quarters away from her.

He wasn't a chubby-cheeked Cupid. This rendition of the god of love was a youth in the first flush of manhood, his lean musculature well defined. He gazed into the distance, his head turned so she could see his firm jaw and straight Roman nose in profile. In a nod to his cherubic roots, Eros's granite head was covered with short curls, and small wings sprouted from his shoulder blades.

"Start from a central point," she muttered to herself. The central point seemed to be his well-developed bum, so she sketched those hard cheeks, adding the thighs and calves, shading as she went.

She'd seen Richard in skin-tight trousers that didn't disguise his ample endowment in front, but she'd never seen him without a jacket, so she didn't know if his backside compared favorably to the statue. She suspected it put the god of love's rock-hard bum to shame.

"There you are." A masculine voice interrupted her increasingly naughty musings.

Richard. He was striding across the crisp green lawn toward her.

She flapped her book closed before he could see what had captured her attention. Not that she had a thing to be ashamed of. She wasn't the one who'd broken her word.

Lady Antonia was still firmly ensconced at Somerfield Park.

"Here I am," she said, determined not to advance the conversation if she could help it.

"The glittering horde descends upon us tomorrow," he said, clearly not looking forward to the arrival of more guests. "The rest of the ladies are in the parlor making favors for the house party."

"How nice. But as it's not my house or my party, I fail to see how that concerns me." She knew he expected her to slide to one side of the bench to make room for him, but she didn't want to. It would be giving in, and she wasn't in the mood to yield a finger width.

Not until Lady Antonia was gone.

"I don't know what you're so testy about." Richard didn't wait for her to move. He crowded onto the bench with her.

She sidled to the far edge. "Don't you?"

"I spoke to Antonia just as I said I would."

"And yet she's still here."

He frowned as if that puzzled him a bit too. "She told me she understood and released me from whatever understanding we may have had. At least, that's my recollection of the conversation. Now that I think about it, I really had to say precious little. Before I knew what was what, she was letting me go."

"How magnanimous of her," Sophie said dryly.

"It was," he said, missing the irony in her tone. "After she was so gracious and harbored no ill feelings, it felt churlish to ask her and her family to leave. Long before she and I kept company in Paris, the Pruett and the Barrett families have been friends. She's only still here to help with the house party and the ball. It's for Ella, really."

Sophie unstiffened a bit. Ella had been giddy with excitement at supper last night. It was hard not to wish her success in her first social outing as an adult.

"Well, that's kind of Antonia, I must say." She flipped open her sketchbook and furiously added more cross-hatching to the cleft of Eros's backside. "If a man threw me over, I doubt I'd have the grace to stay on to help launch his sister into Polite Society."

"You've got your own kind of grace, Sophie."

Before she knew he was going to do it, Richard moved across the bench to her side, cupped the back of her head with his hand, and drew her into a long, deep kiss. Part of her knew she should resist, but it was a very small part.

The rest of her melted into him.

"That's better," he said when he finally released her. Then he looked down at the sketchbook where Eros's bum and legs had taken remarkably good shape. "Ahem. Dare I hope you were thinking of me?"

"Why?" she asked, batting her eyes at him. "Do you feel you're behaving like an ass?"

Richard threw back his head and laughed. "Sometimes, yes. I certainly do." Then he took both her hands in his. "I know things are uncomfortable for you now, but I mean to make this up to you."

"How?"

"On the night of the ball, there will be a toast before we adjourn to the dining room for the midnight supper. At that toast, I intend to announce to the world that you and I are betrothed." He reached into his waistcoat pocket and drew out a small velvet-covered box.

All the air whooshed from her lungs. For the first time in a long while, Sophie had nothing flippant to say.

He opened the box to reveal a charming ring. The setting was a trifle old-fashioned, but it boasted a goodly sized ruby of obvious quality with baguette diamonds twinkling on either side.

"Richard, you can't afford this," Sophie said. "Not when you're trying to get the timber business off the ground. Father always says, 'Build the barn first and it'll build the house for you later.'"

"Wise advice, but unnecessary in this case." He slid the ring onto her third finger. It fit as if it had been made for her. "You'll soon learn that in a family like mine, many things are handed down from one generation to another. This ring belonged to my grandmother's mother. She and my great grandsire loved each other for nearly fifty years."

"Oh, Richard." A thin shaft of sunlight filtered in through the ivy on the trellis and hit the ruby. The stone seemed to catch fire. This ring was far dearer than if he'd taken her to Rundell and Bridge and let her pick out a new one. It carried the weight of the

Somerset marquessate and the solemn joinings of the past, the long line of Richard's noble progenitors. Now he was making her part of that proud line.

Sophie had always striven to be a contrarian. She'd never thought fitting in was a good thing, but something inside her swelled with joy at the thought of becoming part of Richard's family. Yes, the Barretts had their faults, chief among them the tendency to try to manage each other's lives, but what family didn't have that sort of tension in its ranks?

"Gran wanted you to have it," he said.

"You told the dowager about us?"

"And swore her to absolute secrecy. Trust me, the old dear is delighted to be part of the plot." He raised her hand to his lips. "I can't wait to make you mine."

A thrill ran up her arm. "There are only a few days till the ball, so you haven't long to wait. Though if we mean to keep our betrothal secret, I dare not wear this openly yet."

She removed the ring and tucked it into her cleavage. It settled behind the busk that separated her breasts and kept her posture ramrod straight.

"Never thought I'd envy metal and cold stone." Richard's eyes grew dark with desire as he gazed at the ring's hiding place. "Good luck keeping the secret from the help once your lady's maid sees it."

"Miss Dovecote isn't here at the moment. She's visiting her sick aunt, so I'm muddling through with this inconvenient new wardrobe of mine without my maid."

"I'd be happy to help you with it, but I confess I'm more interested in undressing than dressing." He arched a brow at her, and she swatted his shoulder.

Still, the idea of Richard peeling off her clothing one layer at a time made her feel warm all over. "Of course, I could use a valet myself at the moment. Abbot has made himself scarce as well. Don't suppose the two of them have run off together, do you?"

"Why? Has your valet said he's sweet on my maid?" Eliza had regaled Sophie with no end of tales expounding the excellence of David Abbot. It would be lovely to see her attachment returned.

"No. Abbot is pretty tight-lipped about himself," Richard said. "Still, he's a restful sort. I'm grateful Hightower chose him for me. Toby would have talked my ear off."

"Then we must keep Toby and Miss Dovecote apart at all costs. Eliza is perfectly capable of holding up both sides of any conversation. If she ever got together with Toby, no one would ever be able to get a word in edgewise."

"Sometimes, there's no need for words." Richard leaned down to kiss her again, and Sophie lost herself in the swirl of sensations.

After Julian, she hadn't thought she'd ever trust a man again, but Richard changed all that. He was steady and honest. His family might be awash in schemes and plotting, but he was just what he seemed—her knight in shining armor. He was light to her dark, the calm breeze to settle her turbulent sea.

Sophie palmed his cheeks and kissed him back, nipping and suckling his lower lip. He groaned in frustration.

If they had to wait to announce their match to the world, it wouldn't hurt to make him chafe a bit at the delay.

Twenty-two

No matter what the vicar might say, it doesn't seem fair
that the sins of the father are visited upon the children.
Haven't we all enough misdeeds of our own?

—Phillippa, the Dowager Marchioness of Somerset

ROSEWOOD CHAPEL WAS A CHARMING GOTHIC
confection, a miniature cathedral in its rustic setting. Though small by any measure, its spire pierced
the sky above the humble village of Brambleton.
The cross-topped steeple was visible from several
miles away.

"The main part of the chapel was built in the 1200s.
Back then, over one hundred men worked on it for about
twenty-five years," the young vicar told David and Eliza.
They strolled down the center aisle beneath the chapel's
ribbed vault, walking through splotches of color tossed
onto the flagstone floor from the exquisite stained-glass
window. "The village grew up in support of Rosewood.
Its construction was the making of Brambleton."

Since there wasn't much to the little hamlet, Eliza
thought that was faint praise.

"The nave was added during Cromwell's time,"
Reverend Lightbody went on. The man of God was
a thin fellow, all knees and elbows, his movements
jerky. He reminded Eliza strongly of a bespectacled
stork. "You can tell by the difference in the color of
the stone. Different quarry, I'll warrant."

"Yes, that's all very fascinating," David said. "But
I wonder if you might know about the more recent
history of the chapel."

"I've only been serving here for six months, you
understand, but in that time I have made the history
of the chapel my avocation. Of course, I can tell
you about its recent history." The vicar harrumphed
several times, as if affronted that he might not have
the information at his fingertips. "For instance, I
have it on good authority that in the early part of the
1700s, local smugglers used the crypt to store their
contraband, sneaking their demon rum in from the
beach in the dead of night and hiding it here from the
excise men." Lightbody chuckled nervously. "From
the parish records, it seems the chapel was kept in
communion wine by nefarious means indeed."

"We were thinking of something a little more
recent than that," Eliza said. "For example, do you
know of any connection between Rosewood Chapel
and Somerfield Park?"

"Not really, no," he said. "Though a few months
ago, a fellow did come by claiming to be researching
the history of the Somerset marquessate. He asked to
see our parish records. He was particularly interested

in births, deaths, baptisms, and marriages from around thirty years ago."

"But wouldn't the church rolls in Somerset-on-the-Sea be more helpful in that sort of inquiry?" David asked. The village church that stood in the shadow of the estate surely held more records relating to it.

"One would have thought so, but the fellow was adamant. Frankly, he didn't strike me as the scholarly type, but one can never judge by appearances," Reverend Lightbody said, bobbing his head like a water bird wading in the shallows. Eliza swallowed back a giggle. "One must be charitable."

She gave herself an imaginary swat on the nose and abandoned her decidedly uncharitable imaginings.

"We're not scholars either, but we are interested in the history of the chapel," Eliza assured him. "Might we see the records you showed that other gentleman?"

"Certainly. They'll be in the sacristy. If you'll follow me, please."

The vicar led them to a small chamber located off one of the arms of the cross-shaped structure. In addition to the locked cabinet where the communion silver was kept, its walls were lined with shelves holding the parish records in hundreds of calf-bound ledgers. The small space smelled of old leather and dust with an undernote of fruity communion wine tossed in for good measure. Judging from the layers of grime on some of the bindings, Eliza suspected the parish records went back to the time of the chapel's original construction.

"Our previous visitor asked for a range of years, twenty-six to thirty years ago." The vicar ran his long fingers over the volumes and pulled out the appropriate ones. Eliza probably could have picked them out herself, since they were the only ones that seemed to have been dusted recently. Reverend Lightbody laid them on the small table and pulled out a chair for Eliza. "Here you are, miss."

Once she settled, David sat across from her and opened the first ledger, frowning at the small, curlicue script.

"You know, originally I thought the two of you were here because you wished to be married in the chapel," Reverend Lightbody said. "Couples come from miles around to wed here, you know."

Eliza's cheeks heated furiously.

"We're not...well, not exactly..." David sputtered.

"Say no more. You're both young yet. Plenty of time for that sort of thing," Reverend Lightbody said as if he were very much older than she and David. The vicar's unlined face proclaimed him much younger than his thinning hair would suggest. "I'll leave you to it then. If you need me, I'll be in the manse. It's just next door."

Eliza had noticed the vicar's cottage before they had entered the chapel. Homes reserved for the honored clergy were usually impressive, but it seemed all the care and expense had gone toward the creation of Rosewood Chapel with precious little to spare for anything else. It was generous in the extreme to call the vicar's house a manse.

Still, it was a pleasant-looking little home with an arched red door and a snug thatched roof. A thin plume of smoke curled from the chimney.

That would do for the likes of me, providing the right man came with it, Eliza mused. She sneaked a peek at David from under her lashes.

He turned the pages quickly, scanning the entries and moving on. His hands were strong and capable, the fingers thick from work, with square, clean nails. David was no stranger to hard work and long hours, but no lines gathered at the corners of his dark eyes. When his forehead creased in concentration, it was marked with horizontal wrinkles, but they disappeared as soon as his face relaxed.

"How old are you, David?"

He looked up at her and cocked his head quizzically. "Twenty-seven. Guess I'm not supposed to ask that question in return, since it's not polite to ask a lady her age."

"It's all right," she said. "I'm not a lady. I'll be twenty next October."

"My, my. Getting long in the tooth, aren't you?" he teased.

If she'd been a cat, her ruff would have been standing on end. "I'm a good bit younger than you, thank you very much."

"Yes, but men don't age as quickly as women."

"Oh, really?"

"Yes, really. I heard Mr. Hightower saying how unusual it is that Lord Hartley is marrying and him barely twenty-one. Titled gents most often wait till their forties before they take a much younger bride."

"Why is that do you suppose?"

"Something to do with being settled, I guess."

"Or perhaps by then they're tired of chasing every skirt that passes by," Eliza said.

"Eliza!"

"What? I might be innocent, David, but I'm

definitely not ignorant about the ways of men. My mother gave me a stern lecture on the subject when I first left home to work at Somerfield Park."

He leaned back in his chair, tipping it onto just two legs. "What did she tell you about the male of the species?"

"She warned me to guard my purity, because it's all that stands between me and ruin."

He plopped down the chair legs and propped his elbows on the table between them. "Not all men are out to ruin you, Eliza."

She gave a little half shrug. "You're right. You've been a perfect gentleman."

More's the pity.

"It's not for lack of wanting," David admitted, his dark eyes more intense than she'd ever seen them.

Eliza lowered her gaze back to the ledger before him, although she couldn't focus on the crabbed script, never mind that it was upside down and she couldn't read in any case. Her heart chugged as if she'd just run up four flights of stairs. He could have his pick of all the girls in Somerset, and David Abbot wanted *her.*

"Maybe…maybe a little ruination isn't so bad," she said softly. In fact, it sounded like the best thing in the world. She couldn't wait to discover all the delicious doings involved in being ruined.

But David didn't say anything.

When she looked up, she saw him staring in consternation at the ledger before him. He hadn't heard a word she'd just said. Irritation raked her spine. Didn't he want to ruin her a bit? The man was changeable as a weathercock.

"What is it that has you so suddenly fascinated, David?"

"Someone has cut a page out of this book." He turned it around so she could see the clean even edge, tucked so close to the binding one would have to look hard to see that a page had been removed.

"What do you suppose is missing?" Eliza said.

"I'm not sure. But someone went to a lot of trouble to make sure those particular records didn't become known." David closed the ledger. The spine proclaimed it contained the register of marriages in the chapel for the years 1786 through 1790.

"We still don't know if there was any connection with Somerfield Park on those pages," Eliza pointed out.

"No. But the vicar said that other fellow claimed to be researching a link between the chapel and the estate."

"Where does that leave us?"

"Guess you will have a chance to prove you're better than a Bow Street Runner, Eliza. We need to poke around about the estate and discover who might have been married during those years."

"The only one who's been with Somerfield Park long enough to know that is Mr. Hightower, I'll warrant." Eliza's belly curdled with the prospect of impending defeat. She wanted to prove useful to David, so he could get back to thinking about how much he wanted to ruin her. "And he's not the sort to fall prey to light gossip."

"You're forgetting the folk who work at Barrett House. Mr. Porter has been with the estate since I was taken on there as a boy. Perhaps he knows a thing or two." David stood and reshelved the ledgers.

Sunlight shafted in from the western window and crept up the stone wall. It would be dark soon. "Well, it's high time we were getting on to my aunt's home in any case. I can't promise you a feather tick, but I'm sure she'll be able to offer you a pallet by the hearth if nothing else."

"No, I'd best walk back to Crimble. If I go now, I can reach the inn by midnight and be on the mail coach heading back home first thing tomorrow morning. It wouldn't do for us to return at the same time. You know how people talk."

"Especially when there's nothing to talk about," she said, biting back her frustration. It had seemed like they were on the verge of something delightful and dangerous, but then the moment fled. Now he didn't even want to meet her aunt and give her a chance to make him comfortable with some of her family.

He caught both her hands and held them between his. "Eliza, if I thought you'd have me, I'd love to give them something to talk about, but then it would mean that I'd hurt you. A man isn't damaged by that sort of gossip the way a woman is. It's not right, but it's the way things are. I won't be the cause of your discomfort."

If she'd have him? She was shocked into silence. Of course, she'd have him! But before she could unstick her stunned tongue, he continued.

"Once we sort out this mystery with Mr. Clack, I hope you'll invite me to meet your parents because I want to ask your father for his permission to court you."

Her eyes widened. David was finally declaring himself in more than single words. And formal-like too, as if she were a fine lady instead of a recently elevated kitchen maid.

"My father's dead," she said out of habit. She wasn't really sure that was the case, but he'd been gone long enough for the details not to matter. Besides, that was what her mother always said whenever anyone asked about her husband. Mrs. Dovecote took comfort in being thought a widow with a passel of mouths to feed instead of being labeled an abandoned wife.

"Then I'll ask your mother," David said. Then he brought her knuckles to his mouth and kissed them. Eliza was so grateful that Miss Goodnight had given her a small bottle of Olympian Dew. Since she'd been using it faithfully, her hands had lost their red, angry knuckles and actually looked like something worthy of a man's kiss.

And the kiss was worthy enough to make her knees wobble.

But, oh, how she wished he'd kiss her lips.

"I'm sure my mother will say yes," Eliza said breathlessly. Mrs. Dovecote would be delirious to have one of her girls settled with such a fine man.

"And what about you?" David smiled down at her. "Will you say yes if I ask?"

Try as she might, she couldn't get her voice to work. She thought about a vigorous nod but didn't want to seem too eager. Then it occurred to her that he wasn't actually asking. He just wanted to be sure of a positive response if he did ask.

That didn't hardly seem fair.

She managed to stammer, "You'll have to ask me to find out."

"You don't intend to make it easy for me, do you?"

Eliza bit her lower lip and peered up at him from under her lashes. "Is anything easy worthwhile?"

She held her breath as he bent and covered her mouth with his. She'd dreamed of this moment. Prayed for it. Now that it was here, there were a dozen different things she wanted to do at once. She wanted to scream for joy. She wanted to promise God she'd never do another thing wrong in her whole life in order to be worthy of this moment of bliss. She wanted to wrestle David to the flagstone floor and discover total ruination with him.

But they were in a church, and this kiss was a solemn sort of kiss, not one likely to lead to ruination. At least, not immediately. If there was any jumping up and down to be done over it, she'd have to do it on the inside because just now, her feet were firmly on the ground, and her lips were firmly pressed against David Abbot's.

And all was right with Eliza's world.

Twenty-three

When I was young, I lived for intrigue and romance. I was the belle of every ball and had a dozen suitors dancing on the string at any given time. But "Time wounds all heels," they do say. Now I'd just as soon be dealt a good whist hand.

—Phillippa, the Dowager Marchioness of Somerset

"OH, CONFOUND AND BOTHER IT!" SOPHIE WENT through another acrobatic gyration, but she still couldn't reach the trio of seed pearl buttons at that awkward spot on her spine. The red silk gown was simple and elegant, with a bodice that displayed her charms fetchingly without being vulgar. It had no ridiculous flounces or furbelows to detract from its classical lines. The only trouble with the design was the row of buttons down the back. They were too low when she stretched her arms back over her head, and too high if she tried to come at them from below.

The room was dimly lit by a single candle, but she

could make out the bell pull by her bed. Since Eliza was gone to visit her sick aunt, Sophie could ring for assistance, and one of the Somerset maids would come trotting, but she'd been dressing herself since was old enough to toddle about. It felt beyond foolish to need help with something that ought to be so simple.

"And to think I actually spent good money on a dress designed to cause this very predicament!" she grumbled.

When the dowager suggested she needed a new wardrobe that required her to hire an abigail, it had seemed like solid advice. Almost altruistic. It was incumbent on one of her great wealth to provide employment for others.

If old Lady Somerset could see her now, she laugh at her.

No, probably not.

Sophie gave up on the buttons and instead pulled the ruby ring from its hiding place in her décolletage. Since Richard's grandmother had offered this spectacular piece of jewelry to seal their betrothal, she likely didn't have evil motives.

Just inconvenient ones.

She secreted the ring in the jewelry box on her vanity and tried to walk her fingers down from her nape to the out-of-reach buttons again. She brushed a fingernail on the top one but couldn't catch hold of it.

Sophie growled low in the back of her throat. The infernal gown was only part of her problem, only the last frustration in a long string of them this evening. The thing that really bothered her was how her insides had twisted in knots at supper. Lady Antonia had been

seated between Richard and Lord Somerset on the far
end of the long table. Every time Sophie glanced that
way, the lady was chatting and laughing animatedly.
Worse yet, Richard gave every appearance of listening
to her with attentiveness.

Of course, it wasn't Richard's fault he was seated
there beside her. Antonia had seized his arm the
moment his father and mother led the party into the
dining room. Before Sophie knew what was what,
Lord Pruett offered her his arm, and it would have
been churlish not to accept.

If Lord Pruett's plan was to make Sophie feel
isolated, he succeeded completely. Lord Pruett seated
her between himself and Sir Alan Westerling. He was
an aging neighbor of the Barretts', who'd evidently
been invited to help even the number of men and
women. He couldn't hear anything she said to him
without his ear trumpet, and even then, he miscon-
strued half her words. So she ate in uncomfortable
silence, knowing the arrangement shouted that she
wasn't welcome.

Still, she intended to marry Richard, and that guar-
anteed Lord Pruett's enmity, which was inconvenient
for the moment.

"But this gown will *always* be inconvenient," she
muttered. She was just about to give up on the buttons
when her doorknob turned and the latch gave with a
snick. Richard slipped into her chamber, closing the
door behind him quietly.

"What do you think you're doing here?" she whispered.

"Never let it be said I ignored a damsel in distress.
I seem to remember you are without your maid and

wondered if I could render aid." He moved across the room, silent as a great cat.

"This is most improper, you know."

"You surprise me, Sophie. I didn't think that sort of thing mattered to you."

"It doesn't," she said, wishing she still didn't feel that frisson of envy left over from supper. Jealousy was such an unattractive quality. She loathed it in others. She absolutely despised it in herself. "I meant for you. Or do you make a practice of invading your guests' rooms by night?"

"I only invade the ones who need me," he said with a wicked smile.

"And has Lady Antonia needed you?" As soon as the words were out of her mouth, she wished she could call them back. They sounded so pathetic. After Julian, she'd promised herself she'd never need anyone again. It upset her to learn that she'd broken that vow already.

"I doubt Antonia needs anyone," he said. "When it comes to organizing an event, she's a force of nature. All the guests she and Mother invited will be arriving tomorrow. Ella is going to be launched into society in the first stare of fashion, and all the women in the Barrett family are beyond thrilled."

While Sophie could pay for an elegant wardrobe and furnish a home with tasteful art, she couldn't buy the social connections Lady Antonia was born with. Part of her insisted she shouldn't care. None of that mattered to her.

But did it matter to Richard?

"How fortunate Antonia is here then."

He cocked his head at her. "What's wrong?"

Evidently she wasn't adept at hiding her feelings, but she didn't want to voice them either. Richard reached for her, but she stepped back a pace.

"Sophie, you're not upset about Antonia helping with Ella's come-out, are you?"

"I'd have to be a very small person if I was," she said, feeling very small indeed.

"But you're distressed about something."

When did he learn to read her so well?

A slow smile lifted at his lips. "You're jealous."

"I am not." The words scalded as they left her mouth. She was reminded why she was devoted to the truth, even when it wasn't convenient. Lies always tasted terrible. "But if I were, why do you sound like that pleases you?"

"Truly, you have no reason to be jealous. The only thing I feel for Antonia is friendship. You're the one I want, Sophie. You," he said. "But you're right. If you are jealous, it would please me because it's proof that you care."

What it proved was that somehow, she'd begun caring about Richard enough to give him the power to hurt her. When had that astounding event occurred?

"But I can't do what Antonia evidently can," she said. "For pity's sake, I can't even host a simple tea party without things going so badly awry that you became violently ill."

"The less said about that the better." He frowned, uncomfortable being reminded of his desecration of the Barrett House hydrangeas. "Don't fret, darling. I never enjoyed entertaining that much to begin with. I'm sure there will be times when it can't be avoided, but when I think of our life together, all I think about is being with you."

Relief flooded her chest, but it was tempered with a niggling worry. No doubt about it. She was vulnerable. She'd opened her heart to this man. Along with the thrill of love came the risk of loss. She'd been devastated by Julian's duplicity, but she'd recovered. If somehow she lost Richard, she didn't think she would.

He'd touched a deep place in her, a place she'd never allowed anyone to enter before. He'd seen through her bluster to the fragile soul she tried to shield. He could love and protect and nurture her. Or he could destroy her.

When she looked into his dark eyes, she decided loving Richard was worth the risk.

"Now, to business," he said. "I'm still here to play your abigail. Turn around."

"Honestly, I'd have managed on my own." She obeyed him in any case, lifting her hair to one side, so he could find those dratted buttons more easily.

"How? You obviously can't reach these."

"I was about to test the strength of the thread."

He made a tsking noise as he slipped the seed pearls through their small, silky loops. "That'd make more work for your maid."

"The whole point of this dratted gown is to make work for my maid."

"No, it's not." He grasped her shoulders gently and turned her to face him. "The point of this gown is to make every man who sees you in it want to see you out of it."

As if to prove his words, he drew the red silk off

her shoulders and down her bare arms. The fabric skimmed her flesh, followed by the pads of his fingers. Pleasure sparked over her skin. Once the gown cleared her hips, it pooled on the floor by her stockinged feet.

"You're so beautiful, and you smell like…" Richard buried his face at the juncture of her shoulder and neck, suckling the tender skin. "Roses. So sweet I could become drunk on the scent alone. I've wanted to do this since the soup course."

"You showed remarkable restraint," she said as he drew her into his arms. It had been hours and hours since the delicate white soup was served. Judging from his fevered kisses, he really had been saving up. "What did you want to do during the meat course?"

"This." He unfastened the hooks and eyes of her stays. The linen undergarment gave, and she was standing before him in just her shift, pantalets, and stockings.

"Why are you allowed all the fun?" She plucked at the loose end of his cravat, and it unraveled in her hand. Then she peeled off his jacket and waistcoat, leaving him in his shirtsleeves. "Now it's my turn to do buttons. Stand still if you please."

As she undid the row of pewter that ran down to his breastbone, he stroked her hair, pulling out the few pins that still remained in her coiffure.

"I can't believe you're mine," he murmured.

"I'm not. Not officially."

"You know what I mean."

"I do," she whispered. She'd always believed in being direct. This was no time to change. "We both know you're not here just to help me out of my gown and into my night rail. You're here to make love to me, aren't you?"

He drew a sharp breath. "A man can hope."

"But you don't have to hope because I'm going to let you."

Richard needed no further encouragement. He scooped her up and carried her to the waiting bed. He laid her down and then joined her, his hands roaming over her as he kissed her.

"I don't suppose we're the first couple in the world to anticipate our wedding night a bit," she said as she pulled his shirt over his head.

"We're not even the first in Somerfield Park." Richard made short work of her chemise and stared down in dark-eyed wonderment at her naked breasts. "Oh, Sophie, I could eat you up."

He bent and kissed his way down to her taut nipples, suckling and nipping. Sophie arched into his mouth while one of his hands slid over her belly and found her aching mound, bare and waiting in the open crotch of her pantalets.

"Why do you say we're not the first?" she whispered. "Who else is as wicked as we?"

It did feel wicked. And wonderful. And she wondered how she'd lived so long without this man to stroke and tease her like this.

Richard came up for air, and while she undid his trouser buttons over his hipbones, he tugged the knot that kept her pantalets at her waist. When it gave, he slid them down her legs.

"Well, if you check the church rolls, you'll find I was born seven months to the day after my parents were wed."

"Born prematurely?"

Richard chuckled and then nuzzled her belly. "They'd like me to think so, but as I weighed eight pounds at birth, it's hard to believe."

"The wags say the first child can come at any time, but the second always takes nine months," Sophie said with a giggle.

Still, part of her wanted to ask that they take precautions against conceiving. She didn't want a child of hers to be embarrassed about his birth date.

But Richard didn't seem embarrassed about anything. When he kissed down her belly and spread her knees, all rational thought about conception or anything else fled. Instead, only flickers of disjointed ideas floated through her mind.

What's he doing? Surely not. Oh, his tongue. Oh no. Oh…yes.

She'd thought his blessed fingers were magic. His mouth was nothing short of miraculous.

The whole world went wet and warm and wanting. Sophie bit the inside of her cheek to keep from crying out. Who knew how thin the walls in Somerfield Park were? But she was powerless to stop the small noises of need from escaping from her throat. She ached so badly. There was a throbbing bundle of nerves between her legs, and Richard was tormenting each one of them.

She squeezed her eyes shut, but she seemed to be traveling down a dark corridor, looking for the right door. Richard was driving her to it, his tongue chasing her down that hallway, massaging her to white-hot fury. Then, suddenly, the right door opened, and her whole body was flooded with light. Waves of pleasure shot out her fingers and toes, and made her shudder with relief.

But the deep ache still remained.

Then Richard moved and covered her body with his. Somehow, he'd lost his trousers along the way and the thick tip of him was poised at her entrance. Her eyes fluttered open and met his hooded gaze.

"I love you, Sophie Goodnight," he said.

There it was. Plain. Honest. No "may well possibly." Richard loved her. After that shattering release, she didn't think she could move a muscle, but somehow her lips turned up and she rocked her hips against him. "I can tell."

"Good." He pushed forward into her tightness. She expanded to receive him, and the ache was finally stilled. "I never want you to doubt me."

With that, she shoved aside the last of her jealousy and wrapped her legs around him. He began to move, and she moved with him. It was better than the wildest gallop. More heart pounding than a tiger hunt. She hoped it would go on forever.

Richard was hers.

And she was his.

And by the toast before midnight supper on the evening of Ella's ball, everyone would know it.

Twenty-four

It is often said that three can keep a secret provided two of them are dead. As it turns out, not even that will keep some things hidden.

—Phillippa, the Dowager Marchioness of Somerset

"It's right good of you to help out, Mr. Porter, what with all the extra guests. We'd be lost without ye and that's God's truth," Mrs. Culpepper said with a confiding lift of an eyebrow. "Will ye take more tea?"

"Don't mind if I do." Porter held up his teacup for her to pour out for him. She added two precious lumps of sugar and a dollop of milk, just the way he liked it. "Please, Mrs. C, you're embarrassing me with your praise. Think nothing of it. I'm just happy I was here to salvage the situation."

"I should say so. Mr. Hightower would have made a muddle of everything if ye hadn't swooped in at the last minute to save the day." Porter noticed she didn't call the butler "Himself" anymore. Then Mrs.

Culpepper smiled at him. Not the sort of smile she usually offered him, the practiced, no-nonsense one that she gave to everyone who ate her delicious food. No, this smile was almost girlish, despite her years. It was a smile of welcome. Of promise. Of—

"Now see here, Mr. Porter." Mrs. Culpepper's real voice interrupted his idle daydreaming. She sounded neither girlish nor welcoming, but there was definitely a brusque promise in her tone. "I don't know what ye're used to at Barrett House, but here at the big house, if ye don't answer the first time, I won't offer again."

"Hmm?" Porter gave himself a brisk shake. "Yes," he said because it seemed the safest thing to say to a woman armed with a large wooden spoon. Then for good measure, he added, "Please."

Mrs. Culpepper plopped a helping of stew into the bowl before him and moved on to the next servant gathered around the Somerfield Park common room table. With the onslaught of guests pouring into the estate, Porter and Mrs. Beckworth had both been summoned up to the big house to help out. Between the extra Quality Folk to tend to and David Abbot being unaccountably gone somewhere, the servants were all overwrought and overworked.

Were there another eighteen or twenty guests seated around the long dining table upstairs? Porter had lost count. But he and Mr. Hightower had inserted no fewer than six extra leaves into the expanse of mahogany before the snowy linen was laid. When they were done with their meticulous preparations, the china sparkled. The silverware glittered, and the crystal practically sang. Porter could see his misshapen reflection in each shining soup spoon.

"Good thing too," Mr. Hightower had said when he saw the guest list. "Lady Wappington is here."

Even Porter had heard of that lady's waspish tongue. Though her infamous wit often reached the point of cruelty, she was a respected arbiter of correctness and decorum throughout the *ton*. If the dinner party passed her stringent assessment, it would be high praise indeed.

But now that the Quality Folk had all been fed and were enjoying their port and cordials in the parlor, most of Somerfield Park's servants could finally see to their own empty bellies. Porter glanced around the common table. One of the chambermaids was almost dozing at her place, and the housekeeper, Mrs. Grahame, stifled a yawn.

Porter's stomach growled. The quick tea he'd managed to grab hours ago was a slim memory. The aroma of Mrs. Culpepper's stew set his stomach juices flowing.

Mr. Hightower tapped his spoon on his water glass and called everyone to attention. Porter sneaked one more look at his bowl. He wasn't allowed to eat a bite until the butler did.

"Her ladyship wishes me to inform you all that she is very pleased by the efforts of the Somerfield Park staff. Very pleased indeed," he said, his voice gruff but with a grudging smile in the tone. "However, we cannot rest on our laurels. Lady Ella's ball is scheduled for tomorrow evening, and the midnight supper must be presented with such style folk will be talking about it all Season and those who were not present will forever wish they had been among the chosen few to partake of it. Now, Mrs. Culpepper, is everything shipshape and Bristol fashion for the menu?"

The beleaguered cook stopped mid-ladling. She alone of the assembled workers had continued to serve the others while Mr. Hightower spoke.

"Yes, sir, ye needn't worry. I should hope I know my own business," she said saucily. "Mrs. Grahame approved it all a week ago, down to the last petit four." Then she lowered her voice and grumbled as she continued to dish up the stew. "But it don't do me no favors to have to do the work of both Cook and kitchen girl."

Porter knew it was a sore point with her that Theresa Dovecote hadn't proved as willing a helper as her sister Eliza. He wished suddenly that protocol would allow him to rise and hold the heavy kettle for Mrs. C while she served up the stew.

"Oh, thank ye, Mr. Porter," Mrs. Culpepper would say. "What a gentleman. A knight in shining armor, that's what ye are, and no mistake."

Then she'd wrap her arms around my neck, never mind the wooden spoon, and plant a big kiss on my cheek. And if it scandalized Mr. Hightower, so much the better!

"I say, Mr. Porter, aren't you attending?" Mr. Hightower's loud voice jerked him back into the moment. "The parlor bell just rang. Nip off and see if you can help Toby with the last of the after-dinner drinks if you please."

Hightower might have couched his order as a request, but it was an order nonetheless.

"Yes, sir," Porter said with a final longing glance at his bowl of stew.

"I'll take this back into the kitchen and keep it warm for ye, Mr. Porter." Mrs. Culpepper removed his bowl from in front of him.

"Thank you kindly. I always say as you're a woman who knows how to satisfy a man's appetites." As soon as the words were out of his mouth, Porter's ears burned hotly.

Appetites? Oh dear. That could mean... She might think that I... Of course, she'd be right, but...

But instead of rounding on him with that spoon of hers, she chuckled. "Reckon I do at that, Mr. Porter." Then she bent down and lowered her voice for his ears alone. "A few of the petit fours didn't turn out quite as well as I'd like. Maybe ye'll do me a favor by eating one later."

"Gladly." Porter rose from his place at the common table and started for the stairs, but he hadn't made it more than a couple steps when the back door opened. A whiff of the honeysuckle blooming in the kitchen herb garden behind the house breezed in with David Abbot.

"There you are, Abbot," Mr. Hightower said as David took his seat at the table.

"Just in time for supper." Mrs. Culpepper put Porter's steaming bowl in front of the young man.

So much for keeping it warm for me.

"How was your trip?" Sarah, the maid who'd been dozing, looked wide-awake now.

"Fine. Thank you, Mrs. Culpepper," he said before taking a big spoonful of Porter's supper. "Delicious as always."

"Oh, go on with ye. Young fellows like ye would eat the putty out of the windows if they was hungry enough," she said, but Porter could tell she was pleased with David.

Porter, however, was not. Especially his stomach, which rumbled loudly.

As the rest of the servants resumed eating, David didn't elaborate on his mysterious journey, and no one asked, which seemed odd to Porter, since no one seemed to know what it was about. He had come upon several knots of servants throughout the day, all speculating on what might have caused David, who'd never gone anywhere, to suddenly disappear for a day and a night. The cattier ones noted that Eliza was absent from the big house as well, but Porter knew the girl was seeing to her sick aunt in Brambleton and said so to anyone who'd listen.

"Judging from all the carriages parked behind the stables, looks like we have a full house," David said as he liberally slathered a thick slice of barley bread with butter. "If you need me to act as a footman while his lordship entertains, I can do that as well as valet for Lord Hartley."

Still lingering at the foot of the stairs, Porter's heart—and his empty stomach—surged with hope. Perhaps Hightower would send David up to help Toby instead of him, but it seemed everyone, including Mrs. Culpepper, was more intent on seeing that David got his supper than in putting his young hands to work.

Don't know why he's allowed to lark about when the rest of us have more than enough to do.

Porter turned and started up the stairs but froze in midstep. The marquess was coming down.

It was unheard of for his lordship to do such a thing. Oh, occasionally Lady Somerset might venture

below stairs to confer with Mrs. Grahame over something, though usually their meetings were held in
the marchioness's frilly sitting room adjacent to her
boudoir on the second floor. Once or twice, Lady
Petra had wandered into the kitchen to conduct one
of her unladylike experiments. But other than that, no
member of the Family bothered to enter the subter-
ranean regions of the great house.

Until now.

"My lord." Mr. Hightower leaped to attention
and everyone seated around the table followed suit.
Even Mrs. Culpepper stopped ladling. "How may we
be of assistance?"

Even though his lordship was immaculately dressed
for the evening in a dapper tailcoat with a shirt so
white it almost hurt the eyes, the marquess had a harried look about him. Porter noticed a bead of sweat
trickling down the side of Lord Somerset's neck and
disappearing into his elegantly tied cravat.

"Has anyone arrived who was not on the guest
list?" the marquess demanded.

"No, my lord."

"Have you allowed anyone into my study, Mr.
Hightower?"

"No, my lord, of course not. Unless you specifically
request it, no one ever enters that room, except the
maids. Sarah, when was the last time you and Drucilla
dusted the study?"

Sarah dropped a bobbing curtsy. "I'm afraid we've
neglected it of late, what with everything to do for
the house party. We haven't done his lordship's study
since Monday last."

"And the key is still in your office?" his lordship asked Hightower.

"I'd swear to it."

"Don't swear, confound it," the marquess said, his jaw clenched. "Check and make certain."

"Right." Mr. Hightower disappeared from the common room in double-quick march time. Everyone else dropped their gazes to their toes while the marquess stood like a statue waiting for the butler to return.

A statue that nearly had steam coming out of his ears. Though good form dictated that his lordship not show his upset before the help, he was stewing something fierce about someone being in his study and no mistake.

Porter was suddenly glad he usually worked at Barrett House, though most of the time he served merely as a glorified caretaker instead of a proper butler. The Goodnights had been simple folk to care for, and he missed their easygoing ways. Pity they had moved up to Somerfield Park.

Mr. Hightower chugged back into the common room with the key in his hand. "It was on the proper hook as always, my lord."

"I'll take that key." The marquess held out his hand.

"Have you lost yours, my lord?"

"No, but I don't want anyone in the study without my presence from now on."

"It will be difficult for the maids to—"

"When it becomes such a boar's nest I can't bear it, I will allow them in to clean. Otherwise, no one is to enter without my presence. Ever. Is that understood?"

Mr. Hightower cleared his throat. "Is…is something missing, my lord?"

Porter's heart sank to his toes. The worst thing that could happen to a servant was to be accused of theft. Even the suspicion of thievery was enough to cause a body to lose his position without character. He was glad he was standing behind the marquess so he didn't have to meet his gaze. Even though Porter had done nothing wrong, he was the nervous sort.

And nervous sorts tended to look guilty.

"No, nothing's been taken," the marquess said, and there was a collective sigh of relief all around. "Something was…left."

"What?"

Lord Somerset raised a hand to signal the discussion was over. "Never mind, Hightower. That'll be all."

The marquess turned and marched past Porter back up the stairs. For the space of about ten heartbeats, no one in the common room moved. Then Mr. Hightower collected himself and scowled in Porter's direction.

"What are you still doing here? You're supposed to be helping Toby with the drinks."

"Yes, sir, right away." Of course, it was much too late to be right away, but it didn't hurt to say so. Sometimes the suggestion of obedience was every bit as important as the fact. Before Porter had gone two trudging steps, someone caught him by the arm.

"I'll be saving ye that petit four, Mr. Porter," Mrs. Culpepper whispered. "Don't forget."

"No, indeed." The sudden bloom of warmth in his chest made him forget all about the rumbling of his belly, and Porter took the stairs two at a time.

Twenty-five

In the garden, one learns that if one doesn't completely eradicate the root of an unwanted plant, it will assuredly return given enough time. I've found the same to be true of people.

—Phillippa, the Dowager Marchioness of Somerset

"HONESTLY, DEAR, YOU'RE NEGLECTING YOUR GUESTS," Lady Somerset said as her son, the marquess, closed the door to his study behind her. "What's so important that it couldn't wait till after your party retires?" She stifled a yawn. "Or better yet, until tomorrow? Really, I ought to be heading home. I may seem vigorous, but I'm not as young as I used to be. Be a lamb and ring for my carriage, will you please?"

"You're not going anywhere just now." Lord Somerset pulled the cursed note from his waistcoat pocket and tossed it to her. "Once you read this, you'll understand my urgency, Mother."

"I don't have my reading glasses with me."

Nevertheless, she unfolded the missive and held it at arm's length, trying to find the right distance that would allow her to focus on the even script.

"Oh, for heaven's sake, I'll read it to you," he said after several minutes of watching her struggle and frown at the page. He took it back and held the paper so the candles of the wall sconce would light it adequately.

> *"You are not the only one*
> *With sins to hide from day.*
> *What was done, was not undone.*
> *And now you'll have to pay."*

"Ghastly rhyme scheme," the dowager said, fanning herself languidly.

"Mother, that's not important. They go on to say they have incontrovertible proof and we'll be contacted with details of where and when and how much it will cost us to keep them quiet."

"Keep them quiet about what?"

"That's just the thing. They don't come out and say anything really, but I've a sick feeling I should know what they mean." He massaged his temples. "It's so disconcerting not to be fully in possession of one's memory. Sometimes, I feel it's all there, dancing on the edge of my mind. It taunts me, and the closer I come to remembering, the more the memories retreat. However, some more recent recollections are starting to come back."

"What, dear?"

"What happened on the roof. Everything's been

sort of hazy, but now I remember there was another fellow on the roof with me."

"Nonsense, dear. Your footman David told you that, and now you've tricked yourself into believing that you remember."

"No, Mother. David has been very close-mouthed about the incident. Probably because he fears he'll get into trouble for bringing the man up there, but I distinctly remember ordering him to do so. It's one of the few things that are clear in my mind."

"Don't overtax yourself, Son. It leads to wrinkles. How do you think I've maintained my reputation as a handsome woman all these years? I simply refuse to worry about that which I cannot control. Of course, there's precious little I can't." She gave a self-satisfied shrug, rose, and started toward the door. "Come now. Your guests will wonder what's keeping you."

"Don't try to smooth this over and cover it up. Secrets are what got us into this, and we don't need more of them. The man told David to say two words to me."

"And they were?" she asked.

"Rosewood Chapel."

The way her eyes widened told him she knew more than she was saying.

"The words are like ground glass in my ears," he admitted.

His mother cast him a questioning gaze. "And you don't recall why they should strike you that way?"

"No. My mind is a jumble. It's as if I've come upon a mosaic that's been scattered on the floor. I don't understand how all the pieces fit. Images from the past fly at me sometimes, and from far longer ago than my fall off the roof. Faces without names, places that seem significant but are gone before I can get a net around them." He swiped a hand over his eyes. "I'm very much in sympathy with our mad king at the moment."

"Don't be so hard on yourself. Undoubtedly your recovery will continue, and it will all come right eventually."

"But what if it doesn't?" he snapped. "I seem to remember… I was younger than Hartley is now. I'd done something rather unwise, and you and father were furious with me. That much I'm sure of."

"We all do things we regret in this life," his mother said cryptically.

"And what about you, Mother? Have you done something you regret?"

"Almost every day, but I've learned not to burden myself by toting excess baggage. That's what footmen are for."

He paced the room, waving the note in the air. "Don't make little of this. It feels deathly serious in light of… Well, I can only see it as a blackmail threat."

"I fear it is."

"Then you know what the message means?" He stopped before his mother.

"I suspect, which is not quite the same thing." She laid a hand on his shoulder and then took the note from him. "Now, let me make some inquiries about this." She squinted at the missive. "'What was done was not undone,' eh? We shall see about that. In the meantime, notify me immediately if you receive further instructions or demands for payment."

She made a tsking sound. "How very gauche blackmail is, a not-so-small crime for small minds. Vulgar in the extreme."

Lady Somerset turned and slipped out of his study.

"Evidently, I've done something which made me a target for them," Lord Somerset said softly. "Perhaps that's even more vulgar."

❧

The next day, Eliza returned to Somerfield Park, and Sophie was beyond ready for her maid to resume her duties.

"I never thought I needed a maid, but I'm so glad you're back in time to help me with this ridiculous gown," Sophie said as Eliza cinched her stays a bit tighter than normal in order to fit in the bodice of white silk. It was a concession to her mother that she was wearing the pale gown when she much preferred jewel tones. "I hope your aunt is better."

"Better than what? Oh! Yes, it must have been a passing malady," Eliza said. "She was right as rain by the time I left Brambleton. Thank you ever so much for allowing me to go."

"Keeping you from your family when you're needed wouldn't have been fair."

Sophie studied her reflection as Eliza fluffed the gown's gauzy train. The fabric was trimmed with silver and gold thread in a pattern styled after the Egyptian influence. The modiste had warned Sophie that such ornamentation was a decade out of date, but she much preferred the simple geometric embellishments to the flounces and furbelows required of the truly fashionable gown.

She allowed Eliza to fuss over her hair for an excru-
ciatingly long time. Finally, the matching bandeau was
threaded through her tresses in a way that seemed to
satisfy her maid.

"The bodice seems awfully low," Eliza
said doubtfully.

"I've been assured it's all the crack to display this
much bosom for a ball," Sophie said, though her
cheeks did pink a bit when she thought about what
Richard's reaction to her décolletage would be. Since
the arrival of all the new guests, she hadn't seen much
of him except from across crowded rooms. With the
extra people in the great house, there'd been no more
nocturnal ramblings that led him to her chamber—
more's the pity. Well, at least after the toast at midnight, the world would know they belonged together
when he announced their betrothal.

"Perhaps a bit of ribbon at your neck,"
Eliza suggested.

"If you like." Sophie had never really understood
the fascination with fashion. However, if the right
gown made Richard desperate to rip it off her, she was
willing to let Eliza dress her in it.

While her maid pawed through a drawer in the
vanity for just the right bit of satin, Sophie opened her
jewelry box. She drew out the ruby ring and slipped it
on her left ring finger.

"Oh, my lady, that's lovely."

"Shh! It's a secret. And besides, as you're perfectly
aware, I'm no lady."

"In all the ways that matter, you are, and I'll have
words with any who denies it." Eliza met her gaze in

the mirror. "But you're about to be a lady in truth or I'm much mistook."

She took the ring off and secreted it down her bodice. "The ring is a gift from Lord Hartley."

Eliza's eyes sparkled. "A betrothal gift?"

Sophie nodded.

"Lady Hartley." Eliza tried the new title on her tongue and seemed to like the taste, for she beamed from ear to ear. "Oh, my lady, I'm so very happy for you."

Then she launched into one of her running diatribes. This time she waxed poetic about the joys of being a bride and how a betrothed lady's happiness infects everyone around her.

"Sort of like the chicken pox," the little maid said, "only joyful-like instead of itchy."

"Yes, well, Lord Hartley and I will be spreading our brand of pox at midnight. He'll make the announcement then. And I trust general itchiness will not ensue."

Eliza chuckled and then chattered on. The sound was soothing, and Sophie didn't have to be bothered about the substance. Her parents would be thrilled with the news. Her dear father would get his wish—to have wellborn grandchildren. Even though Richard was adamant about not taking her dowry, she'd find a way to put the money to good use for their future children, so her father wouldn't be insulted by his new son-in-law's stubbornness.

Mr. Goodnight might see it as pridefulness, but Sophie was glad Richard didn't want her father's money.

He only wanted her.

She hugged the delicious knowledge to herself, as

Twenty-six

Oh, no, my dear, I never waltz. And don't think to persuade me by telling me the Prince Regent approves of the dance. Anything that young reprobate commends is bound to lead to scandal.

—Phillippa, the Dowager Marchioness of Somerset

SOPHIE'S NEW SLIPPERS PINCHED HER TOES, BUT SHE wasn't allowed a moment's respite. Her dance card was prefilled with every available man in attendance, be he dandy or dotard. In fact, just as the string quartet started a tune in three-quarter time, Sir Alan Westerling started shuffling in her direction.

Sophie checked her card. Sure enough, the half-deaf fellow was the next one on her list. After her last partner trod on her toes several times, she wasn't looking forward to one who had no chance of keeping up with the music.

"Antonia had a hand in this dance card," she grumbled.

"I doubt she planned this diversion from it."

close as the ruby settled between her breasts. Richard loved her. Not her dowry. Just her.

"Oh, my lady, I think I hear the musicians tuning up." Eliza's one-sided conversation finally pierced Sophie's musings. "It's time."

"Indeed." Sophie toed on her jeweled slippers and gave herself one last glance in the mirror. She was done with the bitterness left over from her affair with Julian Parrish. Something new had bloomed in its place. Trust.

Her life was changing forever, for the better, and it would all begin at midnight.

Richard had slipped up behind her and scooped her into a waltz hold without preamble. "Shall we?"

"You're supposed to ask a lady for the pleasure of a dance, you know," she said as he swept her into the turning and dipping throng. They moved together so easily, as if their bodies spoke a secret language and setting it to music only broadened the vocabulary. "*Shall we* could mean anything."

He arched a brow at her. "I like the sound of that. What do you want it to mean?"

Her insides did a slow melt. She wanted him in her arms, in her bed, in *her*. There was that ache again, sharp-edged and throbbing. Richard was fast turning her into a shameless wanton.

"I'll take that blush for a compliment," he said with a grin. "Besides, if I asked for the dance properly, you'd have been obliged to tell me it was already spoken for."

"Yes, I would. Poor old Sir Alan is still looking for me."

"Then he'll just have to keep looking. I intend to keep behaving like a barbarian, flouting convention, and stealing you away."

"Do you promise?"

His dark eyes smoldered. "I do."

As they made another circuit of the room, Richard waltzed her into one of the curtained alcoves and drew the draperies closed behind them. Before her skirts stopped swirling, his mouth claimed hers in a kiss.

"I've wanted to do that all day," he said when he finally released her.

"I wanted you to do it all last night."

He kissed her again, groaning into her mouth.

"Careful," she said, pulling back. "The music isn't that loud, and we've only a bit of velvet between us and the ballroom."

"Sophie, I'm surprised at you." He nuzzled her neck. "You're not turning into a pattern sort of girl, are you?"

"Heaven forbid." His lips on the tender skin of her neck made her eyes roll back in her head. "The idea of fitting in is still repellent to me, but I don't want to spoil Ella's come-out with a scandal, and there'll be one if you and I are caught in an improper situation."

"Improper, eh? I do love the way your mind works." He planted a kiss on her forehead. "And your lips." Another appropriately placed kiss. "And your…" He grasped her bum and pulled her flush against him so she could feel his thick hardness through the layers of clothing separating them.

"Honestly, Richard, when I first met you over your grandmother's roses, I had no idea you were such a wicked rake."

"Even then I wanted to do this." He pressed her spine against the Doric column next to the window and rocked his body against hers. "Now you know the wickedness was there all along, just beneath the civilized surface."

She smiled. "So I do, and I'd better be the only one."

"Always."

Sophie tipped her head back, allowing him to kiss down the bare expanse of her throat to where her bosom threatened to pop out over the top of her bodice. Her nipples ached at the nearness of his mouth, but they were discretely tucked beneath silk and Egyptian trim.

And to think Eliza thought it was cut too low.

◈

From her place on the other side of the velvet curtain, Antonia's cheeks heated. She forced herself to look out over the ballroom with a falsely bright smile. She had plenty of which to be proud. The décor was a classical theme with papier-mâché columns and an exquisite centerpiece on the table featuring a tableau of figurines of Bacchus and his nymphs in the midst of their revels. It was sure to appeal to the prurient natures of some, but with an elegant twist that allowed those with more moral fortitude to give baser desires a wink and a nod.

All her guests were having a splendid time. And she did think of them as hers, since Richard was hers as well—or would be after this. Somerfield Park might not be her home yet, but she would be the marchioness here someday. In the light of this social triumph, Antonia would be seen as the future mistress of the estate by all. Lady Ella was meeting the right people and making a solid impression. Even Lady Wappington, the spiteful old cat, had only good things to say. The evening was an unqualified success.

Except for the fact that the man she intended to marry was in the alcove behind her with that horrid little Goodnight trollop. She wished they'd start talking again because her imagination ran rampant during their silences.

She wasn't jealous of the amorous attention he was giving Sophie Goodnight. Good heavens, she knew what men were. After seeing her mother turn her head and feign ignorance of her father's peccadilloes as a wife should, Antonia was under no illusions about what to expect from marriage to a titled gentleman. In truth, she hoped Richard *would* set up a mistress once they were wed, so she'd be bothered by that sort of attention as little as possible.

But she expected he'd wait until after the ceremony to choose his ladybird. Antonia was not going to be embarrassed by amours being played out under her nose. No wife was pitied over her husband's affairs unless he conducted them in a flagrant manner. Hartley was going to have to behave—if not for her sake, then for his family's. Surely he realized a vulgar affair flaunted in such a public way would stain the Somerset name.

Richard and Miss Goodnight were talking again. Antonia turned her head and leaned back into the velvet curtain as far as she dared.

"The waltz is ending, Richard. We can't stay here, much as I'd like…"

Then the light skirt's voice faded, and Antonia did a slow burn as she imagined what had silenced her. What if Lady Wappington caught them in there? Richard would be obliged to marry the upstart heiress.

Antonia's father had once said in passing that she ought to arrange to be caught with Richard in an indelicate situation in order to force his hand. She exhaled noisily. It wasn't the most elegant of solutions, but it would solve her problems.

"I have to see you. I need to be with you," Richard's voice came again, husky with desire.

Antonia had never heard him like that before. Even though his passion was directed toward another woman, something about the sound of his voice made her toes curl inside her slippers.

"Tonight? After the ball?"

"Sooner," he demanded. "In three dances, there's another waltz. When it starts, slip away and meet me in the second floor parlor."

There was another long pause, some rustling and a low moan.

"Careful, you'll wrinkle my gown. Oh…"

Then Miss Goodnight made a little noise of pleasure that convinced Antonia she didn't give two figs what might happen to her gown.

"I need you, Sophie."

Then there were a few unintelligible mumblings that included something about her being so sweet he could eat her up. It might be undignified, but all the same, something in Antonia wished he'd say that about her.

"I'm desperate." Richard's voice came again. "A quick tryst, love, and then we'll announce our betrothal at the midnight toast."

Antonia never swore. It was ill-bred. It was common and vulgar. For the first time in her life, a ripe curse slipped from her lips.

"Good heavens. There's someone on the other side of the curtain," Miss Goodnight hissed.

"Of course there is. There's a whole ballroom full of people. Meet me upstairs, Sophie. Say you will."

Antonia didn't wait to hear her rival's capitulation. She was certain it was coming. Those *nouveau riche* types had no class, no sense of what was appropriate.

Imagine, slipping off to dally and then coming back to the ballroom to announce their engagement, as if the world were obligated to wish them happy even though their happiness would destroy Antonia's carefully laid plans. Even though—

A way to entrap Richard and foil Miss Goodnight leaped full blown into Antonia's mind like Athena springing from the head of Zeus. It was perfect. All the pieces would work together with the precision of a Swiss clock. It was slightly distasteful, but bold enough to succeed. She couldn't wait to see the look on Sophie Goodnight's face when it did. Antonia hurried to find her mother to put her plan into motion. She already knew she could count on her father's help.

There wasn't much time.

&

"You must pardon me, Mr. Seymour," Sophie said when Lawrence presented himself before her as the next waltz began. Over his shoulder, she spied Richard slipping out the ballroom doors. A little thrill coursed through her. She couldn't wait to join him. "I'm afraid I've overdone myself and need to find the retiring room for a moment."

"Certainly," Lawrence said with a bow from the neck. "Looks like Lady Petra is permanently affixed to the wallpaper next to the punch bowl. I believe I'll go rescue her."

"Ask nicely, or you'll be wearing some of that punch." Sophie found him direct and engaging, but for some reason, Petra didn't seem to like Richard's friend much. Lawrence Seymour was a pleasant change from the stiff and pompous lordlings being encouraged to flock around Lady Ella. The fact that Seymour bypassed the obvious beauty of the family to bedevil Richard's plainer sister endeared him to Sophie.

Not to Petra, however, who complained that Lawrence only wanted to tease her at every opportunity.

A little teasing can be a good thing, Sophie thought as she made her way around the edge of the dance floor. Richard's talented hands teased her in a very good way indeed. How odd that torment could be pleasure, and that the naughtiness she and Richard were about to get into would be socially sanctioned and not naughty at all once they wed.

"Oh, Miss Goodnight, there you are. Slow down and I'll take a turn round the room with you." Lady Pruett practically dashed to her side. "Lady Wappington overheard you tell Mr. Seymour you were on your way to the retiring room. Even though this is nothing like the usual rout, I need a bit of air myself. I do believe I've forgotten which room has been set up for the ladies' use. May I accompany you?"

Without waiting for a reply, she linked her arm through Sophie's.

"Do you know one time at Lady Wappington's town house"—Lady Pruett chatted on amiably—"there were so many packed into her ballroom, if one wasn't on the dance floor, one was in serious danger of asphyxiation from the press of people?"

"Is that so?" Sophie's chest tightened as if she were in such a press.

"Indeed. In fact, I have it on good authority that at least one little wallflower did faint dead away."

"How horrid for her." Sophie glanced longingly at the door through which Richard left. The old Sophie would have shaken her arm free and made good her escape, but if she was going to marry Richard, she needed to learn to be gracious. Especially to people she didn't like, and she sincerely didn't like Lady Pruett at the moment. "Was the young lady embarrassed?"

"Few people ever knew of the incident because, though she was insensible for about half a minute, she remained upright the whole time due to the crowd around her propping her up." Lady Pruett sounded downright gleeful about her ghoulish little tale. "Come now. You and I can have a nice little chat and get to know each other better. At the very least, we'll get away from the music for a while. I say, isn't the second violinist abysmal? I'll warrant the man has been a quarter-tone flat all evening. Tell me, what was the music like in India? I've heard it is the most unpleasant noise imaginable, utterly incomprehensible."

The most unpleasant sound Sophie could imagine was Lady Pruett's voice droning on and on. And unfortunately, she didn't have to imagine it. The woman scarcely drew breath between one rambling sentence and the next.

I'm sorry, Richard. She thought it so loudly, surely he could hear up in that second floor parlor where he waited for her. *Soon we won't have to slip away for a stolen tryst.*

⤬

"Thank you for rescuing me from that awful Mr. Seymour," Petra said.

"Not at all. Thank you for agreeing to show Lady

Wappington your mother's rare art piece," Lord Pruett said as he offered Petra his arm.

"Indeed. Not many Vermeers are extant, and to have one here at Somerfield is something of a minor miracle—not that most of my family members ever trouble to appreciate it. The painting ought to be the focal piece of the gallery, instead of squirreled away in a second floor parlor," she said. "It's not Vermeer's fault he failed to paint a Barrett, is it?"

Lord Pruett laughed as he guided her along the edge of the crowded dance floor. "No, but if it is, we must forgive him. The man was a genius. Now, there's Lady Wappington waiting for us by the door. The second floor parlor, you say?"

Twenty-seven

"Stolen waters are sweet, and bread eaten in secret is pleasant; but…" Why must there always be a but? That small word spoils ever so many promising things.

—Phillippa, the Dowager Marchioness of Somerset

SOMEHOW SOPHIE HAD BEATEN HIM THERE AND WAITED for him in the dark parlor. Silvered by moonlight, she was silhouetted before the window. She was an outline, a dream, a being of such ethereal beauty she ought to have been winged.

And best of all, she was his. A knot formed in his throat so big that Richard couldn't speak for happiness. He crossed the dark room, and she moved to meet him.

Her perfume assaulted his nostrils. He'd have to tell her he preferred that lighter fragrance she usually wore. Funny, he hadn't noticed this stronger scent in the ballroom, but there had been such a press of smells in that place—mingled bergamot and floral, warm silk, warm bodies, and musky undernotes all jumbled into a miasmic soup and liberally stirred by the dance music.

She slipped into his arms, and he found her mouth, but she stiffened under his kiss.

Something was wrong. She didn't taste like his Sophie.

"What the devil?" He staggered a step back from her in confusion. The sharp sound of ripping fabric pierced his ear, but before he could say or do anything else, he heard his sister Petra's voice in the hallway.

"How the family came by the Vermeer is a bit of a mystery," she was saying. "And I'm first to admit we probably don't deserve to have it, but the family legend is that some Barrett in the cavalry was fighting on the Continent. During the course of the battle, he happened to offer mercy to a certain Flemish count. Overwhelmed with gratitude, the gentleman surrendered not only his sword, but also the Vermeer hanging in his chateau. Of course, that tale may be apocryphal. It's just as likely that my many times great-grandfather simply ripped the painting off the wall."

The door swung open, and the light from Petra's candle shot through the parlor, casting stark planes of amber and shadow.

"Oh, I say!" Lady Wappington's nasal whine followed the retreating dark. "Someone's there."

Richard tried to shelter Sophie from the outraged expression on the old gossip's face by standing in front of her.

Confound it! Lord Pruett followed Lady Wappington in.

Being caught in an indiscreet situation might be embarrassing, but it wouldn't hurt him in the long run, especially since he fully intended to marry Sophie.

But Lady Wappington could destroy her in the collective mind of the *ton* with a single raised brow. He cursed himself for insisting she meet him here. There was little hope he could keep Sophie's identity a secret, and even less when she pushed around him to face the others.

Except it wasn't Sophie. In the candlelight, the girl's hair was golden and disheveled and the lacy netting around her bodice had been ripped so that it trailed down one side of her gown like a flag at half mast. Richard's heart dropped to his toes.

"Oh, Papa!" Antonia burst into tears as she hurried into Lord Pruett's waiting arms. "Look what he did to my gown."

"Now see here, Hartley." Lord Pruett handed her a clean handkerchief and patted Antonia's back consolingly. "You cannot treat my daughter like some light-heeled chambermaid. I demand you do the right thing."

"I agree, Lord Pruett." Lady Wappington cleared her throat, an unpleasant sound that reminded Richard of a bullfrog in an amorous frame of mind. "It is the only thing that will answer. The two of you must marry."

"Marry? I can't marry Antonia," Richard said.

Antonia broke into a thin wail.

"You can and you will, young man," Lord Pruett said with a ferocious scowl, "or I'll see you handed over to the magistrate for forcing yourself on my dear girl."

"Forcing myself?" A rake he may have been, but never in his life would Richard dream of such a thing.

"No, that won't do," Lady Wappington said. "A public trial would taint Lady Antonia badly. Better for public censure to fall upon Lord Hartley. If you don't step up and marry the girl, I'll see that neither you nor any of your family"—Lady Wappington eyed Petra meaningfully—"is ever received in any respectable home in the realm. When I'm finished with you, people will cross the street rather than lay eyes on any of the Barretts. The name of Somerset will be anathema."

Again the full weight of the Somerset marquessate descended on Richard's shoulders. It wasn't enough that he'd figured out a way to rescue the family from financial ruin. He had to protect them from social disaster too. In many ways, this was an even bigger threat. One could be threadbare and still be considered acceptable by the *beau monde*. But if the *ton* decided to shun him and his family, no amount of money, no exalted title would protect them from the spiteful cruelty of those who considered it their duty to be the arbiters of correct behavior.

He didn't give two figs for the *ton*'s opinion of himself. But he had three unmarried sisters to consider. And unlike the financial disaster brought about by his father's mismanagement, this debacle was his own doing.

He had no choice.

◈

It was nearly midnight. Strains of the last quadrille died as liveried footmen circuited the room with trays laden with champagne flutes. The toast prior to the midnight supper was almost upon them. Sophie accepted a glass of the sparkling liquid and willed her belly to stop fizzing.

Soon.

She wished she'd been able to join Richard in the

parlor and not only because she wanted a few moments alone with the man. They hadn't planned this very well, and she wasn't sure what she ought to do.

Richard would step up on the dais that now held the string quartet. He'd thank his guests for sharing the evening with the Barretts. Then he'd announce their engagement to the world.

Did he expect her to join him ahead of time or wait until he made their betrothal known?

To be on the safe side, she worked her way through the crowd till she was nearer the dais. Only a few people were between her and the three steps leading up onto it. This would be her first public outing as the future marchioness. She didn't want to ruin things by tripping over her own feet on her way to Richard's side. If she could catch his eye, she'd know what he expected her to do.

She smiled to herself at how much she'd changed in a few weeks. When she first came to Somerfield Park, she didn't care what anyone thought of her. Now, because she'd be connected to a large, influential family, she had to care. Because she was a commoner, the *ton* would assume she didn't know how to behave among the aristocracy. She was determined not to embarrass the Barretts. She didn't want to fail Richard.

The ruby ring seemed to glow warmly in its secret spot over her breastbone. Soon she'd be able to wear it publicly. She'd be able to thank Richard's grandmother for handing it down to them, a treasured token of love from another time. She wished she'd thought to remove it in the retiring room, so she could slip it to Richard. It would be lovely for him to slide it onto her finger before the entire assembly.

She glanced around the room, looking for her parents. This would be such a moment of triumph for her father. Henry Goodnight's hard work would finally make his daughter a real lady, and his future grandchildren would inherit titles just as he wished.

But instead of finding her father, Sophie found Lord Pruett pushing his way through the throng on the opposite side of the room. She caught a glimpse of Richard in his wake.

When Lord Pruett climbed the steps to the dais and raised his hands to quiet the gathering, Sophie's belly tingled as if she stood on the edge of a precipice. She gave herself a shake. This was no time to be fanciful, not when her life was about to change forever.

"My friends," Lord Pruett said once the crowd quieted, "as most of you know, my dear daughter Antonia is the driving force behind this delightful gathering. Her exquisite taste and gracious skills are responsible for the pleasure we've all enjoyed this evening."

He lifted a hand of invitation, and Antonia joined him on the low platform. Her gown was missing its row of ruffles at the bodice. It was an improvement on the pink silk's lines. Sophie had thought the lace netting overly fussy, but now the gown was cut much more daringly than Sophie remembered. At the opposite edge of the dais, Lady Wappington started a tepid round of applause, but others joined in as if their social lives depended upon it. The lady was an unpleasant person to begin with, but she looked even more alarming when her lips parted in a horse-toothed smile.

"Evidently, Antonia's gifts are not lost on Lord Somerset's heir either," Lord Pruett went on. "I'm pleased to announce that Lord Hartley has asked for my daughter's hand, and she has accepted his suit."

The crowds parted to allow Richard to join Antonia and her father.

Sophie's vision tunneled. This couldn't be happening. She was dreaming. She must have fallen asleep on the settee in the retiring room while Lady Pruett droned on and on. She'd wake in a moment.

But she didn't. Everyone was talking at once. Snippets of exclamations forced their way into Sophie's brain.

"Lovely couple."

"So right for each other."

"Not a bit surprised, are you?"

Her mother was suddenly at her side. "Come away, dear," she said softly. Millicent Goodnight put an arm around her shoulders and drew her aside.

It wasn't a dream, but it didn't seem real either. Sophie allowed herself to be led away. She wasn't conscious of putting one foot before the other, but somehow she made it across the long ballroom. Once she cleared the doorway, she sagged against the wall in the corridor, unable to move forward.

She wished she were the sort who could swoon. Being able to slip into mindless oblivion held vast appeal. She expected to feel rage, deep shock, and sorrow. Instead, her insides were numb.

Her father strode into the hall, his steps forceful instead of his usual tentative gait. His coloring, normally tinged an unhealthy yellow, was now a florid red.

About the Author

Mia Marlowe is a rising star whose *Touch of a Rogue* was named a *Publishers Weekly* Top Ten Best Romance for Spring 2012. Mia learned about storytelling while singing professional opera. She knows what it's like to sing a high C in a corset, so she empathizes with the trials of her historical heroines. Mia resides in the Ozarks, surrounded by the beautiful Mark Twain National Forest. For more, visit www.miamarlowe.com.

"I'll bury him," he promised. "Hartley will rue the day he threw you over. By God, I'll destroy him."

She'd never heard her father say anything so aggressive before. Henry Goodnight was wonderful, but he was a man of ledgers and tallies. No one would have ever mistaken him for a man of action, much less one who could take on a fellow half his age in fighting trim. Sweat popped in glistening beads on her father's forehead.

"Father, calm yourself. You'll do no such thing." She took his arm and patted it consolingly. This kind of excitement couldn't be good for him, but she was almost grateful for it, because it meant she didn't have to examine why should couldn't seem to feel anything. "You've never been one to resort to physical violence."

"Who said anything about violence? I simply mean to ruin him, which will hurt a man like Hartley much more than being bloodied. Who do you think his man of business got to invest in that forestry scheme of his? I did it, anonymously, of course, in deference to his sensibilities, but that's over now." Henry Goodnight ground a fist into his other palm. "He's completely in my power whether he realizes it or not. I'll call the note and bring this house down around his head."

"I urge you not to do anything hasty, Henry," Sophie's mother said, then turned back to her. "Come, dear. Let's put you to bed, and we'll discuss matters in the morning."

"I can't stay here." She could barely breathe. If she had to remain under the same roof as Richard, she'd run to madness. "We must go. Leave. At once. And let's not stop till we reach the town house in London."

She'd have preferred taking a ship back to Bombay, but London would have to do.

"I understand how you feel, but that would be impractical. I abhor taking a coach at night. It's simply not safe." Her mother linked arms with both Sophie and her father, and drew them toward the stairs that led to the guest wing and their bedchambers. "Besides, if we left now, it would be cause for comment. You would become an object of pity."

Sophie didn't want that. She didn't want that quite a lot.

"If we stay and hold our heads high, we show the world that the Goodnights can weather anything."

Millicent Goodnight continued to speak soothingly as they mounted the stairs with a slow, even tread. Sophie let her mother's voice roll over her, taking comfort from the sound, but not soaking up the words.

Nothing she said could change anything. Richard was gone. Sophie had lost him as irretrievably as if he'd tumbled off Somerset's roof and not landed on the lilacs.

When her parents left her in her bedchamber with instructions to ring for Eliza, the numbness she'd felt in the ballroom began to wear off.

Her legs gave beneath her. She sank to the thick carpet, wondering how she managed to live when her heart had been ripped out. The gaping hole in her chest left her gasping.

Richard had betrayed her. When she let herself love him, she'd given him the power to hurt her, and he used it to crush her. This was worse than what happened with Julian. Richard knew her. He knew how badly she'd been damaged because she had trusted a man.

He had to know what this would do to her, and he did it anyway.

She curled into as small a ball as she could, hugging her knees to her chest. She was aware of making small keening noises, but she couldn't form a coherent thought.

Some pain was too deep for words.

Twenty-eight

One of the great tragedies in life is realizing that the illusion of free will is just that. Illusion. If one is responsible for the lives of others, one does not have complete control over one's own destiny.

—Phillippa, the Dowager Marchioness of Somerset

BY THREE IN THE MORNING, THE LAST OF THE REVELERS in Somerfield Park gave up and found their chambers. The great house was finally quiet.

Still, Richard waited.

He'd caused Sophie enough pain for one night. The last thing he wanted was to be caught in her room and embroil her in a fresh scandal.

Then too, he wasn't sure what he could say to her. Or if she'd even allow him in. He buried his face in his hands. All he'd wanted was a few stolen moments with the woman he loved. Now a stolen moment was all he'd ever have with Sophie.

How could things have gone so monumentally wrong?

His parents were pleased by the turn of events, even if his betrothal to Antonia came under threat of scandal. Now that he'd sold his first timber contract and Somerset's finances were headed in the right direction, the pedigree of his future bride mattered more to them than her dowry.

Ella was thrilled over the engagement even though the surprise announcement did steal a bit of the attention due her as the reigning debutante. She and Antonia had become like sisters while they planned for that blasted ball. Petra was more subdued about the news, since she'd been present at the horrible moment when Richard realized he had not been caught with Sophie in the parlor. Ariel had been toddled off to bed by her governess well before midnight, too young to know what was happening.

He envied her ignorance.

Seymour wasn't fooled for a moment about Richard's sudden engagement. His sardonic congratulations included a whispered offer to find a ladder, so Richard could escape out a window. The pair of them could run off to chase opera dancers in Paris or take a slow boat to Shanghai.

Richard was tempted.

Two things held him in place. First, there was Somerset. It was his, and more importantly, he belonged to it. As the future marquess, the estate and title's welfare was his duty. It was as dear as his life's blood. He loved the land and its people, and was honor bound to defend them from all dangers.

Even if that danger was the wagging tongue of a vicious old biddy.

The other, even more compelling reason he

couldn't flee with Seymour was Sophie. He somehow had to make her understand what had happened and why. He owed her that.

So after he heard the long case clock chime half past three, he crept into the dark hallway and moved quietly toward the guest wing. There were a few squeaking floor boards to avoid, but he knew where they were. Concentrating on stealth helped him avoid thinking.

Nothing could keep him from feeling.

His chest ached, a leaden throb. When he imagined what Sophie must be feeling, he could scarcely breathe.

When his fist closed over her doorknob, he stopped. He'd never thought himself a coward before, but facing her was the most daunting thing he'd ever done. He couldn't bear to wound her any more.

Perhaps it would be kinder to turn around.

Before he could decide what to do, the door opened before him. Sophie was still in her ball gown, backlit by the moonlight shafting through her window. Her hair hung loosely around her shoulders. She looked up at him, her eyes enormous in the dimness.

There was no hint of welcome in her gaze. There was barely recognition.

She turned without a word and wandered back to the chaise longue. She plopped onto the end of it and knotted her fingers together on her lap. Even from across the room, Richard could see that they trembled.

Richard closed the door behind him.

"Thank you," he whispered.

She blinked up at him questioningly.

"For allowing me in."

"It's your house," she said. "But you're wrong if you think you're in."

Then she glared at him. It was the same dismissive look she'd given him when he first came upon her as she was brutalizing his grandmother's roses. Her eyes narrowed. There was the wall he was expecting.

He crossed the room and knelt before her. "Do you want to know what happened?"

"Would it change anything?"

He shook his head. "But it might help you to understand."

She laughed mirthlessly. "So you think understanding why you broke my heart will make it better? For whom?"

"You're right." He covered both her hands with his, and her fidgeting fingers stilled. "I'm trying to assuage my own guilt. This is all my fault. I never should have asked you to meet me in the parlor. Since you didn't arrive, I assume someone waylaid you."

She nodded. "Are you trying to tell me you were entrapped by Antonia once you got there?"

"Like a stag drawn to a salt lick." He ventured a half smile. "Remember how you likened me to one in the gallery after that first dinner party?"

Her lips twitched. "Thoroughly cornered and beset upon by the hounds, I believe I said."

"And you're the wily vixen who escapes in the confusion, glad her hunt will come another day," he finished.

"But I didn't escape, Richard." A tear trembled on her lashes and then coursed down her cheek to the corner of her mouth. "I didn't escape at all."

"Neither did I. Oh, Sophie."

Words failed him, and he drew her into his arms.

She resisted at first, making small noises, a potent mix of anger and sorrow, that tore at his heart. She pounded his chest with her fist. Then she gave up and melted into him. He tipped her chin up and kissed her, tasting the saltiness of grief on her lips. He'd give anything to take away that taste.

God be praised, she kissed him back. Desperate, heart-wrenching kisses. He could go on making love to this woman's mouth forever, but she finally stopped him by pulling back and putting a hand to his chest.

"You still mean to marry Antonia?"

"I must." Now that they were officially betrothed, the scandal of a broken engagement would be worse than if he'd refused to do the right thing in the first place. His only hope was that Antonia would cry off, though she'd gone to such lengths to entrap him, he didn't think it likely.

"Why?"

There were so many reasons—his sisters' futures, the welfare of Somerset and all the lives attached to it, his own code of right and wrong... But ultimately there was only one reason his destiny was fixed by his past actions. "Honor."

"How can that be? I know you love me, Richard. Is it honorable to wed Antonia when your heart is with me?"

He rose wearily to his feet, walked to the window, and leaned his forehead against its cool surface. Somerset's meadow stretched before him, each gray blade of grass doubled by its own sharp shadow in the moonlight. In the distance, the forest rose up, blocking the view of the sea. He imagined he could hear its breakers pounding relentlessly on the shore, pounding

on his soul, forming him as surely as it formed the rocky coast. Whatever else he was, this land, this title had the prior claim far above his own will. In the end, his honor was all he had. He couldn't turn his back on his duty without denying the core of his being.

"I am not my own. I belong to this place. I will be Somerset. I cannot live to please myself. If I did, I'd take you and flee right now. We'd never look back. But I can't."

"Oh, for heaven's sake," she said, her whisper spiked with irritation. His heart warmed at that show of grit. That was his Sophie. "Do you know how melodramatic that sounds?"

"Yes, but it doesn't change things. I am who I am, Sophie. I was born to protect this place, these people, this family. This time, I'm protecting it from my own folly."

She didn't say anything for a moment. Then she drew her legs up under her gown and hugged them to her chest.

"I understand," she whispered. "When measured in the balance against Somerset, I weigh very little."

"God, no." Couldn't she see she was everything to him—his hopes, his dreams? He hated himself for hurting her. It was as if her pain were his. He couldn't bear it. If he weren't his father's heir, there would be no question what to do. But Somerset, his past, present, and future albatross, dragged him down on all sides. He rushed to her and gathered her in his arms again, pressing feverish kisses on her lips, her cheeks, her temples.

And suddenly Sophie was enough. More than enough. In a hundred years, it wouldn't matter if

Somerset collapsed in scandal, but if he didn't have this woman beside him, he didn't want to keep breathing.

"Damn Somerset," he whispered fiercely. "I can't lose you. Say the word and we'll elope. Now. Tonight. Gretna Green is only a few days away by coach. We'll marry over a Scottish anvil. Once it's done, it can't be undone and devil take the hindermost."

She rocked and hugged him, smoothing down his hair while she whispered his name. His heart surged. She was agreeing.

Then she said in a wisp of a voice, "If we do that, you'll be giving up everything you believe in, everything you are."

"For you. It's a trade I'll make all day." He claimed her mouth, pouring his heart into the kiss. When he finally released her lips, she palmed his cheeks.

"Oh, Richard. I thought I could be that selfish, but I can't." Her face crumpled. "If we do as you suggest, it would be terrible. It might not happen tomorrow. It might not happen the next day, but eventually, you'd hate me because I'd have stolen who you are."

"It's no theft if I give myself willingly."

"You said it yourself. Honor is why you must wed Antonia. I won't take your honor from you." She gently pulled herself from his arms and stepped back a pace. Then she reached into her bodice and drew out the ruby ring. She held it out to him on the flat of her hand. "Give me a chance to have a bit of honor too. I won't let you sacrifice everything you value just for me."

Richard never realized a man could bleed without suffering an outward wound. He forced himself to take the ring from her. "Sophie, you're tearing my guts out."

"Mine too." She forced a tremulous smile. "Especially since it's not in my nature to be noble."

He'd half fallen in love with her smile the first time he saw it. Now it broke his heart. The full weight of all he'd lost crushed him. The long march of years ahead without this vibrant woman by his side loomed before him, empty and joyless.

"Sophie Goodnight," he said softly, "you are the most noble soul I'll ever know."

Then before he succumbed to the temptation to grovel at her feet, begging her to change her mind, he slipped out of her room and made his way back to his.

There was no chance of sleeping. He couldn't rest. His misery was his own fault, and he could see no way to fix it. Until the sun stood on the tops of the distant forest, Richard stared out his window toward the east.

How many more sunrises would he be forced to endure without Sophie?

Twenty-nine

Secrets are like bread. They do not improve with keeping. Surprisingly, the scriptures admonish us to cast our bread upon the water, and we shall find it after many days. This, however, presumes one likes soggy bread.

—Phillippa, the Dowager Marchioness of Somerset

"Richard, my dear boy, I was hoping you'd come."

He rose to his feet as his grandmother swept into the parlor at Somerset Steading. The dower house was grand, a stately home of some thirty-odd rooms. The dowager used her portion from the estate to keep Somerset Steading in fine fettle. The yellow-striped chintz on the matching settees in her parlor looked new, and his grandmother's small army of servants kept the place white-glove immaculate. Whatever financial deficiencies Somerset had suffered over the last few years, it was clear Richard's father had not stinted on his mother's household allowance.

"Sit down, my boy, and I'll ring for tea."

"No need, Gran. I haven't time to stay," Richard said. "I just came to return this."

He offered the ruby ring to her.

"Nonsense." She pretended not to see his extended hand, waving him to the opposite settee and tinkling the bell at her side. "Of course, you've time. If you don't have time, you don't have anything. Sit down while Hobbs brings us a small respite. Cook has baked some lovely butter biscuits, and I know they're your favorite."

"I'm not a little boy anymore." He shoved the ring back into his waistcoat pocket since she didn't seem disposed to take it. "Some things you can't make better with a biscuit."

"Don't be obtuse. Everything's better with a biscuit." She fixed him with a hard stare. "Besides, for what possible reason would you be hurrying away? Never say you wish to spend more time with your new fiancée."

He leaned forward, balancing his elbows on his knees. "No, Gran."

Lady Somerset was right. He could scarcely bear to be in the same house as Antonia, even one as sprawling as Somerfield Park. To be fair, she didn't seek him out at all either, which was probably wise. He was still seething over how she'd entrapped him. Richard wasn't sure how he'd manage private conversation with her, let alone wed the girl. The most civilized option was to hunker behind the distance so common in marriages of the wellborn.

But Richard didn't feel like being civilized. He'd never forgive her. Never.

Most of all, he'd never forgive himself.

"I understand I missed some high drama by leaving the ball early last night," his grandmother said.

Richard had expected to have to explain the whole debacle to his grandmother and was relieved not to have to rehash the events. They still had a nightmarish quality in his mind that wouldn't improve with retelling.

"How do you know about it at all?" Richard asked.

Hobbs, his grandmother's beanpole of a butler, appeared with a silver tea service on a tray balanced on his long-fingered hands. Along with the tea things and a plate a biscuits, a neatly folded letter sealed with a blob of red wax rested on a lacy doily.

"If one wants to know anything, one only need ask the servants. They know everything. My Hobbs is a terrible gossip," she said. "Aren't you, Hobbs?"

"Yes, my lady," came the reflexive reply. "If you say so, my lady."

"There are few secrets from the servants in a great house like Somerfield Park, and since Hobbs collects our supplies from the main house each morning, he is a fount of information for me," she said. "We cannot begrudge the servants their little entertainments. What else have they to do in that pokey little common room but discuss the lives of those who live above them?"

Hobbs's eyebrows twitched as if he might object to this characterization of below stairs life, but he said nothing as he deposited the tray on the low table between the settees.

"I'll pour out myself," Lady Somerset said. "That'll be all, Hobbs."

"Very good, my lady." The butler glided smoothly to the glass French doors and pulled them shut behind

him. If Hobbs *was* a gossip, he'd just lost the opportunity to cower to one side of the doorway and eavesdrop on Richard's conversation with his grandmother.

The dowager poured out the tea, lacing Richard's cup liberally with milk and two lumps of sugar. He normally took his plain, but he accepted the offering without comment.

"You look horrible, Richard," she said, not unkindly. "Try a biscuit, dear."

He brought one to his lips but couldn't bring himself to take a bite. It smelled fresh and sweet, but he knew it would taste like dust in his mouth. He balanced the biscuit on his saucer and set the whole thing back down on the tray.

"Richard, we Barretts are known for our stiff upper lips. You cannot let this get you down. You must simply soldier on."

"Must I?" He rose and strode to the window. He barely stifled the urge to throw it open, leap over the casement, and fly helter-skelter through his grandmother's neatly tended garden. He couldn't seem to make his eyes focus. The colors ran into each other in blurry patches of pink, yellow, and green. "I can't help it, Gran. The sun is dark without her."

"Poppycock. You're being theatrical."

"I'm being honest." He didn't want to argue. He wanted to kidnap Sophie, sling her over his saddle, and run away with her. The only thing that stopped him was that he knew she'd fight him tooth and nail every step of the way. His shoulders sagged.

"Oh my dear," his grandmother said softly. "You really do love her."

He nodded, not trusting his voice.

"Well, Sophie Goodnight is an Original, I'll give her that," she said. "She is not a conventional choice, but I confess, I thought her a good match for you right from the beginning. And not only because of her father's purse."

"She is the other half of my soul," he murmured. "The much better half."

His grandmother was silent for so long he suspected she'd slipped into the light sleep of advancing years even sitting upright, but when Richard turned from the window to face her, she was peering down at the letter that had been delivered along with the tea service. It lay open in her lap.

"What is it, Gran?"

She refolded it hastily and started to put it back onto the tray. Then she stopped and eyed him pensively. "What would you give to have your Sophie Goodnight?"

"Everything." He didn't have to think about it for a second.

"Do you mean that? Truly?"

"If it upended my entire life, I'd consider it a bargain."

She exhaled noisily. "They say the truth is supposed to set one free, but I can make no promises. The lesson of Pandora is that one never knows what will happen when one opens a box of secrets." She handed the missive to Richard. "Read this and tell me your thoughts."

The letter was from a solicitor in London. Richard scanned the neat, round script, hardly daring to believe what the letter contained.

"Can this possibly be true?" he asked.

"I fear it is. Apparently, there was an unexpected death of one of the partners in the law firm at a critical juncture in the proceedings, and somehow, crucial documents which wanted signing were misplaced and never dealt with." She shook her head. "The question is what are we to do with the information?"

"We trumpet it from the rooftops, Gran."

"Speak to your father about it. I understand he has been contacted by unscrupulous parties who hope to profit. It's all so very unsavory. I wish we could spare you." She gave a delicate shiver. "Oh, my dear boy, you do understand what this means, don't you?"

He nodded. She thought it meant sacrifice and self-denial. But to Richard, it meant hope.

❧

"Honestly, Clack, how could you be so irresponsible?" Constance Bowthorpe had asked for the entire day off, something she'd done only once before during her employment at Somerfield Park. She'd promised to return to her duties that evening. Fortunately, what with the house party, there was so much activity to keep Lady Ariel busy during the day, it was no hardship for her employers to be lenient. Constance had taken the early morning mail coach to Crimble. Now she stared at her cohort across the pitted table in the tap room of the sorry excuse for an inn. "Just when I need you to hold up your end, I find you unable to climb out from the bottle."

"I'm *prefectly* fine. *Prefectly*. Don't ye be worrying your head about my end. If anyone's end is up, it's mine. I'll make do." Thaddeus Clack sipped his coffee

and held a hand to his temple as if he willed the dark liquid to make his head stop pounding. "Tell me again how this will go."

"You're to meet his lordship in the Greek folly tomorrow evening at ten. You'll present him with the ledger pages from Rosewood Chapel." She leaned forward and lowered her voice to a whisper. "And he'll give you three hundred pounds."

Clack rubbed his hands together. "That's something like. The things I could do in London with that."

Constance narrowed her eyes at him. "But you won't go to London if you know what's good for you. You'll come right back here, and we'll divvy up the take."

"Half of three hundred ain't near as good." His face crinkled into a questioning frown.

"A third is even less, and that's what you'll be getting for your part in this endeavor. May I remind you that you have not contributed much to this plan? You are merely a courier and, as such, are entitled to a smaller portion."

A lesser woman might have been cowed by his ferocious scowl. Of course, a lesser woman didn't carry a river-smooth rock in her reticule either.

"I know ye're supposed to be the brains of this outfit, but why are we only asking for three hundred?" Clack slurped his coffee. "Seems to me this sort of thing is worth a damn sight more."

"It is. But if one finds a golden goose, one must not take care not to kill it." She skewered him with a purse-lipped frown. "You very nearly ruined all by tossing his lordship off the roof."

"That weren't my fault. He come at me, so he did. A bloke's got to defend himself."

"At any rate, three hundred is what Somerset can spare at the moment. Once Lord Hartley's timber enterprise takes off, we'll up the ante next year." Constance gave a satisfied sigh. "And every year thereafter."

Clack scratched his head, sending his resident lice scurrying. "And why would the Quality Folk keep paying if we give 'em the pages from the chapel this time?"

"Because I have reams of other documents, official sorts of things that would stand up in any court. Then there are the letters." Constance smiled at the thought that the seeds of Somerfield Park's destruction resided safely in the locked box under her bed. "A gentleman like Lord Somerset will pay a good deal to make sure those salacious missives never see the light of day."

"Don't know what sally-ay-shous means, but sounds like his lordship were randy as a billy goat."

"Mr. Clack, you have no idea." Constance sipped her tea. Some of the letters positively curled her toes. She was especially partial to one or two of them and kept them handily on top for when she wanted to reread them. Who would know if she pretended his lordship had written those very naughty things to her? In fact, before she turned loose of those particular missives, she'd have to copy them out for her personal use later.

"Good thing she kept 'em then." Clack's gravelly voice interrupted her decidedly scandalous musings. "My niece was a pack rat and no mistake."

"How would you know? You din't have much to do with her toward the end you said. Come to think on it, how long have you had all these documents and letters and suchlike?"

"Last fall, her old landlord was fixing up the place

where she died and found a small strongbox she'd
hidden under the floorboards. Since I'd paid him the
rent she owed him, he figured he'd send me the chest
as a courtesy."

In fact, the man had threatened to take her to
court to settle her niece's debt. Though it had chafed
her soul at the time, Constance was now grateful she
hadn't been able to afford a lawyer to defend her and
she'd settled with the landlord instead. As a result, the
man had felt honor bound to hand over the small chest
with her niece's name burned into the wooden top.

"Lucky for you he didn't open it," Clack said.
"Otherwise, he'd be the one meeting his lordship
on the morrow."

Or not. Not everyone was comfortable with blackmail. Fortunately, Constance Bowthorpe had no such
scruples. She was done being a governess, too good
for the servant quarters yet not good enough to rub
elbows with the Family on a regular basis. Besides,
chasing after the youngest Barrett brat over hither and
yon was dancing on her last nerve.

Once she got her two hundred pounds, she
intended to give notice and set up housekeeping in
a tidy little cottage in Wiltshire. The White Horse
country had always called to her. She'd invent a past
for herself, something romantic and slightly tragic.
Perhaps a sea captain for a husband who was lost off
the coast of Zanzibar.

And every year she'd refill her coffers, courtesy of
the secrets of Somerfield Park.

Thirty

There are crossroads in life, those moments when one goes left instead of right, and for better or worse, the direction of one's life is permanently altered. It's not often one is able to face that same crossroad again and even less likely that one will make a different choice the second time around.

—Phillippa, the Dowager Marchioness of Somerset

THE APPEARANCE OF BARRETT HOUSE HAD IMPROVED out of all knowing since Richard had come home. The masons he'd engaged to repoint the chimney had finished their work, and new slate graced the roof. As Richard strode up to the freshly painted green door, he noticed that his grandmother's rosebush had filled out. Its fresh green shoots were loaded with unopened buds, just as Sophie had predicted. He'd never considered himself the superstitious sort, but he decided to take the fact that the bush was not dead as a good sign.

He started to push open the door, but then realized

MIA MARLOWE

that even though this was his property, he couldn't be certain of his welcome. The Goodnights had moved back into Barrett House on the morning after Ella's ball. He was grateful they were still in the area. He'd half expected them to disappear into the mist.

Richard rapped the ornate ironwork knocker on the door and waited till Porter opened it.

"Oh, Lord Hartley, good afternoon," the butler said, his eyes darting down the hall as if looking for guidance about what to do next. "Ahem. Come in. May I take your hat? Very good, my lord. Will you be pleased to step into the parlor? In what way may I serve you? However, I feel I should tell you"—he cleared his throat uncomfortably—"that I believe Miss Goodnight is not at home. To anyone."

Sophie had evidently left orders that she would not receive him. He wasn't surprised, but the thought that she was somewhere in the smallish house, knowing he was there and not willing to see him, made his chest ache.

"I'm not here to see Miss Goodnight."

The butler's hunched shoulders slumped in obvious relief.

"I wish to speak to her father."

Porter's shoulders bunched up again. "Oh, my lord, I don't know if... Well, I mean... Are you sure that's...wise?"

"No, I'm not sure it's wise, but it is my wish. Tell Mr. Goodnight I'm waiting for him and I will not leave until we speak." Then Richard reached into his waistcoat pocket and pulled out a sealed letter. "Give this to Mr. Goodnight after I'm gone."

Porter's eyes grew round as a pair of coach wheels, but he scurried off to do Richard's bidding.

Richard sat in one of the leather wing chairs flanking the fireplace and watched the hands on the ormolu mantle clock creep around its face. He tried not to be distracted by thoughts of Sophie, but how could he not when he knew she was so near? If he closed his eyes, he could still taste her. That last salty, tear-stained kiss burned his lips.

Since coming into control of his father's estate, he'd learned to plan. The projected earnings from his new timber interest would put Somerfield Park on solid footing for generations. Now his grandmother had shown him a slim chance to right an old wrong and change everything. But if this new plan didn't work, if at the end of his machinations he still couldn't have Sophie, none of it would matter.

He thrust the possibility away. He couldn't give up on her. Not if there was an ounce of fight left in his body.

Half an hour later, Mr. Goodnight finally shuffled into the room. Richard rose to his feet.

Sophie's father had seemed frail when Richard first met him. He'd shrunk since then. Even though the day was warm, a woolen shawl draped Mr. Goodnight's shoulders. His skin seemed scraped tight over his skull, and its yellowish tinge was even more pronounced than usual. But once he settled into the wing chair opposite Richard, his pale eyes burned with anger.

"What do you want?" Henry Goodnight demanded without preamble.

"First, to thank you for investing in Somerset's timber."

Goodnight's eyes narrowed. "How did you know I was your investor?"

"You are not the only one with business resources. I may be new to trade, but even I know one does not accept funds from an anonymous source—not unless one wishes to risk getting into financial bed with unsavory characters. However, once my man of business confirmed he was dealing with your factor, I told him to allow you the illusion of anonymity."

"Allow me?" Mr. Goodnight snapped. "You insolent pup! I only did it to preserve your dignity."

"And I thank you for that."

"You won't thank me for long," he said, spite dripping from his tone. "I intend to call the note."

"That is your prerogative, but I hope you will reconsider. For your own self-interest, if nothing else. I have promised you a healthy return on your investment, and I'll see that you get it."

"That gives me no comfort. I've seen how much value you put on your promises."

Richard refused to rise to the bait and instead met the man's gaze steadily. "I understand. I'm not here to beg. That would demean us both. However, for the sake of the villagers who are now employed thanks to your investment, I hope you will rethink your plans."

Goodnight shook his head in wonderment. "How you titled folk think the world owes you. It's not enough your family has lorded it over this patch of earth for generations. You think it your right to use my money to continue to do so."

"No, I mean to use your money to lift up those who depend upon my family and put a decent profit

in your pocket while I'm at it," Richard assured him. "Your ideas about what having a title is like are all wrong. While a *Lord* before my name does bestow certain privileges, it doesn't come without obligation. It is my station to care for the needs of my father's estate and everyone attached to it. Everything I have done—everything—is because I am a slave to the title I hold. In many ways, it holds me."

Mr. Goodnight's brows knit together as he considered this.

"Your daughter told me your dearest wish is to have a grandchild who stands to inherit a title. I hope you'll reconsider this desire. It's a pretty conceit to be 'my lorded' left and right, but trust me, it is not the be-all and end-all you seem to think it."

"And that's why you came to see me? To ask me to continue to invest in Somerset and try to persuade me to give up my dream?"

"Partly." Richard leaned forward in his seat. "The main reason I came is to tell you this. Despite all that's happened, I love your daughter, Mr. Goodnight."

"You have a demmed poor way of showing it."

"You're probably right, but whether you believe it or not, I assure you it's true." Richard stood and moved toward the door. "And will be true till I draw my final breath."

❧

Henry Goodnight didn't move from his place by the fire. He was still so angry at Lord Hartley he feared he'd fly apart if he left the confines of the wing chair. How dare the man come begging for Goodnight funds to continue

to flow into Somerset's coffers? Yes, he protested that he wasn't begging, but what else could anyone call it? And those protestations of love for Sophie! If only Henry had the strength he'd left in India, he'd have happily pummeled Lord Hartley into next week.

A board creaked in the hallway outside the parlor door.

"Who's there?" he demanded. "Porter, is that you? Stop skulking and come in."

"It's not Mr. Porter, Father." Sophie appeared in the open doorway.

"I suppose you heard all that," Henry said.

"Some of it. I hid on the other side of the long case clock when Richard left." Her nose was pink. She'd either been gardening without a bonnet or weeping. He hoped she'd forgotten her bonnet.

He lifted a hand to her, and she came and settled on the small ottoman before him. "I suppose you believe him when he says he still loves you."

She lifted her shoulders in a slight shrug. "I wish I didn't."

Henry took her hand between his. He'd give his entire fortune if it would take away the pain he read in his daughter's eyes.

"Being loved is no small thing," he said. "However, you are not obliged to love him back."

"Too late." She stood and paced the room, nervous energy crackling off her like heat lightning. "How do I stop? It's not as if I can snuff it out like a candle. It would be so much easier if I could hate him."

Henry sighed. "Hate is not the opposite of love. What you're looking for is indifference."

"Then I'm doomed," Sophie said. "I can't imagine a world where I could be indifferent to Richard Barrett."

Porter appeared at the doorway, hemming and hawing.

"Don't stand there, man. If you've something to say, say it!"

"Er, yes, if it pleases you, sir, I've a letter here for you from Lord Hartley." Porter presented the missive on a silver tray and then stepped back.

Henry tore open the seal and read the bold script. From the corner of his eye, he saw Sophie frozen by the window, curiosity straining from every pore.

"Do you wish to send a reply?" Porter asked.

"No. I'll deliver it myself. Tonight." Henry rose and tucked the letter into his waistcoat pocket. Lord Hartley wanted a chance to prove his devotion to Sophie. Very well. Henry was curious as to what lengths the young man would go.

But he wasn't about to let his daughter's hopes be raised and then dashed. When she took a step toward him, obviously wanting a chance to read the missive, he raised a hand to stop her and shuffled from the room.

৵৹

The appointed hour had arrived. Thaddeus Clack stumbled through the darkness toward the architectural nonsense called the Greek folly. It was a jumble of tumble-down columns surrounding a small amphitheater.

And to think they built the silly thing to look like a ruin. On purpose!

If he lived to be a hundred, he'd never under-stand the rich.

Of course, once he had his hundred pounds, he'd

be in a bit of the pink himself. Maybe the sense of a folly would become clear to him then, but he doubted it. All Clack knew was that there was a certain sporting girl in Whitechapel who'd help him spend his newfound wealth right enough, and a rollicking good time they'd have of it too.

And they wouldn't waste tuppence on building something that looked as if it were already falling down.

There was no moon, but the starlight was bright enough for him to make out the shadowy shape of his lordship. He was waiting for him on what was supposed to be the stage of the folly. Clack climbed down the sloping sides of the amphitheater and hoisted himself onto the raised platform.

"You got the money?" he demanded.

The dark figure nodded.

"Let's see it."

"First, what are you offering?"

Clack had only spoken with the marquess that one time on the roof. While the voice he'd just heard was similar, it wasn't exactly the same.

"Who are you?" Clack asked.

"Lord Hartley."

"Hmph. His lordship still poorly after his tumble off the roof? Well, guess it's all right for me to deal with you. I figure you're in this business up to your neck, just like your old man." Clack hitched his thumbs under his greasy lapels. "What I'm offering is a chance for you to destroy a certain record what Lord Somerset don't want to surface. Reckon your father's told you what it's about if he sent you on his account."

"Not all of it, though I expect to know the whole

tale soon," Hartley said agreeably. "But what I'd like to know now is how you expect to spend Somerset's money once I break both your arms?"

Then there was a flash of fists. Lord Hartley's punch landed squarely on Clack's jaw and spun him around. He stumbled to his knees but came up swinging. Clack fought back, kicking and gouging with every gutter trick in his bag.

Suddenly a mere one-third of the take for this caper was looking very small indeed.

❧

Antonia stifled a yawn. She still hadn't recovered since the ball two nights ago. It had been hailed a ringing success and more credit redounded to her than praise for Ella, the debutante for whom the ball was given. However, Antonia was plagued with niggling worry.

Since the very public announcement of their betrothal, Hartley had been no more than coldly polite to her when others were around. He avoided her completely otherwise. She'd expected him to be put out at first. No man wishes to be thwarted in the pursuit of his light-o'-love, her father had explained. But she fully anticipated her relationship with Hartley to return to the way it had been in Paris. He'd showered her with courtly devotion and abject adoration at every turn.

Said adoration was not forthcoming. He seemed like another man entirely.

"Have you any idea why we've been summoned?" she asked her father. Her mother was at her side as well, but since Lady Pruett had confessed to feeling guilty over

her part in entrapping Lord Hartley, Antonia couldn't trust her. Only her father had her best interests at heart.

All the Barretts were assembled in his lordship's crowded study. The footman was still bringing in extra chairs to accommodate everyone. Even Lady Ariel and her governess were there, though it was long past the time the thirteen-year-old ought to be abed. The dowager marchioness dozed in a cushioned chair in one of the small chamber's dark corners.

High time for one of her advanced years to be toddled off to her own dower house as well.

Antonia was puzzled by the fact that Henry Goodnight was present and settled in one of the more comfortable chairs before the hearth. Even though it was a warmish night, a small fire had been kindled for the obviously ill man's comfort. Surely since her betrothal to Hartley, the Goodnights ought to be pushing on to greener pastures. Those vulgar cits would just have to look for another lord to use to elevate themselves.

But the truly bewildering thing was that the local magistrate, a Mr. Ichabod Hempsworth, had been called in and was head down in earnest conversation with Lord Somerset. Antonia was even more astounded when the marquess offered the magistrate the throne-like chair behind his massive desk. Then his lordship paced before the fireplace like a caged leopard.

"I've no clue what's afoot," Antonia's father whispered behind his hand.

"David," Lord Somerset said to the footman, "see that everyone who wants one receives a shot of whisky. Or whatever they'd prefer."

"Very good, my lord."

"Make mine a double, there's a good lad." The elder Lady Somerset was apparently not as soundly asleep in her corner as she'd appeared.

Antonia ordered a glass of elderberry wine, hoping it would help her sleep after this bewildering meeting adjourned. Lady Ariel complained loudly when her mother told her to make do with milk.

Then they waited.

There was a scuffle in the hall and Hartley burst in, shoving a scruffy-looking fellow in front of him. The man sported a purpling bruise around one eye and seemed to be favoring his left leg. Hartley's jacket was ripped at the shoulder and his hair was wild, but he himself seemed no worse for the wear.

The magistrate eyed the man. "I assume this is the fellow who accosted you on your roof, Lord Somerset?"

The marquess cast an assessing gaze at the ruffian. "I can't be certain. I regret to admit there are still holes in my memory." He turned to the footman. "David, is this the fellow you escorted up to the roof?"

The young man straightened to attention. "It is, my lord. His name is Thaddeus Clack. However, I wish I could say I had not allowed him into Somerfield Park, much less brought him to the roof, especially after your lordship went flying off the parapet."

"Don't trouble yourself any further on that score. Barring the gaps in my remembrance, I'm right as rain now," Lord Somerset said. "I rely wholeheartedly on David's identification of this miscreant, and you may also, Mr. Hempsworth. Thaddeus Clack is the one who attacked me."

The magistrate looked down his long nose at Clack and then scratched away with a quill on the warrant before him. "Attempted murder to start. Have you anything to say for yourself, Mr. Clack?"

"Murder? No such thing, your excellence." Clack mopped his brow with a dingy handkerchief. "I never meant for his lordship to fall from the roof. Honest, I never. He come at me, fists flyin'." He cut a glance at Hartley. "Sorta like that one there. Both Lord Somerset and Lord Hartley got wicked left hooks. But I tell ye, it were self-defense on the roof. It coulda just as easy been me lying in a tangle on them bushes. He were that upset with me."

"And what had you done to upset his lordship so?" Mr. Hempsworth asked.

Clack started to answer, but then seemed to think better of it.

"I can answer that," Lord Somerset said. "Mr. Clack was attempting to blackmail me with information about an indiscreet incident in my past."

"Blackmail," Hempsworth repeated and inked the word in next to *murder* on the indictment before him.

"Indiscreet incident, ye say?" Clack reached into his grimy waistcoat and drew out a tattered envelope. He handed it to the magistrate. "Is that what Quality Folk call a secret marriage?"

Antonia's nose twitched as it always did at the threat of scandal. The only thing that saved her from a fit of sneezing was that Lady Wappington was not present at this little inquisition.

The younger Lady Somerset, however, was. Surprisingly enough, the marchioness gazed at her

husband without outward show of dismay over the news. Antonia decided if her future mother-in-law wasn't frantic over these revelations, it likely wouldn't bode ill for her either.

Which, after all, was the most important thing.

Thirty-one

At my age, I might shelter behind forgetfulness and no one would dare contradict me. But when memories are etched with such knife-sharp brightness, they are impossible to deny even when it would be more convenient to do so.

—Phillippa, the Dowager Marchioness of Somerset

RICHARD LEANED AGAINST THE BOOKCASE AND HOPED HIS mother had been told what to expect. When his father reached for his mother's hand, she extended it to him.

"I'm sorry to distress you with this, my dear," Lord Somerset said.

"On the day we married, I vowed to stand by your side for better or worse," Lady Somerset said, her voice trembling slightly. "This is definitely worse, but I am still here."

His father bent and brushed his lips over his wife's knuckles. Richard had never been prouder of his parents. His gaze swept the room to see if the disclosures were

upsetting anyone else. His sisters seemed to be bearing up with typical Barrett stoicism, but Ariel's governess looked as if a fish bone had just lodged in her throat.

"Ain't that sweet? When the great and mighty join, it's all hearts and flowers," Clack said. "Only his lordship made the same sort of promise to another girl about seven years before he stood up in church beside you, your ladyship."

"To be honest," Lord Somerset said, "I still have no memory of that day or the young lady in question."

"She weren't no lady, far as I know," Clack said. "She were plain Lyda Mae Saxton."

"At this point, I defer to the document you have before you, Mr. Hempsworth," the marquess said.

Mr. Hempsworth unfolded the page Clack had given him and studied it.

"That's from the parish records itself," Clack said.

"How can we be sure of that?" Hempsworth said. "All I see here is a list of names and dates. Yes, his lordship's name is one of them, but the provenance of the document is spotty at best."

The footman succumbed to a coughing fit before clearing his throat loudly.

"Have you something to add?" Richard asked.

"Not wanting to push myself forward, my lord, but I'm fair certain that page is from the church records," David said. "Miss Dovecote and I looked through the ledgers at Rosewood Chapel and discovered some pages had been cut from the books. I reckon if we take that page back to Brambleton, we'll find the same hand wrote the entries on either side of it."

"Quite enterprising of you, David." Lord Somerset

picked up the page and squinted at it. "It appears I was wed to Miss Saxton at Rosewood Chapel in Brambleton on 20 July 1788."

"But that's impossible," Ella piped up. "Or if it is true, surely that marriage was annulled."

Gran stirred from her place in the corner. "Regrettably, it was not annulled, though not for lack of trying. Your grandfather and I were understandably upset when your father eloped with his young actress, this Lyda Mae person. We immediately set out to have the union set aside and engaged the law firm of Petersmith, Guthrie, and Helzberg to handle the sordid business. Apparently, Mr. Petersmith had the ill grace to die without communicating to his partners that the signatures required for the undoing of this misalliance had not been properly collected. Messers Guthrie and Helzberg had assumed all was well and assured us of it. In fact, it was not." She shifted in the chair and glared imperiously around the room. "Needless to say, their services will no longer be required."

"Father, do you mean to say you've been married to someone else all this time?" Ella dabbed a handkerchief to her eyes. "But that makes us…"

"Bastards?" Richard supplied helpfully. Antonia gasped. He bet she wished she hadn't snared him now.

Lord Somerset nodded soberly. "I was evidently still married to Miss Saxton when I married your mother, Ella."

"No," Gran said with forcefulness. "That's not strictly true. The remaining partners at Petersmith, Guthrie, and Helzberg informed me that Miss Saxton

died a week before your marriage to Lady Helen. Of natural causes," she added quickly.

Antonia sighed in obvious relief. "Then barring a bit of scandal in the distant past, which we can surely all agree to keep secret, nothing has changed."

A potent look passed between Richard and his grandmother. He nodded almost imperceptibly to her.

"You would be right, Lady Antonia, but for one thing," the dowager said, her gaze sweeping the room. "When we tried to arrange an annulment of that ill-considered marriage, we gave the young woman in question a great deal of money, which she accepted in return for her promise never to contact my son again. She lived up to her end of the agreement on that score, I will give her that. Miss Saxton burned through the funds in riotous and, not to speak ill of the dead, drunken excess, but as agreed, she did not send Somerset so much as a note in the following years. However, she refused to sign the annulment documents."

Old Lady Somerset fell silent.

"Go on, Gran," Richard urged.

"As it happens, the reason Miss Saxton wouldn't sign the annulment is that during the brief week when she and my son were playing at being married, she conceived a child."

"They weren't playing, Gran," Richard said. "The marriage was valid."

"Oh, very well. Yes, it was valid. But I didn't learn about the existence of the child until after she died. And I certainly didn't realize at the time that his mother had not signed the annulment papers." His grandmother rose and crossed the room, leaning more

heavily on her cane than Richard had ever seen her. "So you see, our dear Richard is not Lord Hartley. The true heir to Somerset has been fostered quietly by a couple in Wiltshire since he was orphaned. He's been well cared for and educated, but is without knowledge of his true parentage. His name is John Fitzhugh."

"No, Gran," Richard said gently. "My half brother's name is John Fitzhugh *Barrett*."

Thirty-two

The only thing worse than making a mistake is not being given a chance to rectify matters.

—Phillippa, the Dowager Marchioness of Somerset

"HONESTLY, SOPHIE, YOU LOOK LIKE A WASHER-woman. And after your father spent so much on that new wardrobe."

Sophie was wearing her oldest frock, one her mother kept threatening to throw away. The faded muslin was already little more than a rag, but it only made sense to garden in something that wouldn't be ruined by dirt and thorn pricks.

"Mother, I fail to see why I need to dress to impress the greenery," she said as she knelt to yank out a can-kerwort that had sprouted by the rosebush. "Let me worry about what I wear and go on with your story."

"Well, after the revelation that the marquess was being blackmailed over his first marriage," Sophie's mother told her, "your father said the magistrate was

quick to indict Mr. Clack, though Lord Somerset was certain the man had an accomplice."

Millicent Goodnight held the basket for Sophie while she cut a few long-stemmed roses. The bush by the door to Barrett House produced white blooms the size of a child's fist. Their perfume was so sweet that it almost made Sophie dizzy. Or maybe it was just that she had to keep reminding herself to breathe while her mother related the events that took place in Lord Somerset's study last evening. Sophie wished she'd been a mouse in her father's pocket. Instead, she had to be content with a third-hand version of the tale.

"But Mr. Clack wasn't the sort to go quietly," her mother said. "He named his conspirator. It was Miss Bowthorpe."

"The governess?"

"The same. As it turns out, she is also the aunt of Lord Somerset's first wife, Lyda Mae Saxton, and as such, Miss Bowthorpe was privy to the scandal once she collected her niece's belongings."

"But she didn't claim her niece's son?" Even though her mind reeled over what these shocking disclosures meant to Richard, Sophie spared a bit of pity for John Fitzhugh, the child who grew up with no notion of who he truly was.

"No, though Miss Bowthorpe apparently kept a discrete eye on him and bided her time, waiting till the threat of exposure would yield the most return."

Sophie shivered in revulsion. "What a horrid person. And to think Lord and Lady Somerset allowed her to care for Ariel."

"Well, Miss Bowthorpe is paying for her nefarious

dealings now. Unless the new Lord Hartley intervenes on his great-aunt's behalf, she'll be shipped off to New South Wales along with Mr. Clack on the next prison ship going that way."

"Good riddance, I'd say, but then I'm not as nice a person as this John Fitzhugh probably is."

"Nonsense. You're perfectly nice enough for all normal intentions. Besides, no one has any idea what sort of person Fitzhugh is, and I gather it's causing quite a stir. All they're certain of is that he's his lord-ship's heir. The Earl of Hartley by courtesy, and—"

"Mother, stop. This is sounding suspiciously familiar." She rolled her eyes. "Never say you and father are trying to arrange a match between me and the new heir now."

"No, dear. When your father came home last night, he told me he was done trying to live out his dreams through you. It wasn't fair, he said. You have your own dreams, and he hopes they come true."

Sophie snipped another bloom to add to the basket. "Wish he'd say it to me."

"You know how your father is. He feels things deeply, but if he doesn't speak about them, he doesn't have to show weakness." Her mother's eyes grew over-bright. "He just wants to see you settled and happy."

Settled she might manage, but happy? There wasn't much chance of that. Not without Richard.

"Only think of it. All his life, Richard believed he'd be the marquess one day." The title didn't mean much to Sophie, but she ached for his loss. "He must be devastated."

"Perhaps, but that didn't stop him from doing the right thing," her mother said. "As soon as he learned

of his half brother's claim, he was the driving force to make sure it came to light."

A coach clattered past Barrett House, and Sophie looked up in time to make out its occupants.

"Lady Antonia and her family seem to be in a hurry."

"That was the other shoe to drop last night. As soon as it became apparent that Richard Barrett was no longer the heir, Lady Antonia cried off on their engagement. She claimed she'd been courted under false pretenses."

Sophie snorted. "Courted? She all but roped and tied and dragged him into the betrothal."

"True, but the story that will go out is that she is the wronged party." Her mother made a tsking noise. "The Barrett family is beset by scandal all around. Just imagine—a secret marriage, a blackmail plot, and a totally unknown fellow for an heir. I wonder if the reputation of Somerfield Park will ever recover."

Sophie was more concerned about the people connected to the marquessate. Richard had rubbed off on her in that way. He'd always been about his duty to others. It was maddening sometimes, but it was who he was.

And she loved him for it, even after he set her aside for the sake of all those others. It still hurt, but she realized he couldn't have done anything differently, not and remain himself.

She wouldn't change him for worlds.

"Still trying to kill that rosebush?" His familiar voice rumbled over her.

As if she'd conjured him by thinking of him so hard, there he was, dismounting beside the garden gate and looping the reins around a fence post. She'd

never have believed it when she had first arrived at Somerfield Park, but Richard Barrett was everything she'd ever wanted, all she needed. Light to her dark, honorable enough to make up for the way she lived to skirt the rules—the wrinkles in Richard's soul fit snugly into the depressions in hers.

But just because Antonia had thrown him over, Sophie couldn't be sure he was here for her.

"I'll be inside if you need me, dear," her mother said and withdrew. In truth, Sophie had forgotten she was even there. She saw only Richard coming up the walkway toward her. He'd asked her a question, but it wasn't the one she burned to hear. She gave herself a small shake. Oh yes. The roses.

"I did not kill it. As you can see, I was right about the bush. It responded beautifully to my pruning."

"It's not the only thing. You've been hacking away at me since you arrived too," he said with a grin. "And like the bush, I'm still here."

She decided to tease him a bit. "Yes, but somewhat diminished I hear. I can't 'my lord' you any longer."

"Actually, you can. It's true that I'm not Lord Hartley, but even the younger son of a marquess is entitled to an honorific. I'm Lord Richard Barrett now. Still wellborn, if anyone attached to my woefully unconventional family can be counted such, but technically, I'm a commoner now."

"One of us, eh? Welcome to the ranks of the ordinary."

"You are anything but that." He reached up and brushed the pad of his thumb across her cheek. "You've a smudge there."

"One can't create anything worth having without a smudge or two."

"By those lights, we should be spectacular together because I've certainly smudged things up." He took her hand between his and gently tugged off her gardening glove. Her fingers twined with his of their own accord. "Sophie, I haven't any right to ask this of you. I've no title. No wealth of my own. If you accept me, you'd be able to style yourself Lady Richard, so perhaps that will satisfy your father."

"A title has never been important to me."

His brows drew together in a frown. "It is to me. I wanted to make you my marchioness. As it is, my bride will be the wife of a tradesman. My father is not the man he once was. His mind is still foggy at times, so I'm staying on to manage the timber enterprise and estate's finances because my half brother will have his hands full adjusting to his new station. I've been given Barrett House, but it's not nearly grand enough for you."

"Haven't you seen what I've done with the garden?" Sophie leaned toward him. "Wait till you turn me loose on the inside of the house."

"You're making fun of me. We started off all wrong. Now I'm trying to do this properly," Richard said as he dropped to one knee, his soul shining in his dark eyes. "Sophie Goodnight, I love you. I can't imagine life without you, and I'll spend every moment of every day trying to deserve you. Will you do me the honor of becoming my wife?"

"Of course I will, with all my heart." She no longer needed to so carefully guard her heart. Sophie could leave it safely in Richard's keeping. She bent and

kissed him. "And I'll happily do you the honor, but I don't want proper. I want laughter and adventures and a whole houseful of untitled brats. And don't expect me not to make fun of you when you deserve it. If I don't make fun, who will? Oh, let's have fun together, Richard. All our lives."

"We will, darling. I promise." He picked her up and swung her around, her tattered muslin frock billowing out like a banner. "Every day will be golden. Some people go all their lives without realizing what they have. I'm the luckiest man on earth because I know what a treasure you are."

He covered her mouth in a sweet kiss of promise. Then the kiss darkened with passion till her insides throbbed. All his rakish skills were hers now, and she'd never get enough of him.

"We're both lucky," she gasped when he finally released her lips. "But I've got to stop thinking of you as a rake."

"I hope you have another name for me by now."

"Oh, I do. It's love, Richard. Simply love."

Acknowledgments

A lot of loving hands touch my work on its way to becoming a book. Firstly, I want to thank my editor, Deb Werksman. She inherited me mid-project but never made me feel like an also-ran. The most pleasing parts of this story can be attributed to her attention to detail and spot-on good taste. Guess that means the less pleasing parts are mine. Unless I could blame them on my fabulous agent, Natasha Kern. But no. She's been on the Somerfield Park bandwagon since the idea for the series sprang into my head.

Then there are the incredible people at Sourcebooks who take my manuscript and transform it into what you now hold in your hands. Thank you to Susie Benton for keeping me on task and on time. I'm grateful to talented cover artist Dawn Adams, production editor Rachel Gilmer, copy editor Gretchen Stelter, and publicist Danielle Dresser and her crew. Then there are the sales staff, and the booksellers, and I could go on and on.

Lastly, I want to thank YOU, dear reader. There are many things competing for your attention today, and

I'm thrilled you've chosen to spend some time with me and the folk who live in Somerfield Park. I hope you enjoy your visit and return to us often. For more about my books, please visit www.miamarlowe.com.

Happy Reading,
Mia